DUNE BUSTERS

-A SAND DUNES AND DINOSAURS NOVELLA-

SABINE ELROD

SPECIAL HARDCOVER EDITION

Cover designed by Brian Scutt
https://brianscutt.artstation.com

Edited by Ellie Edits
https://www.fiverr.com/elliedits

Sabine A. Elrod
www.nisaryan.com
Halcyon Road Publications

Printed in the United States of America
First Printing: September 2019

ISBN 978-0-578-52974-5

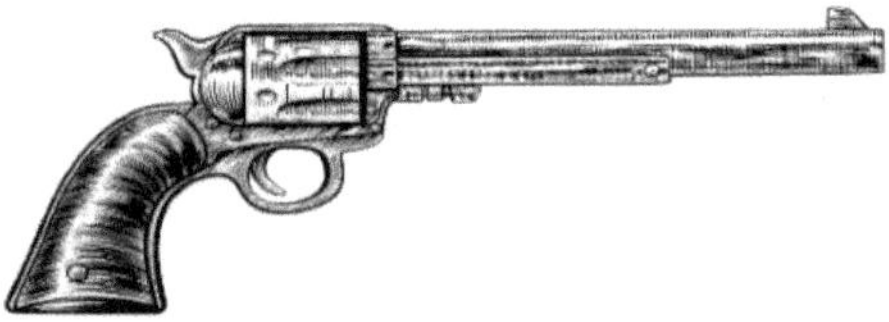

To my dad, who opened the door to fantastical worlds and instilled a love of adventure in a little girl who just wanted to see dinosaurs.

I love the desert and its incomparable sense of space.

- ROBYN DAVIDSON

It'd look better with a satellite dish on its head.

- T. DALE ELROD

SHADY PLATEAU

CHAPTER 1

"*Special orders*. This commissioner asked for you by name even," Camelia said, quirking a finely sculpted eyebrow and lifting her chin. The surprised look on my face made her snicker. *Why would anyone ask for me by name?* I had a rate of 60/40 when it really came down to crunching the numbers. For every few missions in which I'd succeeded, I'd had another handful in which I'd utterly failed. I had suspected this meeting was the one where they would finally revoke my license and send me packing.

I narrowed my eyes, turning my face away to gaze out the window. Lights flickered across the tall jumbled skyscrapers and played with the shadows. Bending light and dark in a display of false grandiose. The tall brick and glass buildings loomed like grey giants over the crisscross lines of streets and knotted highways alike. Citizens strode along the walkways lined with flashing street lamps and neon signs that promised food, drugs, pleasure or sometimes all three. The joyful smiles of streetwalkers, their eyes shielded behind visors with hovering interfaces, hid the secret misery that laced between the buildings with knots of false hope and drug-induced euphoria alike. Cars hung over the littered streets and clogged the inner-city airways, their hovering paths guided by floating, glowing red beacons that directed the traffic. Centrum was the largest and most dynamic city on the planet. Its hazy fog of exhaust and dust the only thing blocking out otherwise bleak and desperate surroundings. Outside the city, walls were nothing but sand, rock, and volcanic mountains that the rest of civilisation had done its best to build around, not that it mattered. This rock was dying. Eventually we'd all need to get out of dodge, but for now, people were mostly happy being left alone to do their thing here. The rest of humanity spread out across the universe in the never-ending search for more resources, more space, and more meaningful existence. If you hadn't found those things here, then you were a better person than half of us by far, and I wished you well.

"Who is it, and why me?" I asked, scratching briefly at the dark stubble on my chin and ran a nervous hand through shorn hair. I turned to meet her eyes. There was no emotion there, her face was flat as ever. Sometimes I wondered if she was human at all or rather, I often wondered if her face was synthetic. In the years I'd contracted with the Imperial Commission, Camelia never aged. No wrinkles, no errant grey hair, no deepening of the voice or thinness of the lips. Her skin was bright porcelain against ice-blue eyes and pitch-black hair. Too perfect for human.

"You know I don't have the permissions necessary to divulge that kind of information, Grey,"

[She doesn't want to tell you]

I nodded as the smooth voice of Kato, my skyeye cyborg, entered my mind. Somewhere outside, probably perched on a building nearby so that our sensors stayed within range, the skyeye sat and watched and listened. His body in the shape of a barn owl. Our joint communication link allowed him to hear every word. He specialised in keeping one eye in the sky and the other to the land. It was somewhat useful in various situations.

My lips twitched.

Of course, Camelia wouldn't tell me anything. I don't even know why I bothered asking. Shoving my hands into the deep pockets of my worn leather duster, I rolled my shoulders into a shrug as an irritated smile crossed my face, "So, where am I headed then?"

[Wherever they don't want to go themselves. Isn't that how it always is?]

[Kato. Quiet, or I'll turn off the feed. Got it?]

Silence. I turned my attention back to Camelia as she flicked her cigarette into the ashtray. A stream of blue smoke, like incense, wafted up from the glowing red end. Steeling her fingers together, her pale face leaned towards me across the large black desk. In the darkness of the room, she looked like a ghost with her oval face bobbing like a lantern. The thought crossed my mind that she probably could devour me, and would, if given a chance. Her face came to within inches of mine and, for the first time, I could remember in a long while, a smile turned the corners of her lips upwards. It didn't meet her eyes, they stared like dark blue holes of animosity.

Sliding a file across the desk, she said "You should already be very familiar with this little dust bowl of a town," her eyes bored holes into my head. The smile was still there as she watched me take the file and flip through the pages before I coughed out a curse. Camelia's laughter was sharp and dark as my face shifted from confusion to one of dismay and then anger as I read the file. She relished my reaction, I could tell. Her eyes flicked down to my throat when I swallowed, clearing my voice before replying with a candid, "Oh?" I slid the file back. It disappeared into the dark recesses of her desk.

Camelia continued to laugh long and hard. Throwing her head back so that the black strands of her hair seemed to blend in with the dark space behind her. Her pale face took on a hint of a rosy glow. She swiped a finger beneath each eye to catch the tears that glistened along the dark lashes, "I'm very interested to see how this job works out for you Grey, please keep me informed of your progress as per the contractual agreements," she said a laugh still on her lips, making them tremble, "You have eight days."

She was terrifying. It was eerie to hear her laughter, and it continued to echo behind me as I took my leave.

Stepping out of the elevator, I passed through the stark white and empty lobby. Only a flat-screen television on one wall and a desk, complete with a bored receptionist, sat directly across from it gave any sign that this place was used for anything other than an elevator entryway. I stood outside and waited. A brush of cold air against my face and a vice-like grip on my shoulder let me know that Kato had arrived. Resting on my shoulder, the cybernetic owl flapped his wings once before settling comfortably against my neck. His large black eyes glowed with an unnatural light. It was the only thing that gave away his true nature. [I'm sorry, Grey. I dislike Camelia; she gives me the creeps.]

I nodded in agreement,

[I know, but this time it's personal for me.]

[Why's that? Who is it?]

I let out an audible sigh, glancing at Kato as I headed home to pack a bag before catching a late-night ride at the Blimp Station.

It wasn't the most ideal way to travel, but it was quick and would carry us over the rusting Dune Sea faster than a skaali would,

[It's not who, it's where. We're going to an island in the Atolls]

[You've been there before, I gather?] Kato asked, blinking his large eyes slowly.

I shrugged, [I was born there.]

CHAPTER 2

Two days later, I stood with my back to the wind and sand swirling around my boots. A wide brim Stetson hat shielded my eyes while a cloth bandana was tied against my face for protection. I took a moment to shove a saline syringe up each nostril and pinched my nose to make sure the liquid didn't run back out. The dry air tended to give me nose bleeds, and I didn't feel like dealing with a laundry bill. Having packed a small bag of only the necessities, I carried it now, slung over one shoulder with Kato resting on the other as we entered the hotel. A dingy little place called *The Harpoon*. The only hotel and, coincidentally, also the only full-service bar in this shit-hole of a town called Shady Plateau. Which was a hilariously bad joke because it was neither shady, nor was it on a plateau. The craggy island was surrounded by several days of hot, barren wasteland that was nothing more than cracked clay and sand that swept over the small city, coating everything with rust-red dust.

The only safe way in or out of this pustule was by the Imperial Blimp aero-system, and even then you still ran the risk of the occasional air-pirate.

The only way to board the blimp was to be an Imperial citizen or someone endorsed by the Imperial Commissioner Office, fondly known as ICO. Luckily enough, my contract gave me the clearance to take advantage of the aero-system, a network of transport towers spread throughout the continents. Otherwise, you were looking at several weeks of walking along the Halcyon Road, a stretch of broken highway leftover from the early days of Terrafirma V. It ran from one end of the lesser continent of Caldura to the main continent of Oceana where Centrum was located snuggled up against the edge of Last Ocean. Aptly named Last Ocean because it was quite literally the last of the surface water. Clustered around its shores were several cities and towns, most notably Gardenia where you could witness the last of the remaining greenery on the planet struggling to survive.

On the Halcyon Road, you'd be facing dehydration, starvation, and desert carnivores. And that was if you were alone. If you travelled with a caravan, you'd most likely end up being taken by the raiders who camped out among the dunes and preyed on travellers.

There were rumours that they were cannibals.

Or, if you were wealthy enough to buy one, you could ride a skaali or hire an Evanescent Defender cyborg as an escort. The skaali were giant lizards, similar in looks to the ancient dinosaurs from Earths prehistoric record. The most popular ones, raptors, were bred and augmented for riding. Only on Terrafirma V, thanks to genetic meddling and doses of medicated who-knew-what, they grew to be the size of a horse with wickedly curved talons on their hind feet that were as long as a grown man's forearm. They were expensive though, especially if you wanted one with all the cybernetic enhancements that were all the craze these days. *Goddamned cyborg dinosaurs with lasers in their heads.* I'd had more than a few run-ins with the occasional skaali turned wild. Maybe it had something to do with lousy wet-wiring, but occasionally one would go hay-wire. Didn't matter how or why it happened, if a skaali went over the edge they had to be put down before they tore apart more than just their owners.

The young man behind the counter was scrubbing its thick wooden surface with a threadbare rag. Making wet soapy circles as he hummed a tune. His head was shaved, but his face was not, the shade of new stubble made his jawline dark against already darkly tanned skin. He looked up as he heard my footsteps and the swoosh of the leather duster jacket I wore despite the heat. Better to be hot than burnt to a crisp by the twin suns. A trail of sand rushed in with the wind as the door beat against its frame before clicking shut behind me. His brown eyes shot up to his missing hairline then dropped to the badge dangling around my neck before his brows plunged downwards so low they buried his eyes. Setting his jaws, he frowned.

I knew that look well enough.

"Hullo, law-man. We're all booked up for the night, apologies," he said. I understood his avarice. I once hated my kind as well back before I learned better. Back before I finally found a way out of this place. I put on a smile, reaching into a pocket and pulling out my wallet, I began to flip through the crystal-clear bills that lined the inner fold. Narrowing his eyes, he was opening his mouth to say something when a hand slapped down on the counter with a loud *thwack*. We both turned our heads to find a woman, portly and greying with lavender-blue eyes and a broad smile. She pressed her thick hands into meaty hips,

"My word, Christopher Grey. I thought you planned to never come back here, boy?" she said loud enough that it made me flinch and Kato flapped his wings. Digging a finger in an ear, I returned the smile and nodded. I knew this woman. The inn-keep, Rosie Langham. She had been here working this inn since before I was born, and each year her hearing grew worse though she'd always deny it.

"No, ma'am. I'm not back. I'm just here for work," I said, turning my body so that the badge dangled within view of them both. Rosie's eyes grew wide before narrowing into her scrunched face, she waved the boy from behind the counter and motioned for him to take my bag. He started to protest but the look she shot him made the and I both quiver. If you ever got on Rosie's bad side, you'd regret it soon enough. She'd make sure of it.

"Forgive Tyler, like all of us here we just–I mean well, you know, before you, uh –" she stuttered to a stop. I nodded. I understood well enough. Before I had joined the Imperial Dune Busters, I was just like Tyler. I didn't want anything to do with the city, with the Commissioners, with the Imperials. None of it. I was fine living here in the sand and dust just doing my own thing while avoiding my dad on his worst days. It wasn't until I met Natalie that my life began to change. Natalie was the one, I was sure of it, so when she applied to attend the Arboreal Academy in Gardenia near Last Ocean; I knew I had to go with her. But I was three years younger and ten times dumber. My thoughts were interrupted as Tyler yelled for me to follow him as he'd be taking me to my room,

"I thought you were all booked up?" I said with a smirk. The boy's shoulders hitched up to his neck, and his back stiffened. He looked over his shoulder at me, both hands wrapped around the strap of my bag,

"Nah, mister. I just don't want any trouble for my aunt. That's all, I didn't mean nothing by it," the words fell from his mouth in a heavily accented jumble. Nodding I let out a sigh. I knew what he meant.

The room was small. The door banged against the base of the bed when I opened it. Inside were just a bed and a desk with a lamp. A PDA display screen was mounted on the wall, encased in protective plastic, but it was so small you'd have to stand up to see anything on it. There was barely two feet between the edge of the mattress and the desk. It didn't matter, I wouldn't be here longer than I needed to be.

Closing the door behind me, I dropped my bag onto the desk and reached up to my shoulder, Kato stepped onto my hand, and I lowered his feathered body to the foot of the bed where he perched. His round face bobbed as he took in the room, eyes flashing as the lens' dilated and adjusted to the sudden darkness.

I reached up and swiped a finger across the PDA screen to turn it on, sliding the volume up so I could listen as I pulled off the sun-warmed duster and draped it over the back of the chair; sand fell from the folds to form miniature dunes on the floor.

"Another High Commissioner was found dead this morning. The victim is none other than the Commissioner of Ricia, Cassidy Florence. She was found unresponsive in her office at 3:00am this past –"

I flicked the screen off and sighed.

This wasn't good.

A dead Commissioner happened here and there, the chance of assassination just kind of came along with the job. But a High Commissioner was something else.

[This is it?] Kato flapped his wings as I dropped my weight onto the bed. It creaked in a way that told me I was going to wake up in the morning with a sore back and maybe a broken neck, [Afraid so, but it used to be home] I thought and let out a sigh.

[You used to live in a hotel?]

"Of course not, smart-ass, I meant I used to live on this island," I said aloud, [Oh, you didn't like it?] he hooted softly, and the sound of it soothed the rough edges of the room. Kato didn't have a replicated voice box, so even though he could hear me and understand, he could only speak to me via our linked communication device or commlink as we liked to call it for short. It was one of the few augmentations I agreed to receive as part of my work as an IDB. I didn't like cyborgs, the idea of metal and skin knitted together creeped me out. Joints upon joints, wire and tendons, bleeding together. Who was in control after a certain point, the man or the machine? It was desperation and the need for a purpose that drove me to pursue work with ICO.

"No," I said as memories I had tried to erase flooded my thoughts. Memories of my dad with his hard words and the even harder beatings. He was more monster than man by the time I left this place. His body riddled with alcohol, Roid, and second-hand augmentations he had earned on the black market. Scrunching my face up I scowled. Even after all these years, my body still remembered the sting of the metal buckle biting into my back as he struck me and this tiny room rung of familiarity. I wasn't in the mood for more questions. Turning the joint audio feed off I settled back on the bed, crossing my hands over my stomach and propping my feet up on the end of the wooden frame, I pulled the wide brim of my hat down over my eyes.

"Get some rest, K. We've got business in the morning."

CHAPTER 3

[Kato, you got a read on our target?]

I was standing on a dusty metal pathway that arched over the central main street of the island. Looking down, dozens of people passed beneath me. They were a colourful stream of reds, blues, greens and various hues between. Most of them were, like me, wearing hats or a facemask to keep the sands from settling in our lungs. Rust Lung was a genuine threat out there among the islands and the dunes. Breathing in too much of it and you'd literally find yourself filling up with the stuff, slowly suffocating to death as the broken-down rust particles buried themselves in your guts, giving you a nasty case of tetanus. It might take a few weeks or even a year or more, but you'd suffer the entire time. The first signs of Rust Lung were coughing, wheezing, severe shortness of breath before you finally started to get the trembles. Your whole body would seize up in spasms, joints locked in place. Immobile. And then one day you just wouldn't wake up.

Kato's voice echoed through my thoughts again as I continued to scan the people passing beneath me,

[Target is confirmed, Grey. I'm trailing her now. ETA is three minutes]

[Too many people. Use your adverbs, Kato]

I noticed as a pair of rare sabre-toothed Kit'th with fur shining like gold as they walked beneath the archways. The tall cat-like humanoids wore tan and brown loin clothes and were armed with twin scimitars and a rifle of Kit'th design. If you saw a Kit'th, you knew they were guarding someone. They weren't cheap and only took work from humans if it was as a mercenary or a bodyguard and only if the pay was excellent and mostly came in advance.

I wondered about that.

Who would be rich enough, or notorious enough, to need a pair of Kit'th guards on this little shit-hole of an island? I was pondering this when Kato cut into my thoughts again, [She is here. Brunette wearing camo pants and a yellow crop-top], he said as his shadow passed over the bridge.

I scanned the crowd below.

A flash of yellow caught my attention.

I was struck. The woman's bobbed hair and tawny skin contrasted wildly against the yellow top and denim camouflage shorts that rode so high you'd think she was wearing underwear. Keeping her in my sight, I reached out to the skyeye, [Watch my back] I said as I made my way towards the spiral staircase that led down to the street, taking it two steps at a time.

Meandering my way through the crowd, I pushed people aside as I went. If they protested it only took a quick glance at the badge around my neck to send them running. With a smile, I approached the stall and, standing next to the girl, asked the cyborg behind the counter for a skewer of meat. Sinking my teeth into it, I glanced at the brunette next to me as she finished speaking with the vendor. They were obviously familiar with each other, smiling easily and chatting about various things. The girl herself seemed oddly familiar, but I couldn't quite place why. She seemed too young to have known me when I was a kiddo.

I tried to listen in to their conversation, catching snippets about repairs that were needed and new orders that had been placed or received. However, my presence didn't go unnoticed by either of them as they exchanged glances, and their chatter turned to hushed whispers. I continued to chew the meat stick and was about to ask a question when the girl turned and ran, "Dammit, they always run," I said with a growl, tossing the half-eaten meat into the trash bin as I leapt to action.

Feet pounding on the ground, dodging around moving carts and shoving my way through groups of pedestrians, I ran after the yellow flash of fabric. With my heart thrumming in my ears, I felt sweat begin to trail down my temples and the small of my back. The mask made it hard to breathe, but it was that or risk catching Rust Lung.

[K, she's on the run. Be my eyes,] I commanded. Kato replied instantly, [on it].

I blinked, and my vision was flooded with an overlay map of the street in front of me. It began to fill in with more details, the names of buildings, shops and shop owners, homes and the people residing within. Features that most people didn't even know we, the ICO, had access too.

With Kato guiding the way I ran. I leapt over street debris, ducked around carts laden with goods, and dodged groups of people as I chased my elusive prey. A carriage rolled between us, *Shit*, kicking off the ground I leap over it, tucking in and rolling across on the other side with my duster jacket trailing behind like a bizarre cape. I was on my feet in an instant. The girl turned and our eyes locked for a moment as they went wide with shock and I grinned. As if a fucking cart could stop a Buster from pursuing his quarry. She skipped back a few steps and then twisted to the side, disappearing into an alleyway that was overhung with colourful awning and planks of wood to keep the sun at bay. I skidded to a stop at the entrance of the alley and frowned as I observed the long corridor of shadows and light. Plants, their long vines reaching down to the street, were rare glimpses of green in this otherwise beige and brown hellhole. Trash bins lined both sides of the alley, they were heaped with garbage and old machinery parts. You could easily hide behind them. Kato's shadow passed overhead, above the awnings, making the light flicker in a pattern of dark and light.

Slowing my pace to a walk, I listened as I entered the alley. Water sloshed somewhere beneath me; I could hear it running through pipes that were nestled beneath the streets carrying pumped water in from miles away. That's how you knew you shouldn't be living here. Humans, I mean. If you needed to have water pumped in, and taxed by the tablespoon, your species didn't belong here. The metal hooks that plants hung from creaked in the light breeze as I pressed further into the alley; it was noticeably cool here. A blessed reprieve from the heat outside. Closing my eyes, I sensed the current as it suddenly changed direction and jerked my head back.

My eyes snapped open just as a small fist passed half an inch away from my nose. Reaching up, I grasped the attached arm and pulled, jerking my bounty from her hiding space. Throwing my elbow up, I rammed the sharp end of it into her stomach. With a grunt, she toppled over my shoulder and to the ground. But she wasn't going down that easy. Rolling away, she leapt to her feet and stood, staring at me with defiant green eyes that flashed with fury. *Wait, weren't they brown?* Sliding one long leg back, she rested her weight on it and brought her fists up, taking a boxing stance. I only had a half a second to laugh about it, *What the hell, I must weigh at least eighty pounds more and stand a good six inches taller,* before she hit me with a volley of blows. Hitting fast and hard, she glanced me with multiple punches to my gut and chest before uppercutting me in the jaw, my teeth smashed together with an audible click.

The taste of hot iron flashed across my tongue.

I stumbled in surprise and winced against the pain that laced my lips with profanities that dripped to the ground along with bright red blood. I ran a finger over the cleft of my jaw. Tonguing the laceration inside my cheek, I knew it'd be sore in the morning. *I wasn't expecting her to move so goddamned fast.* She went to hit me again, but I threw an arm up to block her, stepping to the side as her fist passed harmlessly by. Keeping a tight grip on her wrist, I twisted sharply and felt something pop, with a cry she swung around, attempting to chop me in the neck with her free hand, but I managed to grab that as well and, with both her arms now crossed over each other, I pressed back. Forcing her up against the alley wall, "Enough," I commanded, my voice dark, "Doctor Samantha Adele Cowell, my name is Chris Grey, and as an Imperial Dune Buster I've been ordered to place you under arrest on orders of the Imperial Commissioning Office of Centrum, I've been contracted to take you in for the crime of, *oof*–" her knee jerked up into my groin, and she grinned with satisfaction that quickly faded when she realized it had little effect, "Yeah, I like to wear a bit of extra protection in cases like these. I don't know what it is with you ladies and always aiming for the groin," I said with a triumphant smile as I pushed harder, feeling our bodies press together against the wall. She gasped as furious tears began to fill her eyes. Averting her gaze, she continued to struggle, but I could feel the bones in her slender wrists as they ground together beneath the pressure. Wincing in pain, she hissed between clenched teeth,

'Let me go, you've no idea why they even want me. You're just hired muscle with zero brains," she yelled and spat at me. *Gross.* I turned my head to the side and ran my cheek against my shoulder to wick the moisture away. "You're right. I don't know all the details, but I do know how to do my job so, we're going back to your place, and you're going to give me what I came here for. I'm sure you know what it is or you wouldn't be running," I intoned while slipping a hand into my jacket long enough to pull out a set of cuffs. Snapping them around her wrist, I turned us around and marched out of the alley.

As soon as we stepped amongst the crowd, I felt her chest expand as she sucked in a deep breath and then released the most ear-splitting scream her tight little body could muster. People stood and stared as she raged against the cuffs and began to twist and kick at me, stomping her heel into my foot and grinding it, "Shit, hold *still.* You're just making this harder on yourself," I hissed into her ear. They always struggled in the end, though. She sucked in another breath and screamed, *'Fight the Commission, fight Centrum! Don't let them fool you, those augmentations are ticking time bombs!"* I rolled my eyes and sighed as I pulled my pistol, hidden within my jacket, out of its holster, "*I know, I built –*" and slammed the butt of it against her temple. Hooking her on my arm before she could fall to the sandy ground I hoisted her up over my shoulder and flashed my badge around so the growing crowd would disperse before I scanned her identity chip for an address. Usually, the people I was hired to track down didn't have anything registered. No address, no contact info of any type. It was just safer that way. Surprisingly she had a registered apartment though the name was wrong.

Either a fake ID or a friends place.

Taking note of it, I headed in that direction with Kato's map as my guide.

[Hope I can find what we need here. Keep an eye on things, I'll be on standby,] Kato answered an affirmative as I weaved my way through the crowd, cargo slumped over my shoulder.

CHAPTER 4

This was the part I hated. Usually, they were awake when I had to pat them down and search for hidden weapons or other contraband. Ms Cowell however, was out cold, and the purple bruise stretched over the welt on the side of her face clued me in that maybe I'd hit her a bit too hard. Either way, I had to search her, it was protocol. As a professional and went about it quickly and with great care The welt on Ms Cowell's temple made me wince. I didn't want to have hurt her. I never did. With the body search complete, I left her resting on the bed and waited.

An hour had passed when her eyes snapped open, and she leapt to her feet and stood looking down at me from atop the bed. Her breasts had just the right curve to them. With slender shoulders and wide hips with legs thick with muscle, firm calves and ass. Dark brown hair was cut into a bob and hung against her jawline, the cuts messy edges a clue to her having cut it herself. Her luminous green eyes flashed in the sunlight that filtered through the window slats.

"What do you *want*?" she asked, straight to the point. Curling her hands into delicate fists at her sides, my eyes flicked down to the bruises forming on her wrists. I needed those hands. Or more accurately, my contractor required them. I sat on the edge of her bed as she stood above me. Spreading my legs, I draped my arms across the padded thighs of the denim jeans I wore. The many pockets sewn into their length were pretty damn convenient as well.

"You've seen my badge, Ms Cowell. You know what I'm about or you wouldn't have tried to run. I've been commissioned to bring you back to Centrum."

Leaping down to the floor she used a foot to kick around the piles of clothing that were strewn across it and found an acceptable bra and panties. I turned my head away, closing my eyes as she began to change but I couldn't help a quick glance.

As she reached behind to hook the bra clasp, the muscles of her back and shoulders knotted up. All toned strength and whispered danger. I tore my eyes away, looking out the slatted window at the passing shadows of people as they went about their daily lives. She found a shirt and began to pull it over her head,

"Yes. I get that. But why and what for? I've done nothing wrong," she asked, her voice muffled by the fabric as she wrenched it over her face and tugged it into place around her trim waist. A sleeveless black tank top–it suited her. After that, she found a pair of jeans, the knees worn through, socks and sneakers. *More comfortable to run in, no doubt.* She probably traded a fortune in artefacts and cash to get those. That, or a few illegal repairs and adjustments I'd wager.

Snorting, I replied, "Really? You ran, that tells me you've done something wrong." She looked at me, sourly. Ignoring the gorgons glare, I continued,

"I'm not privy to that type of information. All I know is that they want you. I was asked to take good care of you, protect you, ensure you aren't hurt in any way. Think of me as more of an escort," I said. She smirked, "Well, you already failed in one aspect," she said as she brushed a hand over the welt on her temple and winced.

Pulling her pants up, I looked pointedly at the long fingers that played with the zipper. She looked up and met my eyes, "Don't get any funny ideas," she said, "I'm sure you had enough fun while I was knocked out," she said with anger edging into her voice. She flashed her teeth at me and spat into the rusted sink nearby. I raised my hands in mock surrender though my eyes were still glued to her hips.

"Not at all. Not interested," I said, "You'd better start packing. I plan to leave first thing tonight. Hop the very next blimp outta here,"

She stopped then and looked at me, cocking her head to one side as her eyes stared into mine. I wore a mask of calmness, but I could feel my heart drumming wildly in my chest as my skin prickled beneath her scrutiny. I was actually very interested, but she didn't need to know that and besides, I was working. Her brow drew in, forming a subtle crease between her eyebrows, "Wait. What was your name again? I *know* you," she said. I let out a sigh as soon as I heard those words. It had been long enough since I'd left that most people wouldn't recognise me. But, in certain circles, my name still floated around, and for good or bad, I had a reputation of sorts. Making a face, I shook my head gently, "No, you don't."

She pulled back, crossing her arms over her chest and leaning back to rest her butt on the edge of the empty dresser. It had to be empty, all her clothes were on the floor or strewn across the bed or hanging from clotheslines that crisscrossed the narrow hallway to the toilet. The edges of her hair bounced as she shook her head, "Like hell, I don't. I was there when you left, you son of a bitch. I watched you climb on that blimp without us," she said, spitting the words at me with an anger that turned her eyes into emeralds on fire. One edge of her lip curled up as she glared, burrowing her eyes into me and daring me to deny anything and everything.

"I've no idea what you're talking about," I said with a wave of my hand.

"Yes, you *do* Christopher Daniel Grey. I was there, my brother was there. You left him behind to save your own ass. If you think I'm going to come peacefully then you can fuck right off," she said, low and dangerous. I had no idea what the hell she was talking about, how the hell did she know my name? Making a face, I thought back on the day I left, trying to remember the details. It'd been nearly fifteen years. I couldn't be expected to remember one furious girl.

And then I did. *Fuck.*

My head shot up as I looked at her, *really* looked at her. The defiant green eyes, *though I was sure they'd been brown*, the stern jaw with a hint of a cleft, tawny skin with dark hair and a scar, grown smaller with time, that bisected the flesh of her collar bone. If I remembered correctly it from that time she tried to use a broken screwdriver to open a can of corn.

"You're Jack Espen's sister, Samantha Marie Espen. Long-time no see, Sam," I said casually, furrowing my brow as I ground my jaw. She didn't deny it, nodding her head and crossing her arms as she shifted her weight from one leg to the other.

Fucking hell, no wonder the name rang a bell.

Her lips curled into a smirk, "I was ten years old when you ditched us," she said.

My shoulders heaved as I sighed.

I had forgotten about her.

As for her brother, "*Fuck*," I breathed out the word in a whisper, laden with regret. I was fifteen when I had finally hopped that blimp, sneaking up the huge magnetic claspers that held the blimps into place and wriggling down between the dual keels to keep the defence system from finding me. Many a would-be hitchhiker had ended their brief journey jettisoned off the side of a blimp.

Or electrocuted.

Sometimes both.

It had taken Jack, Samantha, and I months to figure out and program the codes the defence system ran on to create a radio pattern that would sync with it so we could ride without fear. Reach Centrum. Take on new identities if we had to. Sam and her brother were a large part of that. That day, the blimp we caught wasn't headed for Centrum, but I insisted we hop it anyway. I had to get off this suffocating rock no matter where it was taking us. The armed guards should have alerted me to the fact that this particular blimp was headed to Watchtower Plateau with fresh meat for the prison pits. *If only I'd waited a few more days.* Standing I reached over to one of the shelves mounted above the window and picked up a small figurine made of twisted metal that'd been welded together. It looked like a ballerina.

There was a time when Sam loved to dance, but I never had time for it, and neither did Jack. She was always tagging along after us, begging us to play. From a young age, Samantha had a knack for building things. Making something out of nothing. She'd score the trash heaps and junk piles in search of things she could use and, as she got older, she started dabbling with more advanced science. Messing with chips and bio-filaments, cyber-filaments and nano-tech whenever she could get access to it. She was a real Doctor Frankenstein.

I thought Samantha would have been long gone from this place. I thought she and that brilliant brain of hers would have gone off to Centrum, or Gardenia at least, where she could set up her own shop and make a killing repairing or modifying cyborgs and synthetic body parts. Instead, here I was to bring her in for information theft and illegal manufacturing.

I put the figurine back in its place, feeling her eyes on me as I did so, "So, it's Cowell now. You married?"

"What does it matter to you?" she asked, her voice smooth as I turned and flicked my eyes over her, "Nothing really," I said flatly and shrugged, "Just curious was all." I took in her small home. An engineering genius she might be, but she was no lady. The place was a mess with clothes strewn across the floor and bed. Bottles of shampoo and lotions had lined the small sink in the bathroom with its broken mirror. The kitchenette held only a few plates and glasses. No signs of anyone else living with her. *A widow maybe?* Or she had changed identities for some reason. Or tried to anyway, we found her quickly enough.

I should have known that the only reason they'd send me to Shady Plateau was for Samantha. There was nothing else here worth a shit.

"Your brother was a good man," I said. She whirled on me with fists raised and eyes flashing, "I don't need *you* to tell me that," she said, eyes flashing with anger. Turning her back to me, she began to open and empty the cabinets. Dumping the contents onto the already dirty floor. I didn't know what she was looking for, but right now, we were wasting time. I had a hotel to check out of. I stood and rested a hand on the pistol at my hip and held up the cuffs, "Come on. You're dressed. Time to get going."

"I'm not going anywhere with you," she said again while tossing aside a few magazines that fluttered noisily to the floor. The pages scattered, images of well-dressed socialites with fancy hover-cars and guns splashed across the leaves in colourful neon prints. I heard the sound of a lock sliding open and a latch being opened.

"Found you!" she declared, and when I looked up again, I was staring down the black pits of a thirty-inch, double-barrelled shotgun. It was outfitted with a sight, and archaic runes were scrawled up and down the metal barrel and down the wooden stock. The markings twisted in an intricate web of binding spells.

A rune-gun.

How in the hells did she get a rune-gun? I wondered, *dealing in illegal arms, that's another box to check on her booking papers.* I didn't know if it was loaded and I didn't particularly care to find out. Rune-guns were deadly and occasionally unpredictable, and in these close quarters, we'd be lucky if either of us survived. She'd be very stupid to pull the trigger. But I wasn't going to chance it. Lifting both hands into the air, I stepped back and tilted my head to one side, surrendering.

It was my fault.

I had fallen into a false sense of security, having searched the room while she was knocked out and finding nothing. Of course, she'd have secure areas I couldn't reach – trap doors with coded access, and the like – I'd have done the same. I should have had Kato come in and run a scan over the apartment beforehand. My bad.

"You seem surprised, Grey," Sam said, her green eyes alight with arrogant smugness, "What, did you think I'd just go willingly? Just fall into your arms? Is that how all the other girls do it?"

I shrugged, my hands still raised with fingertips brushing the low metal ceiling, "Well yeah. Generally, they just fall right into my arms," I agreed, trying not to smile; my face twitched from the effort. Sam's lips turned into a pout as she considered my words, trying to decide if I was serious. I continued, "But they only want me for my body. I need a deeper commitment than that."

The weapon dropped just a fraction of an inch as she narrowed her eyes and scowled at me. That was all I needed, I leapt to the side but slipped on some loose paper, kidding into the wall. Quickly regaining my balance, I ducked beneath the barrel and reached out towards the weapon as Samantha took another step around me, lowering the gun towards my head with her finger hovering next to the trigger my hands shot up over my head instinctively when the entire place began to shake. A loud boom followed by another rumble made us both lurch to the side. I thought we were done for, that spell bullet would tear us apart and half the building with it. But nothing happened. I sat there in confusion. Samantha lowered the weapon as I breathed a sigh of relief.

The floor lurched.

Our eyes met as a tremor rippled through the place again, and we nearly collapsed to the floor.

"*The hell?*" we said in unison. Confusion reflected in both our pairs of eyes as the ground buckled again and lurched to the right, so roughly the floor shifted beneath our feet, tossing us to the left. Sam shoved the weapon into her waist belt and spread her legs wide, her arms spinning like windmills as she tried to keep her balance, "An earthquake?" she wondered aloud. I shook my head; this didn't feel like an earthquake.

From the window, a bright light filtered into the room casting us in alternating stripes of shadow before flashing and then fading to grey and back to tepid daylight. Motes of light swam across my vision as I blinked, rubbing my knuckles against the lids as I waited for the sparks to fade. A lock clicked behind me, and I turned to see Sam throwing open the door as another tremor sent what remained on the shelves scattering across the ground. I stumbled after her, one hand shielding my eyes while the other reached out to grab her elbow, crushing her against my side just as a neon sign crashed to the ground. The entire place erupted in explosions as the island seemed to split down the middle and the base shifted. Sand began to well up between the cracks, "Fucking hell," I heard Sam gasp and followed the direction of her eyes.

Buildings burst and split part, sliding away like a great knife had spliced them in half. One half crumbled away into a land-slide, the rubble tumbled down the side of the island and sloshed into the gritty sea of sand waiting below. Rust red sand and smoke billowed up into the air, blinding us as we ran. The sound of rocks grinding against each other made it impossible to hear anything else, and the pounding of my heart thrummed in my head fuelled by adrenaline. Yanking the bandana up over my mouth and with a pistol in each hand and worn duster trailing behind I blazed across the remaining street. The very earth seemed to groan as another shudder rolled beneath my feet, momentarily lifting me up into the air before plummeting back down. I tucked and rolled across the pavement, sliding to a stop with guns at the ready. Tracing the outlines of the buildings I took in the lay of the land, or at least what remained of this end of the small desert island. This wasn't natural. Something was coming up from below, and I had to find it before it destroyed everything. Shit hole it might be it was still my home.

"Grey, over here!" I heard Sam yell from somewhere to my right and charged in that direction, boots pounding against the hard road as debris clouded the air and grit stung my eyes. The ground suddenly dropped sharply away, and I held my arms out to balance as I teetered on the edge of a gaping hole. Sparks from severed wires snapped at the air like snakes, twisting their plastic-sheathed bodies into knots. Water and sewage pipes spilt their contents into the maw that went down so far, I couldn't even see the bottom, only inky blackness. I lifted my eyes to the row of buildings on the other side. As my ears adjusted to the noise, I could hear screaming as people ran in panicked circles, not sure where to go or what to do.

We didn't get Earthquakes in the Atolls.

I stepped back from the canyon and frowned, wondering if I could jump the crevice before it grew any wider when a man barrelled past me. Reaching a hand out, I snagged him by the back of his jacket, knotting the fabric in my fist and yanking him back; saving him from plummeting to his death in the space of a heartbeat. The man stared at me, his jaw hanging slack at an odd angle with eyes glazed. Blood, wet and sticky, stained his greying hair and plastered it against his face and neck. His skin was red with dust and more blood. He began to tremble, his shoulders shaking so hard I could hear his teeth rattling together as his eyes bulged. Leaning down, I reached out a hand to assure him that I meant no harm.

But it wasn't me he was terrified of.

A shadow engulfed us; the man screamed and ran.

I turned, raising an arm to shield my eyes from the glaring sun that cut through the clouds of dust and turned the sky a hazy orange. A shadow, ominous and enormous, wove through the air. Dark and serpentine it passed between what was left of the buildings.

"Shit," I hissed through gritted teeth as the golden scales of an enormous desert viper slithered into view. Its wedge-shaped head reared above me as it's cotton white jaws opened wide. Sharp silver fangs glistened in the dust cut sunlight. They were as long as my arm and dripped with milky white venom. A small nick from those fangs would be enough to send a man into a spasming death. Unnaturally gold eyes stared into my face. The pupils were barely there; tiny slits in the giant orbs that glowed brilliantly. I couldn't look away, I imagined that if Camelia had a spirit animal, this would be it; terrifyingly beautiful but also profoundly unnatural. This wasn't an ordinary desert viper; this was an Evanescent Destroyer. A cyborg built from both cybernetic and living genetic materials beefed up on a bedrock of Roids and adrenaline; made for speed and destruction. They could be custom built to almost any shape or specification. Usually, the popular ones were the typical humanoid; they blended in better. Perfect for guard duty.

But occasionally people with too much money and time on their hands got fancy and went a little design crazy. More importantly, though, *what in the bloody hells is it doing here?* Evanescent Destroyers weren't your typical cyborgs. You didn't just send them out to wreak havoc. They always had a purpose; *what was this one here for?*

"Grey! Get the hell out of there, why are you just standing there staring at it?" Sam's voice cut into my thoughts, "Gods, you fucking idiot, *run!*"

[I'd listen to her Grey, get your ass in gear] Kato cut in and swooped down low, the tips of his wings pummelling lightly against my face as his talons tugged at my shorn hair before gliding back up to the safety of the skyline. Blinking hard I shook my head as the aura of the beast finally broke, and I ran.

CHAPTER 5

Spinning on the heel of a boot, I bolted up a slab of broken pavement that lay angled up into the air with one end rammed against a metal balustrade. Leaping up onto the railing, I ran horizontally away from the enormous viper. Its head turned in my direction. I stopped, bending my knees and taking aim with my pistol, held my breath for just a moment before breathing out and squeezing the trigger, the viper flinched as the bullet sunk into one of the thick scales that lined its nostrils.

Its forked tongue flicked in and out of its mouth as it tasted the air and caught my scent. Rising up on a coil of muscle and scale it burst into action as I turned and flew down the railing, leapt to the empty street below, and down an alley crowded with terrified people. Dodging past a line of crushed stalls with their bright awnings hanging in shreds I took another turn, recalling the hairs-breadth spaces between buildings that gave a quick escape from the law in my teens. Breath ragged and lungs screaming, I forced my body to keep moving. It was hard to breathe in the bandana, and the moisture of my breath made the fabric heavy. I yanked it off my face, letting it sag around my neck.

Dust burst in clouds from every direction as buildings crumbled while the viper worked its way between them. Its sinuous body slamming left and right leaving a trail of falling rubble and bursting metal archways that sent hapless passer-by falling to the street below. Where the alleys were too cramped for it to squeeze through it slithered over instead, the loops of its body crushing everything beneath its weight. Approximately two tons of cyborg snake came crashing after me, but even with the fear of being ground up in the gut of that cyborg behemoth, I knew I couldn't keep this up forever. *Why is it after me?* I didn't have a bounty on my head I was an Imperial Dune Buster. Slamming into the wall of the alley, I pressed my back against the cold stone.

The vines that hung around me stirred in the hot breeze, and I was grateful as the colder air wrapped around me, the deeper I went. Hard to believe I'd visited this place twice in one day but, Shady Plateau wasn't exactly the largest island in the Atolls of the Dune Sea. Over the decades most of the island itself had eroded away from harsh wind and the weight of the city on top. I tensed my shoulders and wrapped my fingers tightly around the pistols grip as the breeze changed direction, and the sliding of scale over concrete made my breath hitch.

It sounded like a knife on a whetstone and brought back memories of my father, back when he used to sit on the porch and run his bowie knife up and down the stone in the palm of his metal hand.

The viper entered behind me as ducked behind some crates and held my breath. I tilted my head back as its tapered snout hovered directly above my head. Its forked tongue dipped in and out a few times before it turned and left the alley. It wasn't after me if it was I'd already been dead. *Then who?* I ran an arm over my forehead, *Sam*, the scent of her had been all over me. The mist in the air must have washed it away. *Fucking hell.*

[Grey, we have a problem] Kato began.

I frowned and spun around, quickly [Yeah, I know. We got a pretty big fucking problem. Where am I going?] I asked and followed the skyeye's directions. Not that I needed them. All I had to do was follow the trail of destruction left in the wake of the giant viper, but if I kept doing that it will have already found Sam by the time we got there.

[K, find my girl. Where is she?]

[Your girl? I hardly think she would appreciate such language]

[Kato, find her for me before the viper does or I'll silence you for two weeks]

Kato went quiet, but I could hear his grumbling thoughts through our connection. Call me psychic, but for whatever reason, I was always able to quickly and deeply connect with my skyeye. The moment I activated Kato after purchasing him from the second-hand shop, I knew I'd made the right choice. He wasn't the newest upgrade, and he wasn't useful for much more than a GPS, but he was mine. He wasn't just a cyborg he was also a companion, my friend even, and I'd come to depend on him as much as he depended on me to maintain his charge and keep his gears well oiled.

Rounding the damaged corner of the Imperial Blimp Station, I frowned. It looked like Samantha already had the bright idea to catch a ride out of here, which meant she already knew that that thing was after her. But I had no idea why. A block of crumbling cement forced me to step away from the walls of the building, the sand polished marble of the vaulted roof had collapsed in on itself and stood in mockery of the Imperial Commissioner who had built it. The entire structure had been broken up from the vipers thrashing, and large chunks of marble and cement blocks were scattered across the central courtyard that rests directly in front of the station. On cooler days, which were rare, the yard acted as a gathering place for the locals and occasionally holiday performances might use the space for morale so long as the Commissioners had pre-approved the festivities. I shook my head when I saw the magnetic blimp tracks, embedded as they were in the polished stone that followed the length of the island before arching upwards and away to the sky above. Periodically, an extra-strong magnetic pulse would work to repel sand particles that gathered around the metal rods the blimp keels glided over. I could tell immediately by the gathering sand that they had been rendered useless, we wouldn't be getting out of here on a blimp. We needed a Plan B. But first, I had to make sure I even had a job to complete.

A deafening explosion erupted nearby. I dropped to the ground, hands clamped over my ears. Sand and stone were tossed up into the air, arced over my head, and came crashing down all around the piazza. Throwing my hands over my head, I held my hat on and shoved my pistol into my waistband and ran for cover as boulders slammed into the ground and shattered all around me. The air was thick with orange dust [Kato] I coughed, pulling the bandana up around my nose. But even the bandana wasn't keeping the finer particles from being sucked into my overworked lungs. The air grew hazy, making it difficult to see. I reached out to Kato again, mentally screaming, [I need visuals, I'm blind down here]

No reply.

Kato always replied. *Shit, this ain't good.*

I blinked my eyes, trying to clear my vision. This wasn't from the explosion. The grey cloud was most likely the dusting of magnetic particles from an EMbomb; sometimes used by the ICO Military and lower-level authorities to put out riots. It worked as a dampener field that jammed communication devices and worked to slow down the synaptic conversation between muscle and machine. It worked by shutting down an augmented individual, or in this case an augmented desert viper, forcefully. Perfect for breaking up gatherings of dissidents or the stray cyborg skaali.

I didn't know where it came from, but it didn't matter. The important thing was that it was doing its job as the giant viper slid into the centre of the courtyard and wound around its coils, its head weaving back and forth and tongue flicking like crazy as it tried to gather its bearings. One of the few weaknesses of the Evanescent Destroyer and Defender class robots was that they were easily reprogrammed and easily jammed. Often times, their creators pumped more time and money into their offensive aspects and not their defensive ones. It left them weaker than they seemed. This beast was no exception. It was blind in the cloud. Unfortunately, the bomb was also affecting communication between Kato and me.

Stumbling through the thick fog I made my way towards a row of shops that lined the far end of the courtyard, it was the only thing that seemed relatively untouched. The viper snapped its head up, and the golden orbs focused on me. It wasn't after me, but that wasn't going to stop it from taking me out either way now that is was in a foul mood.

I spun on my heel, drawing my pistol, and squeezed the trigger. And kept on squeezing.

Breathing out as I counted each spent round.

One, two, three.

Welts raised up on the skin of its serrated lip as purple liquid trickled down the sides of its jaw as it slithered towards me. *Purple nano-blood, definitely augmented.* I could see down the dark gullet as its throat fluttered in expectation and could practically hear the gears ready to grind me into mince-meat.

Four, five, click-click, *shit.*

I slid a hand into a pocket and withdrew several additional rounds of ammunition. Spinning the cylinder open and popping out the empty shells, I continued to step away from the viper, but for every foot, I gave, a foot it took. Achingly slow. Its pupils were tiny pinpoints of red light in gold that traced my every move and the sharp edges of its scaly lips were upturned in a strangely personal sneer, but I didn't have time to consider that further as I popped in the last of the rounds and raised the gun to fire.

Ka-boom!

My ears rang. My teeth rattled in their sockets. Blinding light and a deafening roar made me drop to one knee and squeeze my eyes shut. I curled in on myself. Lifting my eyes just enough to see past my knees. *What the hell?* Flames of white shot through with blue engulfed the viper as its head was slammed into the ground with an unseen force. The viper's body thrashed wildly, twisting itself into knots as the flames rippled across its body and ice burst along its skin, ripping it apart. The blast was both burning hot and freezing cold in alternating waves. Golden scales turned scorched brown and black as sections of skin sloughed away to reveal the separate parts of smooth bio-plastic shell wrapped around an adamantium skeletal frame. Recovering quickly despite the wounds, the viper reared up and swung its snout in the direction of its attacker. As it moved, I could see its face had been mostly torn away to reveal a sickening mixture of flesh and reinforced bone. The glint of the metallic pistons of its jaws pumped as the fangs snapped open and closed rhythmically, their springs broken. Poison foam bubbled out one side of its mouth and the forked tongue sagged through a gaping hole in the underside of its slender jaws. Sputtering, the viper scuttled forward, its body undulating across the rubble in a jerking motion; nowhere near as smooth as it was only half a minute ago. Whatever that weapon was, it was fucking powerful. But the viper was still deadly even in this wretched condition. A glint of light caught my eye, and I traced it back to the same direction the viper was now headed, leaving a trail of steaming venom and other body fluids in its wake. Sam knelt on a stone rampart; one arm was thrown around an exposed rebar wire to keep her balance as she held the shotgun up. That was one hell of a blast from a gun like that, even one with bind runes carved into its side. The rune-guns were powerful sure, there was a reason they'd been outlawed. But even a rune-gun wouldn't make an explosion like that.

As the last of the grey mist began to drift away Kato's voice began to cut through the static,

[Be careful] he said [not just runes] he screeched as his shadow passed overhead. Circling down he landed on my outstretched arm and tapped his beak anxiously on my shoulder, even in such close proximity the aftereffects of the magnetic smoke screen was still making it hard to communicate.

[Spells, she has spell bullets, powerful ones. You need to get out of the way] my eyes went wide as his words sunk in and I flicked my head up to the slender woman as she waited for the viper to get closer. The twin barrels glowed a pale blue as the runes etched on their sides began to activate again, a disk of archaic symbols with filaments of psychic prana bloomed outwards as the round entered the chamber, changing to a purple glow tinged with orange and red. There wasn't time to act, [Shit, Kato, hang on] my mind screamed as I quickly grasped the skyeye in both hands and curled my body around him, tucking him protectively up to my chest as I hunkered down as tightly as I could. Despite having my eyes squeezed shut the blast of white light, blinded me and my ears hummed with the subsequent explosion. I couldn't hear anything. My body felt heavy, numb, *frozen.*

When I opened my eyes, I realised the blinding whiteness wasn't from light. Snow fell around my shoulders. Swirling through the air, it rested in thick and frozen clumps over the ground and covered the ledges of buildings and the ruins of the train station in crystalline ice cycles. I stood and looked down at Kato. He rested on his back in my hands with his talons curled up in the air and eyes large. He blinked slowly up at me and looked so ridiculous I couldn't help but laugh, "That was one hell of a blast," I said, grateful that the bandana disguised my smile. [No, shit. I wanted to warn you. You're lucky it didn't fry your face off, but then, it might be an improvement]

[Hey, not nice. But, your sense of humour is expanding sort of] I said. [Thank you, I try] he replied as I placed him back on my shoulder.

It was true, in the last several months since getting Kato his personality matrix had expanded exceptionally fast considering he was an older model, and second hand to boot. I sometimes wondered what he was like with his previous owner, *Nah, it doesn't matter, he's mine now, and I'd never give him up.* Besides, having had his data wiped before the sale, we would never know.

Snow crunched beneath my feet as I stood and walked towards the massive form of the viper, covered in snow and ice, the inky nano-blood had formed a frozen puddle around its head and parts of its body. I tapped it with the metal toe of one boot before following the sinuous shape the rest of the way to its head. A slight movement in the snow made me jump back, instinctively raising my pistol only to see Samantha as she dug in the snow. I nodded to her in recognition and lowered the weapon, but only by an inch. Sam sat on her knees in the ice with a scowl on her face as she examined what was left of the vipers' skull. It was huge. The flat of its head was as long as I stood tall, roughly six foot two, with jaws half as wide. It must have slithered up through the sewage system to reach the surface of the island without being seen. My eyes scanned the ground, I didn't see the rune-gun, but I approached Sam cautiously either way, "Where's the rune-gun?"

"Up there somewhere," she said, waving a hand towards the ledge she'd been perched on when the viper took the full blast of a spell bullet to its face, "It's useless now. I don't have any more spell shells for it." I nodded, didn't matter; it was dangerous and was highly illegal, and I didn't believe her for one second. Spell weapons imported from the Herth Kaddîska homeworld were often unstable, prone to exploding or worse, creating a temporary vacuum that sucked everything in till collapsing in on itself. Sam was lucky the damn thing didn't blow up in her face, or I'd be hauling her ass around in a bucket of melted ice and entrails.

I sent Kato off to collect the discarded rune-gun. Standing beside Sam, I wrinkled my nose in disgust as she suddenly thrust a hand into the skull, edging her way around the plastic eye-socket. She forced her arm in all the way up to her elbow, causing one giant golden orb to pop out and roll across the melting snow beside her thigh, tethered to its host with a bundle of goopy wires.

I kicked the eye aside and knelt down next to her, "So, what're you doing?" I asked, trying to sound casual and nonchalant despite the churning sensation in my stomach as fluid and flesh squelched around Samantha's elbow as she worked further in. She grunted with the effort, her sharp teeth grit together as she gripped the ridge of the socket with her other hand for leverage. I pulled down the bandana still wrapped around my face for just in case I couldn't hold the rising bile back. The acrid smell of snake musk and seared flesh attacked my nostrils the moment I did so, and I regretted the choice, turning my head and spitting on the ground to keep from vomiting.

Voices and shouts of surprised joy echoed across the snow-covered courtyard as people began to realise the danger was over and materialised from their hiding places. Some walked with their hands and tongue out to catch the last of the icy flakes as they drifted to the ground among the rubble. I noticed then the Kit'th guards I'd seen before standing at the edge of the ruined blimp station. Their mistress was standing with her arms crossed and steel gaze levelled on me. I narrowed my eyes; I was sure I knew this woman or I'd at least seen her somewhere. *In Centrum perhaps?*

Her blonde, nearly silver, hair was plaited in a long braid over one shoulder, the leather armour she wore was polished to a soft sheen and moulded to her skin. Decorated with cabochons of brass and gold. With leather, lace pulled taught across her bust. From the pauldron of her left shoulder drifted a caplet of bright red fabric. The Kit'th stood with their black noses twitching in the air with whiskers drawn up to fan around their faces. They seemed uncomfortable, and for a good reason, their species abhorred magic. Ever since the Sydian Wars of 4506c. Kit'th swore off all magic and cut all ties to their deities, overthrowing their religious leaders and bringing the production of rune-guns and the magically charged spell bullets to a halt. Rumour has it that Spurtown was still in a good supply of the rare weapons, but no one was positive.

Over time, the further the Kit'th drifted from their home planet, the more quickly magic was abandoned. Remarkably few Kit'th exhibited the trait to wield magic these days, and those that do are either abandoned by their family at birth or put to death, they didn't want to risk breeding the trait back into their colonies.

The snow was already melting in the oppressive heat and children ran to dash through the wet slush while others gathered buckets to collect the precious liquid while it was still frozen. Shady Plateau was mostly rubble, but it was more or less intact. The infrastructure seemed to have survived most of the damage, and it wouldn't be long before the people rebuilt and got on with their lives. It's what you did out here. You either kept an eye to the future, or you died with the past.

Sam continued to dig around in the viper's skull, and the squelching noises continued. Thick purple goo and strings of something yellow gushed around her shoulder, soaking the shirt she wore and splashing across her breasts, she ignored me.

I coughed, “Seriously, what the fuck are you doing, Sam?” I pressed a first to my chin, trying not to gag.

“I’m trying to confirm something,” she said, ducking her head down to look up into the space she had carved out, “Son-of-a-bitch. I *knew* it. Those bastards, what the hell were they thinking. As if I wouldn’t know.”

I quirked an eyebrow, “Pardon?”

“I can’t believe this shit,” she said and with a grunt began tugging on something deep inside the skull. There was an audible *pop,* and when she withdrew her slime-covered arm, she held what looked like a piece of brain tissue roughly the size of her palm. It was cylindrical in shape with strings of cyber-filaments that hung down, their ends still twitching as they continued to fire synapses. She grimaced, the edge of her lip curling up as she picked the brain matter away until all that was left was a small clear capsule, no bigger than my index finger. There was something inside. The filaments seemed to originate from the capsule until Sam twisted each one until it snapped off and then, with both hands straining, twisted the plastic pill open and dumped the contents to the ground. It was filled with a series of microchips and other micro-machinery; a tiny red light was blinking. Clearly, it was a signal of some type, but I wasn’t sure why or for whom it was intended.

Kato returned, the rune-gun dangled in his firm grip, and I took it from him, breaking it open and confirming that the rounds had been spent. I held a hand out to Sam, “The spell bullets, hand them over,” I said. She didn’t even look at me as she reached into her thigh pocket and handed me a single bullet. It was heavy, the pointed end carved with runes and other symbols. Otherwise, it looked like a standard bullet.

Samantha continued to dig around the vipers' guts as I pocketed the shell.

[Kato are you recording this?] I asked as his talons dug into my shoulder. He turned his body around for a better look. Perched next to my ear, I could hear the whirring of his parts as his cyber optic eyes focused on it [Got it, Grey. I'll run a scan and see if I can locate who the signal is intended for.] I nodded, "Good boy," I said aloud, and Sam tilted her head back to look at me funnily as she began to use the melting snow to scrub clean her arms and hands, "Not you. Kato. He's my skyeye. He's recording everything for posterity," I said. She looked at me and then Kato as if noticing the cyborg for the first time, "Good. Record this, I want them to know I won't go down without a fight," she said, squeezing her hands into a fist. She slammed the heel of her boot into the mess of wires, twisting her ankle back and forth until the chips and tendrils had been all but ground to dust, "Takes care of that. For now, anyway," she said and rested her hands on her hips and grinned. But when her eyes met mine, she dropped the smile. Remembering again who I was and what I was there for when I lifted the cuffs into the air. I step towards her, "Do we really need to do this again?" I asked, hoping against hope that for once just one of them would come peacefully. Tilting her head to one side, she pushed back the long strands of her bangs and tucked them behind her ears. Green eyes flashed as she looked me over before nodding, "Alright. I give up," she held out her hands, palms down. I narrowed my eyes in suspicion, tilting my head to the side as I scratched at the scruff of beard along my jaw. Red flags went up in my thoughts. *She's up to something.* No one changed their mind. They always ran, always.

Samantha continued, "But once we get there, you'll be clearing my name and making arrests you'd never dreamed of," she grinned and wriggled her fingers at me as if waiting for a damn ring. I smiled back as I snapped the cuffs around her slender wrists and cocked my head to one side, "I highly doubt that," I said. Samantha snickered and winked an eye. She seemed to be in good humour considering an Evanescent Destroyer had just taken down half the plateau to try and kill her. I was starting to wonder why the viper was after her but cut the thought off, *not my business*. My job was to retrieve her alive and bring her back to Centrum then collect my pay and get on with my life. End of story. But fuck it all was I wrong about that.

CHAPTER 6

Untying the bandana from around my face, I snapped it in the air, sending a cloud of dust across the desk before stuffing it into a pocket and slumping onto the hotel bed. Briefly, I wished I had just gone ahead paid the extra coin for a bigger room. But, based on Tyler's continued hostility, I got the feeling that no matter what I'd spent, this was exactly the room I'd get. The kid was none too happy about my presence here, especially when I had walked back through the doors with a cuffed and grinning Samantha.

"Hey there, Tyler," she had said brightly and waved at him with a cuffed hand. The boy had raised his brows as his jaw dropped in shock before his eyes shot up to mine and he sneered, "Hullo Sam," he said, but his eyes never left mine, "Lawman," he greeted me with an incline of his head. "See you around My-ty," she quipped as I pushed her past the counter and back towards my room. Tyler leaned over the counter to watch as we entered the room, shouting, "You scream if he tries anything, Sammie."

I shook my head. The problem with being in a small town like this was that everyone knew everyone and everyone's business. I was positive that young barkeep was running his mouth off to anyone who came through those doors. The entire town probably already knew an Imperial Dune Buster had come to bust someone.

Samantha settled on the small chair at the desk, the cuffs clinking against each other as she crossed her arms as best as she could, "So, you wanna know what that thing was right? Why it was after me?"

"Nope," I said, pulling my duster off and tossing it onto the desk. After today events I would be more than happy to get the hell out of here before some other insane thing could happen. But seeing as how the blimp station was destroyed that wasn't going to happen anytime soon. Sam frowned, "Really? You're not curious at all?"

"Oh, I'm curious alright, but it ain't my business and I've no intention of making it my business," I said with a snort, falling back on the bed and pulling my hat down over my brow. Kato sat on the foot of the bed, his eyes trained on our enthusiastic prisoner. [She's up to something Grey, I know it.] I nodded beneath my hat, the smell of the old hide and shampoo filling my nostrils, [You don't say?]

[That signal, Grey, I was able to track it down. It was from the Imperial Commissioners Office] he said. That made me pause, I titled the hat back enough to look at him. *Why would the ICO hire me to come and collect her but also take the time and money to wire a cyborg for the job?*

That was highly unusual. [Hmm. Keep an eye on her Kato, we'll be heading out at first sign of daylight] Kato hooted gently in reply, and I heard the sound of Samantha shifting her position in the chair.

Kato hooted softly as he said,, [How? You can't hail a blimp with the tower down. They wouldn't come anyway without a dock.]

I nodded without a word slipping my face beneath my hat and closing my eyes, [Don't worry. I'll figure something out. I always do, right?] I said. Kato tapped his beak against the bed frame, [Knock on wood] he chuckled.

A smile broke across my face as I laughed unconsciously.

"What are you two talking about? Don't be shy," Sam interrupted. I lifted my hat to glance out the corners of my eyes at her. "We're discussing how we're going to get out of here. I'll probably hire a ride with a caravan," I said, "But no telling how long till the next one arrives, and I'm on a deadline."

I didn't like the idea of waiting around, much less take a caravan. The caravans were often targeted by dune raiders and rouge skaali, but it was generally accepted as one of the safest ways to travel the wastelands. Sam crossed her legs and huffed, tossing her head to the side to swing her long bangs out of her eyes, "You could, or I could save you some time and money. I have a better idea,"

"Really now?"

"I happen to own a shop here you know, or did they not tell you that I specialise in reptilian augmentation?"

I slid my hat all the way back, letting the sandy-blonde strands of my bangs hang over my eyes. Now I was interested. Propping myself up on my elbows, I motioned for her to continue. I knew I shouldn't get involved but, "I'm assuming then that the viper was your work?" I asked. She nodded, pulling her legs up onto the stool she sat crossed-legged, "Bingo. Around four months ago, I was hired to wet-wire and augment that viper. The client asked that I enhance its speed, strength, tracking, the usual spy type stuff. I always install a tracking device. The capsule you saw," she continued, "But, what I don't tell them is that my little tracking device is also continuously sending information back to me, you know, just in case I need some data to cover my ass," she grinned like she was a fucking genius. She wasn't, she was fucking insane. It was as illegal as hell to record information without another's knowledge. And the political climate of Terrafirma V it was a life sentence of servitude in the prisons of Watchtower Plateau.

Not denying that others don't do it all the time, but generally, no one would be stupid enough to admit to it, especially not to an Imperial Dune Buster. I shook my head. I could already figure out the rest of the story, it didn't take a genius to figure out Sam had been caught collecting information she shouldn't have, and the employer turned her creation right back on her. With a sigh, I settled back down onto the hard mattress and closed my eyes. Samantha waited a moment silently when I stopped probing for more info. The cuffs clinked together as she moved, sucking in a breath she said, "I have a garage full of augmented skaali."

The night went by quickly enough with Kato waking us up as soon as the twin suns rays made their first splash across the rusty sands. As we left the hotel, avoiding Tyler's evil eye, the heat slammed into my body like walking into a stone wall. It was already making me feel miserable, and I'd only been up an hour. I'd been spoilt living in the continental cities, with their giant fans pumping cold air between the buildings. Large cities on the mainland, like Centrum, had the advantage of accumulated wealth that allowed for publicly accessible luxuries like that. Mainland meaning the last vast expanses of earth that weren't covered in dust and dry heat, raised above the deserts as they were. I was born and raised in the Atolls, but I didn't miss them. I'd be grateful to land my feet back in Centrum where an apartment with easy access to clean water, a hot shower, and cold air awaited my return.

With Samantha in the lead, we worked our way towards the aft end of the island where a series of warehouses lined the central road. Stopping in front of one, she lifted a cuffed hand to the electronic door pad. It scanned her hand. The lock popped open with a click and, reaching down, she rolled the sliding metal door up and into the roof,

"Hello babies, I'm home!" she called out and was answered by the roars of several very hungry sounding skaali. They were velociraptors. Their distinctively shrill cries set my heart to pounding as the blood drained from my face. There was a reason we let these things die out and yet here we were today, using old technologies combined with new ones to re-create fucking dinosaurs for the sole purpose of riding them off into the desert and praying they didn't decide to eat you. I stood just outside the garage door, rooted in place, "You didn't say they were raptors," I said, my voice accusing. Samantha smirked, grabbing ahold of my elbow and pulling me inside, she slapped a button, and the door rolled back down behind me, "You didn't ask," she said with a grin. Sam held her cuffed hands out to me, "You mind? I can't work like this."

I frowned. Sam tilted her head to one side, "Really, Grey? I said I was coming willingly."

I nodded, "Okay. But if you run I've got no problem putting a bullet through your calf. They said to bring you in alive and unharmed, but even that has its limits," I said, an unlocked the links, shoving them into my pocket. She busted away, and the roads grew louder in response.

Kato's eyes focused on me, [Careful Grey, she might have more rune-guns. This place has been reinforced with a magnetic dampener. I can't scan it] he warned. I shooked my head, [Doubtful, those things are rare. I've only seen one other in my lifetime] I said, leaving it at that. I didn't want to discuss the past right now. The butt of the rune-gun rest against my shoulder alongside the modernised Winchester rifle I favoured. Kato flew off my shoulder and settled in the rafters of the garage, [Oh, my] he said and hooted loudly.

I wrinkled my nose. The smell of reptile mixed with hot air and hay was tangy. I pulled the bandana down as I stepped further inside. My eyes winced against the musk of the beasts. "Fucking hell," I breathed out, the entire garage had been outfitted for performing augmentation surgeries. On one side of the warehouse, a series of desks with computers and a series of machines lined the wall. I could identify and autoclave, thermocycler, a centrifuge, a whole series of microscopes and literally hundreds of glass beakers, bottles and pipettes in neat metal compartmented racks. There was an operation table, its porcelain sides stained pink from years of surgery, in the centre of the room. It was oversized, made for large animals. On the wall nearby hung wicked-looking instruments along with rubber aprons and gloves, a few pairs of goggles. A gas mask for working with harsh chemicals, its filters as large as a fist rest on the swivel chair pushed back beneath them. It was completed with a cold storage cooler, and walk-in freezer with clear glass allowed me to see that she had been stocked with a series of blood bags and various medicine bottles and vaccinations.

Samantha was definitely outfitted for more than the run of the mill bio-mechanic chop-shop. She was the real deal.

Yup, Frankenstein.

The opposite side of the warehouse was lined with six holding units, square-shaped with thick metal walls and shatterproof glass on the front. Its transparent surface was scratched in places, especially around the ventilation holes. Only three of the units were occupied, and Sam was already pressed against the door of the first one. She knocked on the glass, the raptor stood with its head a good three feet above Sam's. Its long and feathered tail wagged like a dog as slender three-fingered hands clicked together in excitement while the large sickle-shaped back toe-claws trembled, causing them to tap on the hay covered cement floor in an erratic rhythm. From the looks of them, they were more cyborg than a dinosaur, you couldn't even call them a dinosaur really, hence the reason people took to calling them skaali.

[Kato, let's be careful here] I said. He hooted in response, saying [I'm already speaking to this one. She is thrilled to see Samantha. They are hungry.]

I frowned; three hungry skaali couldn't be good, [These things can fucking speak?] I asked, incredulous.

[Not like I can. It's a series of images and impressions shared over our established commlink. She cannot understand human speech, and she is most likely incapable of the level of interaction that I am] Kato finished. I nodded, that made more sense. These things were rigged with communication implants and no telling what else, *interesting.* I stayed back, clenching my fists nervously. I didn't like skaali. I'd heard of and investigated the aftermath of, what happened when one of these things went crazy. It wasn't pretty. Worse cases were the skaali who'd been fully augmented with weaponry. And not just lasers but also things like a poisonous bite and claws of adamantine that could cut through flesh like a knife through a cake, maybe a cannon or two hidden somewhere in their metallic and bone frames. Mainly the raptors were used for transportation. But that didn't make them any less formidable.

Sam pressed her hand onto the identity pad in the wall nearby, and all three doors clicked open. I took another step back as my fingers fluttered over the grip of my pistols. On my back. The skaali all screeched. It echoed off the walls of their units as they rushed out, surrounding Sam. They circled her and bobbed their heads as they ran their metallic lower jaws over the top of her head, nuzzled her shoulders and hands. Their noises soon settled to a deep purring sound as they settled down, wrapping their feathered tails around where she stood and forming a protective circle.

All three sets of eyes turned and stared at me, I could see the irises twisting open and closed as the bionic mechanisms within focused on me. The shallow holes along each side of their lower jaws told me they were armed. The skaali watched me, wary, and were most likely already searching databases for information. Unconsciously I reached into my jacket, moving slowly, and felt my badge resting in my upper breast pocket of the vest I wore beneath. What they didn't know wouldn't get me killed.

Samantha tapped a spot on her neck that looked like a mole, just beneath her earlobe. A small red light began to glow from beneath her skin, accessing her commlink, she spoke aloud. It was for my sake more than anything as I stood with my back against the garage door.

"Alright, settle down. This is my friend. He's here to help us," she said and then looked pointedly at me, "Even if he doesn't know he is," she smiled. The largest of the skaali stood and rested its narrow chin, the metal teeth glinting, on Sam's shoulder. The sharp rows of alabaster and silver resting only an inch from her face, all it would take was a quick snap, and that'd be the end of Samantha Cowell.

She smiled and rubbed a hand over the skaali's neck, scratching its mottled brown and red hide affectionately, "This is Ruff," she said, "Alright then, let's get ya'll fed and tacked. We've got a long way to travel."

CHAPTER 7

The skaali waited patiently as Sam saddled each one and adjusted the specially made bridals around their pointed snouts. Strands of beads clicked together around their nose, eyes, and ears to keep the flies away. The saddles were laden with storage packs and a sealed case for supplies. I watched as Samantha checked on each raptor personally, making sure the leather tack was comfortable, and their saddle blankets weren't riding up beneath the seats.

The stirrups barely reached their knees. Samantha vaulted up onto her skaali with familiar ease, her legs spread wide over its barrel chest. I tried hard not to stare as the denim shorts she'd insisted on changing into rode uncomfortably high into her butt crack, exposing more cheek to the sun than the wide-brim hat on her head ever would. The brown leather vest she wore over a black bandeau top was snug over her breasts, and her slim waist was wrapped with an ammunition belt that didn't take anything away from each curve. On the back of her saddle, affixed to the rounded cantle was an umbrella with its hood tied shut with twine. Her long legs were bare except for the boots laced up past her calves, the metal toes shone in the sunlight despite having started to turn black with age. I coughed, "Don't you think you'll get a little sunburnt like that?" I asked. Sam grinned and resting her hat on her skaali's head, she reached into a sack, unrolling a long bundle of tan fabric that she pulled over her head. A poncho. It covered her all the way down to her knees. Adjusting it, she winked as she placed her hat back onto her head, "You done staring?" she asked. I turned away, denying that I'd been looking. She'd grown into herself over the years, and I wasn't so cold as to not appreciate that.

The skaali, Ruff, reached back to snip at Sams' booted foot playfully and ruffled the crest of red feathers that trailed from the top of his head to stop between his shoulder blades. Nervous at first, I climbed into the saddle of the larger female raptor Sam had assigned to me. She had seemed the most curious about me, and when the communication link information was exchanged, and I was able to access the data flow, I immediately transferred the info to Kato as well so that the three of us could stay in touch and share information. It was strange, feeling a skaali in my head.

Unlike Kato, she didn't know how to control her thoughts, and the constant flow of images and raw emotions bounced over my own. It was annoying at first. I really didn't need an update on every time she needed to take a shit. Which was surprisingly often. After a while, I began to filter out unnecessary commentary to focus on the important stuff. Such as that she liked to be scratched in the small pin-feathers behind her ear holes where the bridle irritated them and that Samantha called her Tweet because of the low whistling noise she often made.

"Tweets' a good girl, you'll like her. Plus, beneath all that scaly skin and feathers she's running on a fully integrated adamantium frame laced with sensors, cyber-filament nervous system and dual mini-cannons in the nasal cavity and a large-bore shotgun mounted in the roof of her mouth. It's a rune-gun, FYI," she said with a wink, "so don't waste it, they ain't cheap," she said.

I shook my head in amazement, "How the hell did you mount a rune-gun in a skaali? What about the spell bullets? How the hell do they eat?" I asked as my eyebrows shot up to my hairline. With hands wrapped tightly around the reigns, I guided Tweet out the garage door.

Same chuckled, "That's a trade secret. The rune-gun is limited though. Tweet can only use it once, just two rounds," she said. I nodded; it was an emergency weapon. Made sense but still I'd love to know-how in the hell she managed to get a hold of enough rune-guns with their highly coveted spell bullets to be wasting them on goddamned skaali augmentations. It's probably part of why the ICO wanted Sam brought in on such strict terms and why she's so damn desperate to see them. I'd never had a prisoner who actually wanted to be turned in, and all my senses were telling me this was going to end badly. *Not your business, Grey. Just check-in and then check right out.*

Once we were good and ready, we continued down the main road, people gawked but moved aside, usually sporting an uneasy smile as they nodded at Sam and I. The third skaali was loaded down with more supplies and his reins tied to the horn of Sam's saddle so that he was kept close by.

She refused to leave him behind since she couldn't guarantee that any of her folk would come and feed the skaali.

"What's that one's name?" I asked, she looked over at the bag laden raptor and reached out to scratch his chin. He was a bit smaller than the others, maybe still a chick, he might not have augmentations even, she smiled fondly at the smaller skaali, "Oh, that's Jimmy," she said and continued to scratch its chin. I made a face, "Jimmy? Really? What was he named after, an old boyfriend?" I asked, the sarcasm causing my voice to drop an octave as I peered at Sam from beneath my brow. Sam nodded again, "Maybe he was, what's it to you? Jealous?" I scoffed and shook my head as she gazed at the purring raptor; scratching around the massive scales surrounding his eyes. Exhaling loudly, I snapped my reins, "Alright then, Jimmy. Ruff. Tweet. Let's mosey on along now."

With that, we set our skaali to a loping gallop down the main street, through what remained of the blimp station court, and towards the edge of the plateau. Sam waved at a few people, blew a kiss to one, and I tilted the brim of my hat politely while tugging on my bandana. I made sure it was tight enough to keep out the blowing sand. Sam did the same. On our foreheads, beneath the rims of our hats, rest the dark lens of goggles specially designed to protect our eyes from the sand, winds, and the harsh desert sun. You didn't want to be out in the wastelands without something to keep the dust from clogging up all the holes in your body.

The main street ended abruptly at a cliff-side but a path tread by many feet over the decades had been carved into the side of the cliff. I remembered when I was a kid, we used to stand on the edge of the plateau and stare out over the rolling sand dunes. It felt like we were at the precipice of the world. A neat line that separated our lives from the oceans of dirt and cracked earth but all the dangers of the wastes didn't seem so bad when you were living with someone that made sure, every single day, that you knew your life was in their hands. My Pa was a cruel man.

One day, after an unusually hard beating, I sat at the edge of the cliff. Fuming with unspent rage. My face stung every time I touched it, and I was sure my nose was broken; it was swollen, and the straight line of it wasn't so straight anymore. My knuckles were scratched and bleeding, and my knees banged up after he'd shoved me down. I'd rolled over and kicked him square in the balls only, he didn't drop like people said they would when you did that, nope, instead, it was like dousing a fire with kerosene. He was all fury and fumes, and I'd paid for it dearly. I could feel things shifting inside that I knew shouldn't be moving around. I had run off as quickly as I could manage, leaving him behind screaming and cursing up a storm until I'd come to the edge and wondered how much easier it would be to just step off the side and let the desert take me. But then there was Natalie. And she'd convinced me otherwise.

That day, as I sat on a ledge of rock that jutted out over the path below, Nat found me. I kept inching closer to the edge and had just about decided to jump when she had gripped my shoulder so tightly, I thought it was my Pa come to shove me off. I wasn't about to let him make this choice for me. I yelled out in anger, raising my fists defensively when Natalie jumped back and grabbed both my wrists, pulling me into her and wrapping her arms around me. She stood there on the edge of the plateau with the wind tearing at her dress and hugged me tightly. My chest felt like it had exploded by the time I was done shedding all the tears I'd held back. Tears for my dead Ma and the wretched situation my Pa had put us in. I breathed in the scent of Natalie's hair, her skin, and I knew then that I wanted to be with her forever. Natalie was my first love, my first *everything*.

And then she left.

Samantha turned to me and smiled as the breeze that gusted up over the side of the plateau made her hair lift up and away from her face. Like a shadow of that pivotal day. Her tawny skin was already sparkling with sweat and gave it a copper sheen that begged to be touched. Sam inclined her head, closing her eyes a moment to enjoy the only breeze you could find in Shady Plateau. "Penny for your thoughts?" she asked, sliding her eyes to mine. I pressed my lips together and shook my head, tearing my eyes from hers and trying my damnedest not to look guilty. She'd gone from ugly duckling to swan over the years, and I was confident she knew this, "I reckon I've more thoughts than you've got pennies and, once we're in Centrum, you're going to need all the pennies you have," I replied turning the mood sour. Sam tilted her head back and looked at me down the bridge of her nose, "You really think so, don't you? Huh, you're a looker, Grey. I'll give you that," she said with a snort, "But you're dense as hell," she put it bluntly and snapped her reigns. As she pulled ahead of me, she chuckled to herself, "It's always the pretty ones."

Scratching the feathers of Tweets neck, I grinned, "Aint that the damned truth," I agreed, earning a double-take from Sam.

Guiding our skaali rides around wind-swept boulders and steep inclines, we rode. The rusty ground growing closer by the hour as warm air gushed around us. It swept from the base of the island and up the side of the cliffs, carrying dust to settle over the small city above. At the bottom of the path was an encampment of men and women who guarded the road against would-be raiders. The guards maintained both the entry gate and the watchtowers set in a ring that was spread out roughly two hundred feet or so all around the island. If raiders or stray skaali attacked, they'd light the beacons in the towers to alert the island residents to prepare their defences. It worked out well enough. I couldn't remember suffering any attacks in my time.

The sun was still high by the time we reached the bottom. Here, on the backside of the plateau, the sun was mostly hidden by the island itself lending shade to the series of buildings that made up the guard compound. After a quick talking to and a flash of my badge, they let us through the gates with a warning about sightings of sandworms and wild Tyrants. That piqued my interest. The random raider party or two was pretty much the usual news, but a large skaali like a Tyrant was something to pay attention to. We stopped long enough at the package store to double-check our supplies before turning our noses to the wide-open space that was the Dune Sea of Terra firma V.

THE DUNE SEA

CHAPTER 8

I rolled my eyes for the hundredth time as Kato continued to complain, buried in the folds of my duster, [I knew this was a bad idea, Grey].

With my bandana up, goggles down, and my hat pressed down tightly over my head, we walked with our flanks towards the wind that gusted through the area, tearing at our clothes. I knew that later we'd find sand in all the places you didn't want it to get. The three skaali blinked their large eyes slowly, the transparent membranes of their second eyelids working to maintain their vision despite the clouds of sand and dirt rushing by. Still, we continued on, and when the winds finally died down, we were left in the sweltering heat. Lifting my goggles, I shook my head and sand that fell from the wide brim of my hat. I unwrapped my bandana long enough to shake it clean before wrapping it around my neck. This far out the winds had died down, and Rust Lung wasn't as much a threat. Kato wormed his way out from his hiding spot. Settling down, he proceeded to groom the filaments of his feathers and rearranging them.

From out of the sand the rusted shell of a ship, the metal hull long turned from silver to a red and brown patina rose like a monument to the past. It rested on its side, and the large flat surface of its flight deck had been ripped open, most likely by a dune worm looking for food despite the carrier having been a rusted heap of junk for centuries.

The Dune Sea had dried up nearly two hundred year ago on the surface, beneath the ground was another story, but that didn't stop the worms from searching every old-world rust bucket they found. Their blind eyes relying on sound and touch to tell them what was edible or not. Most things were edible to those damned worms. Thankfully they were a rare sight as they stayed mostly deep underground where moisture and underground streams could still be found.

Samantha pulled the reins, and her skaali snorted as he pawed the ground, his sickle claw tapping with impatience. Looking up, Sam shielded her eyes with one hand and scanned the sky. A lone sand-kite with its wings spread wide made lazy circles in the distance. "We should set up camp soon, the shade of that old tanker will do nicely," she said. I looked at it doubtfully.

[It is roughly two-point-three miles away. We could get there in twenty-five minutes at our current luxurious pace] Kato said. "Alright, I need to check my map and get our bearings while there's still a bit of daylight left anyway," I agreed and, picking Kato up from my shoulder, tossed him into the air. His white underbelly flashed as his wings caught the warm updrafts. I watched his small form glide towards the ship to perch an a piece of metal that jutted up from the sands nearby. I needed to get a hold of Camelia to request an extension on my contract time. Now that I was relying on travel by skaali, this was going to take me a few extra days, and with three days already gone, the deadline was going to be tighter than I'd have liked. I glanced over at Samantha. With her goggles and hat hanging around her neck she stood up in her stirrups, a hand shielding her eyes as she observed the horizon. I kept my face neutral and reached out to Kato.

[K, link me up with the ICO rep office. I need to speak to Camelia] I said as our skaali continued towards the rusted ship with its promise of shade. He was silent for a long moment, [Kato?]

[Apologies, Grey, I appear to be unable to make a connection. It might be interference from that metal relic your insisting on camping beneath. I will try again in three minutes] I nodded, [Do that. I don't want my ass getting handed to me if I can't deliver the girl in the next five days. I'd like to keep my license] I said with a nod. Kato grunted, [Honestly, Camelia has had it out for you since the beginning. Who expects a contract in the wastelands to be completed in only eight days?]

[Camelia does. ICO does. And I intend to deliver.]

[If you say so, Grey. I've got my opinions.]

[Don't even get into –]

"Your whispering about me again, aren't you?" Sam chimed in, breaking my thought stream. I turned around in my saddle too quickly, causing Tweet to jump as I tugged the reigns with an unpracticed hand. I wasn't new to riding skaali, but it wasn't exactly something I did every day either. I looked at Sam, "You're just a mighty bit too perceptive for my comfort," I stated. I was beginning to wonder if she had a hack device that allowed her to hear our private communications. Without direct access or permissions the only other people who could listen in where the random drop-ins by ICO authorities and even then it was rare. But, in the past, more than one person had been taken down by information gained over a hacked commlink.

There was one particular case I dealt with several years back where some poor sap had been hacked by his own girlfriend. She gave him a nasty virus that periodically reset his internal clock by a year, in the past, his brain was literally going back in time as it began to delete his essential functions. It's a risk you run when you decide to go full cyborg but also part of why integrated electronics is so heavily regulated, restricted and the laws reinforced. In a matter of a month, he'd gone from one of the most feared names in Solace to the saddest grifter you ever saw. These days the man sits in a catatonic state, his entire consciousness self-deleted. Last I heard his old buddies were using him as a centrepiece at the bar they frequent, a living statue. If you could call that living.

Samantha shrugged her shoulders with palms up, "No sir, I'm just good at reading the air," she smiled and gave me a slow wink, managing to be both sassy and sexy. *Fuck*. I narrowed my eyes at her and opened my mouth to say something when Kato alerted me to a message, [Grey, it's Camelia] I held a finger up to Sam, "One moment. I've gotta take this call, and yes, it's about you," I said and turned away.

[This is Grey, I've a request to make]

[Grey, I'm hurt. Not even a hello, how are you Camelia?]

Camelias voice came smoothly across the link. Yet over the membranes and cyber-filament connections, I could hear the steel in her voice and the dead smile she always wore.

[I know the situation Grey, your spyeye informed me of everything, and we've confirmed it virtually. Unfortunately, the deadline is set on this one,] she said, [Your commissioner was particular about this case.]

[Was?]

Camelia's voice hitched, [Is, Grey. Don't be pedantic. You have five days remaining.]

Grinding my teeth, I flicked a glance at Kato. Even from his perch in the distance, I could see the flash of his eyes as he followed along with the conversation. I knew he was taking notes and recording everything. They couldn't ever claim he-said-she-said logic with Kato at my back. Camelia sighed; I heard the sound of her lighter clicking as she lit another cigarette. The music of her breath flowed over my thoughts like the smoke she held in her lungs. I smiled. If there weren't a bit of wiggle room, she would have hung up already.

[Alright Camelia, the deadline sticks. Can we at least request some transport?]

Laughter echoed through my brain, and I winced, screwing my eyes as the beginnings of a headache began to pound at the base of my skull, the pain crept up across my scalp and my skin prickled with goosebumps despite the dry desert heat.

This wasn't good.

Camelia didn't laugh, not like that.

She sounded nervous. And she was still chuckling when she spoke, [Oh, Grey. I will miss your wicked humour,] she said and sucked in another drag of her cigarette. My eyes popped open, and I pulled back on the skaali's reigns, "Whoa, wait up," I said out loud, the shock of her words snapping me temporarily off my commlink, furiously I focused my mind, willing it to reconnect.

She was still on the line. Laughing hysterically.

[With all due respect madam, but what the hell does that mean exactly? *Will* miss my humour?] I asked, trying to keep my voice steady despite the thoughts that were bouncing around my skull. Camelia didn't answer, she only continued to laugh before signing serenely, [Again Grey, don't be pedantic about it. Just do your job, and I'll do mine. The deadline stays in place, you've five days left to get here with Samantha Cowell in cuffs. Good luck, Grey. I hope you make it,] she said, and the connection dropped.

Kato stared at me with his large eyes and seemed to shrug. I had no idea what Camelia was trying to imply, but I didn't like it. The hull of the ship was well within reach and with a "*Kyah*!" I forced Tweet into a gallop. She let out a surprised chirp that sent Sam trotting after me astride Ruff with Jimmy in tow. The sun and the heat were only working to make my foul mood all the worse, "Grey, wait up!" I heard Samantha call from behind me, but the steady *thump thump*, of the skaalis canter, drowned out much else. Kato spread his wings and lifted into the air, spiralling upwards on the hot currents of air with little effort as cleared the wreckage.

"Grey, wait!" I heard Sam yell again. The shade of the vessel was just within view but, heading her call, I yanked on the reigns. Tweet let out an angry whistling screech that reverberated against the dunes. Stomping her clawed feet, she shook her entire body, and I had to hang on or risk being bucked off.

"What is it?" I finally asked, irritation turning my voice dark. Sams' skaali caught up to mine, and the three beasts chortled at each other, banging their snouts together. "They don't like to be separated, much like people they prefer to travel in family groups," she said. I made a face, rolled my eyes, and turned my skaali back around, "You've gotta be kidding me," I said with a snort, "What happens if they are separated?" I asked, more to humour her than anything. I didn't really care what happened so long as they did what I needed them to. If there were even the smallest sign that they were going haywire, I wouldn't hesitate one damn second to put every last one of them down. Sam glanced at me, placing a finger on her chin she began to tap it thoughtfully, "Nothing really so long as they can find each other. But then," she paused a second, rolled her eyes up to the sky as she thought about it, "Well, Tweet is liable to wrap her metal-reinforced jaws around your head and put that shotgun in her gullet to good use," she smiled, "Though I'd hate to see those shells go to waste," she finished with a wry smile. I shook my head in disbelief. I asked, "And the little one, Jimmy, what's he gonna do? Bark at me?"

She shook her head, "Jimmy is the worst of them. He'll explode," she said. Her face was dead serious, not a hint of humour tickling the corner of her lips and her eyes stared into mine. I stared back, almost a moment too long as my eyes flicked down to her mouth again waiting for the smile to return that told me she was joking.

She wasn't.

And then my eyes dipped down to her breasts, pushing up over her vest. Sweat had cut trails through her dust encrusted skin and pooled into her cleavage. It was distracting. The entirety of Samantha Cowell was distracting. She had always been a headstrong girl, and if I hadn't of been so wrapped up in Natalie I might have noticed her a bit more, but then, when we were kids, she was small and gap-toothed with hair cropped too short against her skull, matching her brothers. He was her hero, and I had killed him. More or less. I tore my eyes away and turned back towards the ship hull.

"Let's just get to that relic and bunk down, I need to get some coordinates and see where we are," I said mildly. But this time we stayed together. Samantha might be making it all up to keep me close for safety, but something told me she wasn't entirely lying either. I've seen skaali before, and there was definitely something different about these three. I couldn't place a finger on it, but there was something a little disconcerting. Especially now that we were riding with the three of them head to head. They kept turning to look at each other and at Samantha, making noises, Tweet with his bird-like chirping like they were plotting something. Whatever they were discussing amongst their selves, I was effectively cut-off from. Tweets stream of consciousness had melted away from mine for the time being.

The ancient hull was rusted out to the point that if you touched it, it'd probably fall apart. Crumbling away to leave flakes of red across the dunes that would quickly consume them. That or it might just fall over and crush us all. But we needed the shade. It was nearly high-noon. The twin suns, Rosa and Raina, were especially harsh this time of year and the heat was all the more intense for it. It'd only get worse once we made it to Halcyon Road, but at least there we would have more chances at finding shelter. The entire road was littered with old relics like this one making it easier to find refuge on the hottest days. It still had its dangers, though. They would just be easier to hide from.

[Kato, I need a map] I sat, legs crossed, with my back resting against Tweet. The raptor sat crouched down in the sand, and her tail whipped back and forth as the smallest one snipped at it like a kitten. Sam sat similarly with Ruff splayed out behind her, his head bobbed up and down as the wind whistled through the rusted holes of the ship. His large, luminescent eyes were wide with interest.

Katos' claws sunk into the thick padding of my shoulder armour as he landed and fluffed his feathers, [On it Grey, I've scanned the area and have plotted out the most efficient route]

I nodded and closed my eyes as he transferred the data, and an image was implanted in my head, as I opened my eyes the readout projected across the sands from my retinas. Kato couldn't send large files or a constant stream of images like the newest and most expensive skyeye could, but I was okay with that. I wasn't a cyborg and couldn't support a massive inflow of data.

My entire life I'd been pressured to upgrade. To become less human and more machine. But it just didn't settle right with me. I was okay with my naturally born self and only paid for the augmentations necessary to survive daily life and maintain my career. Namely an implant for essential communications, a mental image conductor, and a few other small but minor adjustments. I could display images on my retina and save them in my thoughts which allowed me a decent enough navigation when we didn't have access to full GPS. I brought up the picture Kato sent and concentrated on it, bringing it to the forefront of my mind. We'd need to leave the hull and cut upwards in a south-westerly direction to reach First Camp just outside the Atoll.

First camp, a way station before fully entering the worst of the wastelands, was located at the junction between my home of Shady Plateau and Yellow Plateau. With the path set, I was ready to go. But, as I rose to my feet, I felt the ground shake. The raptors all popped their eyes wide open and leapt to their feet in alarm, whistling quietly. Tweet chirped at me, and the flood gates of communication flung wide open as images and words collided in her fear.

[Grey, we should leave now] Kato said, his voice a whisper even though I was the only one who could hear him. I held out a hand to stay the raptors as Tweet stamped the ground with her feet.

"Sam, let's get out of here," I said. She nodded, a startled look on her face, and silently jumped in her saddle with a practised leap. Brushing her hair away from her face, I saw her skin grow pale, and her eyes grow round. Jaw trembling with nostrils flared her mouth gaped open. Ruff growled, lowering his head, his feathered mane bristled in a colourful display as his growl turned into a hiss.

I had one hand wrapped around the saddle horn and one foot in the stirrup, slinging the other leg over Tweets back, when I noticed the look on Sams' face. Quirking an eyebrow, I turned to see the enormous snout of a skaali peering around the hull. It stared at us for a long moment with yellow eyes topped with short bony horns surrounded by small red and yellow striped feathers. The harsh sunlight glittered along its back in flashes of green and blue over the exposed scales that faded into the feathered upper body and head. Long jaws, heavy with muscle and filled with rows of serrated teeth, parted as it breathed in our scent and flexed the short arms that hung from its chest, its rear legs were long and powerfully muscled with wide feet splayed out in the sand up to its ankles. A thick tail waved back and forth.

It was the last thing I ever wanted to see out here in the dunes, a tyrannosaur. Tyrant as we called them. Most likely one of the older escaped ICO militia tyrant tanks. I could see the gleam of plastic and metal beneath the thinner flesh of its underbelly, coils of membrane guts churning fluids through its body. Over each eye, a scope had been mounted, the short antenna pointing forwards. The circular lens gears rotated as the skaali scanned each one of us, its nostrils flaring. I wasn't even sure what information it could gather with such outdated equipment if anything at all. Its back was studded with the rusted remains of grommets and metal plates used to secure Gatling guns to each side. The .50 calibre mounted turret and handlers' seat was long gone, but some of the thick belts that would have been used for extra security remained, the webbing worn in places where it cut into the tyrants' skin, chaffing scales and rubbings it's exposed under flesh raw.

Kato took off, and the giants head followed him for a moment, tracking his movement with its nose up in the air before lowering its head back down towards us.

The wide jaws parted.

It roared.

I'd never seen the back of a Tyrannosaurs' gullet before, and though I'd never really wanted to, I could appreciate being able to check it off my bucket list. But only for a moment. The beast launched into action, all teeth and terror.

Sand flew up into the air as the tyrant churned its heavy clawed feet, pumping across the ground, moving faster than I'd have thought a monster that size could. Eyes flashed and teeth clicked together so close to my head that I had to force myself not to stop and look back. The tyrant roared again, its bright red snout coming into view as it attempted to slam the side of its head into my raptor. Tweet leapt forward and out of reach just in time as I heard those terrible jaws snap shut over empty air way too close to my head for comfort. We raced ahead, Kato guiding us, towards First camp. If we could make it to their gates, the guards should be able to scare it off. Most of the skaali were afraid of only two things, fire and deep water. So, you had two choices when you had a beast like a tyrant after you. You either found water, which was never going to happen this side of the Dune Sea, or you set it on fire. Usually, this could be done in the form of specialised flame throwers mounted in the watchtowers of most larger towns for just this kind of emergency. The flamethrowers worked an excellent eighty per cent of the time. The other twenty per cent of the time the Tyrant was just too damn hungry to give a fuck. I hoped that this one wasn't in the latter twenty per cent.

Over the dunes, we fled.

Sand pummelling our bare faces but I'd rather risk Rust Lung than end up in some cyborg reptiles stomach to be shat out three days later.

[Not far now, Grey, you're almost there] Kato encouraged us, but it had already been nearly an hour, and this tyrant was not giving up. I could smell blood in the air as flakes of dried sputum laced with red lined Tweet's jaws. She had been running hard. Beneath the saddle, I could feel the steady swelling, in and out, of her chest cavity as thick thighs bulged with an additional flush of steroids and adrenaline. Her augmented adrenal glands worked overtime to keep the pace up. But even fine-tuned machinery could give out. Beside us Ruff and Jimmy kept pace, their clawed feet throwing sand up in puffy trails behind us; the only clouds you'd ever see in this barren wasteland. Like Tweet, their muzzles were flaked with red, and this only spurred the tyrant to keep up its pursuit as the smell of blood drove it into a frenzy. I couldn't imagine we'd get much further and for a moment –

"*Grey, watch out!*" I heard Sam yell too late as Tweet went tumbling into the sand, and my body was lifted into the sky. Air rushed over my body and sent my hat flying like a leather saucer to land half-buried in the sand.

The impact was hard.

My right shoulder crunched as I landed, tumbling to a stop face down on hard, burning hot, ground; solid beneath me. Something didn't feel right inside, but there was no time to check for injuries. I turned my head left and right, the worn white paint dotted down the centre of the pavement teased a grin out of me despite the pain.

We'd made it. The last remnants of the Halcyon Road.

Pulling my legs up beneath me, I felt a pop and crunch followed by a rush of warmth and more pain as I shifted my body and forced myself to stand. On days like these, I wished I had invested more in the variety of augmentations offered by ICO to its employees, some pain reduction surgery or adamantium bones perhaps. Maybe something to consider in the future.

Iron raced across my tongue as I flicked it at a loosened tooth in the back of my jaw. Stinging pain followed by motes of light swam across my vision as the shadow of the Tyrant loomed above me, I kicked back across the ground, my palms stinging wherever they made contact with the burning hot pavement. *Fuck, this shit.* I thought and reached for my pistol as the beast slammed a foot onto the concrete and tarmac. It dropped its jaws and roared. Pelting me with a blast of hot air laced with the smell of rotten meat.

CHAPTER 9

The tyrant lifted its head, bellowing out a victory call as it climbed up onto the road, talons scraping against the hard surface. Reaching into the sandy folds of my duster, I wrapped my fingers around the hilt of my sidearm. It wouldn't do much to a tyrant, but it was better than giving up. "Grey," Samantha shouted from somewhere to the right of me. My vision was blurred with pain. Reaching over my shoulder, I fumbled for the rifle secured on my back alongside the rune-gun. I briefly considered the weapon, *if only I had the spell bullets for it,* when the tyrant turned its head away from me.

The sound of tires screeching made us pause our deadly dance.

In the distance, growing closer by the second, a cloud of black fumes and sand trailed the dune buggy that ripped across the sand and onto the road. A massive engine mounted on the front of it was nothing compared to the size of the cannon on its enclosed roof; my hands were over my ears before the sound of the blast came.

Flames engulfed the tyrant as the rocket slammed into its side, searing feather and scale as the skaali briefly became a moving ball of fire. I got my teeth against the skull-splitting roaring as it stomped its feet in fury. It was like watching an absurd dance as it kicked through the sand and ran blindly across the road. My nose burned with the acrid smell of burning flesh and reptile musk as the great lizard let lose its scent glands in panic. As the tyrant thrust its head against the sand, trying to extinguish itself, I leapt to my feet and found the rune-gun.

With hands trembling I loaded the only round we had and hefted the weapon to my shoulder, I peered down the site at the oncoming buggy.

Took aim and squeezed the trigger.

I held my breath as the twin barrels lit up, the carved runes amplifying the spell bullets effects as the hammer struck home. A disk of swirling patterns rippled outwards from the cold metal and sent the projectile spiralling out in a flash of light. I threw an arm up over my eyes as the shot trailed a steak of glittering blue behind it. The buggy swerved, I could hear the engine revving, tires scraping on the tarmac. Two men leapt out and were sent rolling off into the sand, but it was too late for the driver.

Ice crystals splintered across the hood of the vehicle, cracking glass and bone alike as the poor sap was torn to shreds, his body frozen in pieces. The tyrant turned and galloped toward the melting ice, and the ground shook as it began rolling its burning body across the buggy, crushing it in its desperate attempt to soothe its blistering skin. The two survivors had regained their footing and were backing away slowly, avoiding the lashing tail and claws of the monster as it nosed its body through the quickly evaporating puddles. [Kato, is everyone okay?]

[Yes, Grey. But your skaali are in bad shape. They need rest unless you plan on walking the rest of the way to First Camp…]

[How much further?] I asked. Now that we were on the Halcyon it shouldn't be too much longer before we reached the camp, assuming we were headed in the right direction anyway. Samantha, mounted on Ruff, skidded to a stop next to me, "That was my last spell-bullet. You should have used it on the tyrant," she scolded, pulling the gun out of my hands and shoving it through a loop on Ruff's saddle. "But I'm glad you're still alive," she said, leaping down from her skaali her arms slid around me in a brief hug before shielding her eyes against the sun to watch the tyrant rolling on the moist pavement, "That's not going to keep it busy for much longer. We should get going," she said. I nodded in agreement. Placing her fingers in her mouth, she let out a whistle, and in moments, all three of the raptors were with us again.

[Kato? How far?]

[I don't know Grey; my sensors are being jammed, but I can see that we've more company on the way. You'd best move on, posthaste.]

I ran to grab my hat. Dusting the sand off it, I placed it back on my head and cursed. Kato was right. I could see more smoke cutting a black scar across the sky, "Shit, we better get moving. If we're lucky, the tyrant will take care of them for us," I said. Sam nodded, and we began to walk away, leading the raptors, trying not to catch the attention of raider and tyrant alike.

A gun fired.

The sound echoed across the dunes like slow thunder.

A voice, sounding gruff and annoyed, cut the air behind us,

"I don't think so," it said, "Hands up where I can see them. On your knees. I'll be confiscating them weapons and your skaali," the click of a hammer being cocked for a second shot reverberated from behind us. I turned my head to glance over my shoulder. A single-action pistol, the silver barrel shinning in the sun. Two raiders, having survived the ice blast, now stood behind us. A gun in one's hand and a pair of rusted scimitar blades in the others. All three of the raptors began to hiss, their jaws wide open and clawed hands curling in agitation. They were tired and hungry and walking the razor edge with eyes large and pupils tiny. I noticed the twinging of muscle in Ruff's thigh and knew he would attack at any moment.

Bang! Bang!

I dropped, hands over ears and forehead against the burning ground. The heat searing a layer of skin away. I lifted my head just enough to look, *dammit.* I hadn't even seen the third man, lying prone with sand over his back, watching and waiting for his chance.

Ruff lurched to one side, hissing as another *bang* interrupted his screech of rage. Teeth and claws flashed as he leapt.

Tweet on the ground, and Jimmy next to her. A dart of silver with a tuft of bright red feathers sticking out of one end was embedded in each of their necks. *It's just a tranquilliser. They aren't dead.* I had to tell myself.

Samantha screamed and ran to her raptors. I was on my feet again in a flash, ignoring the sinking in my gut and the buzz of images in my head as confused raptor thoughts tumbled over mine a moment before going silent with sleep.

A raider, the one with the swords, stepped forwards and yanked Sam back by the hair, forcing her to the hot pavement and ignoring her screams as she thrashed and kicked, rolling like a crocodile. Her teeth clenched and fingers clawed at the raider's arms and wrist until rivulets of blood trailed down his dirty skin as her nails and fingers were stained with it. She spat at him and hissed between gritted teeth as the raider forcefully searched her, digging in-between places that made the heat rise up my neck. With a gun to my temple, I had to fight back the urge to run to her rescue. I couldn't do anything for either of us if I were dead.

Finally, he shoved her onto her side, "Abe. She's clean," he said. I bit the inside of my cheek to keep from saying anything as the third man clambered out of the sand, slung his rifle over his back, and began to pat me down, taking my pistol, rifle, the rune-gun, ammunition belt, everything. The bastard even had the gall to reach up and take my hat, placing it atop his own head and exposing my shaggy sand-coloured hair. The sun on my scalp was making me sweat more than my beat-up leather Stetson ever had.

Abe stood in front of me. I couldn't figure anything about him. A heavy executioners hood had been pulled over his face and goggles covered his eyes where the holes were, "Are you gonna tell me that you don't have any more weapons hidden?" the muffled voice said. I shook my head, "Nah, I got plenty of weapons," I replied and smiled. The raider stood still. I couldn't see his face, but I could tell by his eyes he was trying to figure out if it was trick somehow. I reached my thoughts out to Kato, circling above us somewhere. [K, the raiders now, where at and how many?]

[They are almost here, there are approximately twelve, Grey. Four vehicles total and three raptors, what's your plan?]

[Ain't got one. Stay safe. I'll call you later]

Kato didn't reply, but I knew he'd heard me. For now, I needed someone with their eyes in the sky. We couldn't afford for Kato to get captured if I had any chance of getting us out of this mess.

As the raider began to search me, I slipped out a laugh, and Abe snapped his head back to look up at me, "What's so funny?" he asked. I shook my head, "Nothing. I'm just ticklish," I replied and cracked a smile, "Oh, and this," I said and jerked my knee up into his jaw. He stumbled backwards but regained his senses faster than I'd hoped, steadying himself he lifted his head. Blood mixed with purple fluids trickled from within the hood and down his neck. *Shit, he's been augmented.* With an angry roar the man raced at me with arms spread open. He rammed me, wrapping his arms around my waist and squeezing tight, lifting me off my feet as I was wrenched to one side. The ground met my face and my vision blurred with stars as my ribs, already bruised from my previous ordeal, screamed in protest. It was getting hard to breath. I twisted, forcing myself onto my back and lashed out with my legs, landing a boot heel on his lower jaw. I heard the sound of something giving, a crack, a gush that spattered over my chest and face. Red and purple soaking into the bandana dangling around my neck. Abe went reeling off the road and into the sand. The rifleman that stood guard next to Sam laughed, shifting from foot to foot in excitement as he beat his swords together, sending sparks into the air.

A roar echoed behind us, and I turned to see the dune buggies had arrived. The tyrant turned in circles, growling and snapping its jaws as the vehicles spun around it, kicking up dirt and blowing smoke. Pissing the giant skaali off even more than it already was. The men on the raptors leapt off their mounts, leaving the smaller skaali to tease the tyrant away from the road. A few men snuck up behind it, lassos with heavy metal hooks on their ends glinted wicked sharp. A quick observation told me the hooks were live and would deliver several hundred volts of electricity once they'd snagged onto the Tyrant.

The rest of the men began to approach us.

One vehicle, more significant than the rest with a round satellite dish mounted on top, broke off from the group and rolled up behind the footmen. The vehicle was mounted with two Gatling guns, and the men that sat on the installed seats were bent over them, ready to let rip at the drop of a hat. The footsoldiers were armed with various types of weaponry and, similar to our new friends, wore goggles and various amounts of mismatched armour. Bandanas or strips of cloth was tied around their faces for protection against Rust Lung.

"You've had it now," Abe said as he got up on his knees. Reaching up, he yanked his goggles down and removed the sack from his head. Spitting a wad of blood on the ground along with what looked like some teeth.

He wasn't pretty.

His face was covered in sores surrounded by rings of swollen, angry, tissue and his bald head had skin peeling back in sheets. The newly broken nose certainly wasn't helping. I snickered as he wiped sweat and blood from his face with one hand as he stood. Lifting a hand, he gave the barest of nods, and the swordsman grinned. Brandishing his weapons, he twirled them through the air, as he approached me. I took a step back and narrowed my eyes, letting him come to me.

I dodged, twisting my body to one side, and narrowly missed the rusted edge of the blade. My ribs ached with the effort.

Another jab.

Another dodge.

We danced around each other fists and blades flashing.

I winced as the blade caught me on the forearm, slicing through the skin easily. Like it was nothing. A needle of fear threaded its way up my back and lodged into the back of my brain.

If I had my sidearm, he'd already been dead. I don't fool around with blades. My fingers twitched at my hip out of habit, instinctively trying to reach for a gun. I reached out and wrapped a hand around his wrist, jerking him towards me. Guiding the blade beneath the crook of one arm, slamming our bodies together. Clenching my arm around his, I balled up my free fist and began pounding his head till I felt him go limp and dropped him like a sack of potatoes to the ground. Abe stepped up to the plate.

Narrowing his bloodshot eyes, he leaned in and thrust a punch, two more punches, straight to my gut in rapid succession. He was fast, and it caught me off guard. I took the full brunt of both blows. It hurt more than I wanted to admit as the air left my lungs in a groan as pain radiated from my bruised innards. Abe laughed as I hugged my waist and doubled over, "Woohoo boy, I like a fighter. You just earned yourself a date with the eminent Bombasta," he grinned. Half his teeth were missing, and the ones he had were green. That name flickered with recognition briefly in the back of my head. I knew it from somewhere. Samantha, back on her feet with hands neatly folded behind her head, glanced at me, catching my eyes, and the look on her face told me she knew who this Bombasta was. She mouthed a word at me, but I couldn't read it because the butt of a gun was bashed against my temple, and I was busy trying not to pass out and failed miserably.

When I next opened my eyes, my ears were ringing, and my head felt like it weighed a ton. My heartbeat throbbed between my ears as my stomach lurched. I thought I might vomit. Sitting up, I winced as my head banged into something hard. *Dammit.* Massaging my scalp with one hand, I realised two things. One, my hat was missing. That asshole had taken it. Two, the laceration on my temple hurt like hell and was most likely the source of my pain as memories came flooding back. Brief snatches of being bound and trussed on the back of a raptor, Sam with her wrists tied being led along behind us over the sand. The Halcyon Road growing distant as we moved away from it. Away from First Camp. Engines so loud just thinking of them made my heard hurt worse. I cracked an eye open.

It was dark out. After a few moments of focused concentration, I began to make out shadows and stars on the horizon. Voices and laughter and the smell of something cooking. There was a flickering fire nearby that people sat around but not close enough to really hear what they were discussing. My stomach grumbled in response, tongue thick and dry and lips chapped. I could feel rather than see a presence close by, and a steady trickle of water was poured over my head. *So thirsty.*

I tilted my head back to let the water splash across my tongue. Bitter acid and something else.

It was pungent.

It was piss.

I coughed. Spitting on the ground to the sound of wild laughter. "Fuck you," I managed to grind out of my throat. I craned my head back just enough to take in his face. Remembering his features; sun-bleached hair, green eyes with one gone milky white, a scar from the top of his head that slashed across his dirty face and down his neck to disappear beneath the ratty shirt. I'd make him pay for this later. And then behind the laughter, I heard a low whistling. I turned my head to the noise, *Tweet?* My brain was still trying to wrap around all that had happened, and I was feeling faint again. *Gotta stay awake. Samantha? Shit, where is she?* I twisted around in the cage and tucked my body in, knees pulled up close to my face, and began to kick with all my strength which wasn't much but at least they knew I was alive and angry. *And maybe Sam could hear me.*

The pissant continued to laugh as he finished his business, tucked himself away and kicked sand at the cage. I now realised I was in. "Fuck off," I said again, more forcefully. Snarling, I asked, "Where's the girl?" but my voice was weaker than I hoped it would be and this elicited more laughter. The pisser chuckled to a friend standing beside him, face blurred beyond recognition in the flickering shadows of the torch he held. His teeth flashed white as he spoke, one eye glittering as he leaned in to stare at me, "Your girlfriends doing just fine, lawman," he said, holding up my ICO badge. He waved it in my face before jabbing the sharp corner of it into his mouth, picking at his teeth with, he gnawed on the hard plastic and growled. Sneering.

I sneered back, allowed my head to fall against the bars, and then kicked the bars again. Hard. The entire cage rattled, and the two men leapt back, their eyes held a stroke of fear. I laughed. Spitting at me, they both turned heel in the sand, marching back towards the fire.

I had no idea how I was going to get out of here.

Hours passed, and I was still thirsty, hungry, and stuck in a cage, and none of my ideas was helping solve those problems. *Think Chris. Gotta get out of this, find Sam, grab the raptors…where the hell is Kato?* There was a sudden twinge in my gut, a miasma of sadness I couldn't understand. I didn't know where it had come from. And then a long whistle, tinged with sadness, reached my ears. It was Tweet.

I could feel Tweets rising anger seeping into my bones as images passed between us. The twitch of nostril, the churn of the gut, the saliva brought on by the smell of something roasting. The scent was familiar to the raptor, but I couldn't tell what it was. Tweet didn't like it.

It was musky. Charred. Burnt.

I pushed the thoughts away and kicked at the cage again. If I kept on kicking it'd have to give way eventually, right? This thing looked rickety as hell but damn. I kept on kicking and then paused. Someone was crying soft feminine wails.

"Sam? Samantha!" I called out; voice hoarse but loud enough to carry over the sound of laughing raiders. I hoped. After a few moments, I heard her voice. She was close. Somewhere behind a stack of wooden crates and rubbish to my left. Her voice was tight when she replied, "I'm here."

I pressed my face up against the bars, trying to see if I could make out her shape through the cracks between the wooden stacks. "Did they hurt you?" I asked, my voice a low growl *if they touched her. If they hurt her. There'd be a reckoning. Hell, there already will be.*

"No. I'm fine, but…they killed him, Chris. They're eating Ruff," her voice ended in a moan. Strangled and weak. I could hear Sam shuffling around in the cage, the bang of bars as her knees and elbows, like mine, jutted at odd angles, trying to find a comfortable position. My stomach lurched, and the bile rose before I could stop it.

Tweet.

The smell.

That's what Tweet was so upset about. I could feel it now. She was angry and fearful at the same time.

Another wave of sickness rolled over me, catching me in the undertow, and I had to pull back, pull my thoughts away from Tweet before her reptilian emotions overtook me. I needed my thoughts to be mine. I couldn't let instinct ruin my better judgement. Samantha had been linked to Ruff in the same way Kato, and I was. Apparently, Tweets' link had grown stronger as well.

Samantha had suffered through Ruffs' death. Feeling every wire as it was cut, disconnected, every fibre as it was squeezed between pliers. Plugs pulled. Liquids drained, "Sam, I'm sorry," I said quietly, "I can't even imagine how that must feel. I could hardly imagine life without Kato."

I sat back in my cage, ready to kick it one last time for good measure.

The door swung open, barely a noise.

I sat bolt upright, banging my head into the bars I winced and groaned.

[Quiet, idiot!] Kato's voice flooded over me. A welcome addition to the other thoughts and feelings tumbling through my head and pulling at my guts and instincts. [Kato! Your safe?] I said as relief washed over me. I reached out and pushed the door open the rest of the way, uncurling my body from its cramped position. I must have been sitting here longer than I thought because my entire body ached and tingled with sleep it didn't want to wake up from.

[Of course, I'm safe but if you don't quiet down none of us will be for very long,] Kato said. I heard him hoot lightly from somewhere to my left, followed by the sound of Sams' cage door opening as well. He must have either picked the lock or stolen the key. Creeping around the side of the crates, I found Sam still in her cage, and it took a few moments for me to coax her out. We sat a moment in the sand and held each other while I kept an ear out, listening for the laughter to continue. I ran my hand over Sams' hair and smoothed away the wet strands that were plastered to her face, damp with sweat in some places but crusted with blood in others.

[Over there, they keep the supplies on the other side of the camp] Kato said, alighting on my shoulder where his sharp claws dug into my skin. Without my leather duster jacket, the flannel shirt offered little protection. I ignored the sparks of pain and pulled Sam up to her feet. I whispered in her ear, my face so close to hears I could feel her breath on my cheek, "I know it's tough, but I need you here with me right now, okay? I said. She nodded slowly and rubbed her eyes with the palms of her hands. When she turned to me, her face was a blank wall, the sadness there bricked up behind a wall she'd have to tear down later, but for now, it was what we needed.

Under the cover of darkness, we moved, slinking around the crates and piles of rubbish. I was grateful that the flickering of the fire made it easier for us to see them as we crept along the perimeter of the camp bathed in shadows.

"Grey,"

[Grey]

Sam and Kato said in unison. I went still, keeping my body rigid. A sleeping raider, his face cast in shadow, was resting against a vehicle, his back propped up on the hood. His head kept lolling to the side, and he'd snort, straighten up only to fall back asleep again, starting the cycle over. I glanced over at Sam. Kato didn't need me to tell him what to do. His wings barely made a sound as they scooped the air and sent him into the darkness above.

[He's alone but armed,] his voice echoed in my thoughts. I nodded to Sam, and we both skittered across the sand, leaving one shadow to pass into another. Pausing behind the dozing raider and his vehicle. I looked it over briefly but could already tell there was no way we'd be taking this, not without the key for the ignition. Sam tapped my shoulder, but I shook my head, mouthing the words '*we can't take the buggy*'. She shook my shoulder, earning a glare, but her finger pointed over my shoulder and towards the fire.

In the centre of the circle, I could see remains of Ruff hanging over the fire. Most of his body was gone. All that was left really was the metal frame, wires and silicon. A heap of parts resting beside the campfire was all that remained after the meat had been carved away. I felt a shudder. It was hard to remember sometimes that the skaali weren't real. That my skyeye wasn't real, either. Or at least not in the way I would think of it. Skaali and skyeye and many other cyborgs were different from the people who, like me, had parts installed for various reason. They weren't born, they were created.

I reached a hand back and squeezed Sam's fingers, but she slapped me away and thrust her index finger out again. This time I followed her directions, my eyes peering past the ring of fire with its laughing guests. There were Tweet and Jimmy, cramped together in a cage barely big enough for the two of them. They were still alive and sat quietly in the cage, staring at us expectantly.

CHAPTER 10

It was too easy. I reached across the hood and wrapped my arms around the sleeping guards' neck, a hand clamped tight over his mouth, and twisted. The pop of his spine was so quiet I turned it again just to be sure before guiding his body down to the sand. Sam and I pulled him beside the buggy, searched his pockets, and rolled him beneath the carriage. Sam nodded as she handed me the rifle and a belt of ammo. She kept the bowie knife, snaking the sheath through her belt loops.

[Kato, which way? We need to get Tweet. She's our only chance out of here] I asked, relaying the conversation to Sam. Keeping our heads low, we made our way to a row of buggies lined up in a neat row. Their rear bumpers pressed up against a wall of rusted sheet metal. I looked up, following the edge up above our heads. A hooting sounded from the top of it, and Kato's eyes glowed briefly as they caught me in his sights. [It won't be so easy, Grey. The whole compound is surrounded by walls like this] he said. [Show me] I replied and opened my mind, an image of the raider compound sinking into my thoughts and imprinting over my vision when I opened my eyes. Kato preened his wings as he continued, explaining the map to me, [The gates are heavily guarded. They've got this place on lockdown. See the gate here?] A dot began to blink in my retina, marking the main entrance to the raider compound. Focusing on that spot the image zoomed in, Kato continued, [That's where we need to go, but the barricade is too high, and they only open it when raiders are coming or going, I haven't seen it open again since we arrived yesterday].

I slid around the front bumpers of three vehicles, continuing our way around the compound.

Pop! I looked down, expecting a bottle of booze.

It was a bone. A human bone.

Stumbling back my elbow banged into a crate, my knee catching the edge and I bit back a curse as the wood crashed to the sand and broke apart. It was filled with bones. Samantha slapped her hands over her mouth, her eyes large and startled as a skull rolled up against her ankle. She reacted without thought and, with a strong kick, sent it flying to bang up against a slab of sheet metal where it shattered. I turned and glared at him, biting on the edge of my lip to keep from saying anything. She shrugged and shook her head. Rolling my eyes I knelt down and scanned the fire again, no one moved.

They continued to laugh.

Sam reached out and grasped my fingers, squeezing them, we advanced our way around the stacks and canisters that lined the rest of the perimeter. Ducking behind them where we could.

[Grey, we've a problem,] Kato said. His map zoomed into our location. From the end of the stacks to the skaali cage, the space was wide open with only the wall behind us. We'd have to either follow the wall to the gate and hope we could get out and away without the raptors or, we'd have to cut through the fire. I relayed this to Samantha and, of course, she refused to leave her skaali behind. I knew she wouldn't. "We'll get them out, I don't know how but we will," I assured her. To Kato I said, [Shit, any bright ideas?] Kato chuckled in my head, [Take them out? Hope you can outrun and outgun them?] he said. I smirked, [Very helpful, thanks. Any other ideas?]

[Ask Sam to seduce them?] I turned my head and glanced over my shoulder at Samantha. *That might actually work if she'd do it.* I scanned the fire pit again; the bastard Abe was sitting with my hat perched on his head and mt duster wrapped around his shoulders. *I bet he's got my guns too.* I motioned for Samantha to follow me, and we regrouped in the shadows, pressed up against the compound wall, where we discussed our next move.

"You hear that?" one of the raiders asked, leaning back on the crate he was using as a seat. He wiped his mouth, wet with melted fat, on the edge of a stained sleeve and stood. Tilting his head back, he stared up at the sky. Abe chimed in, "It wasn't nothing Jesse, sit yer ass back down." Jesse nodded, scanning the dark space above. The moon rings of Trion weren't visible tonight, making the sky dense with millions of tiny specks of light.

I thanked my lucky star for that as I sat with the rifle, an old-world Winchester 62, ancient in its own right, perched between two crates as I counted the rounds that slid between my fingers and down the magazine tube. Twenty

.22 calibre shots. It wouldn't be accurate if I pumped it fast, but it'd do some damage, and that might be all I needed. I settled down with it aimed at the men sitting around the fire. Kato was hovering somewhere overhead, keeping an eye on the raider's movements. His visuals told me that a few of their men were outside the compound, circling it in a small vehicle built for speed. We'd have to worry about them later. While the rest of the men were inside the walls. There was an area sectioned off, a large oval like an arena with rows of makeshift seats and stacks of cages. It was most likely used as a fighting pit, the type my dad frequented decades ago. In a corner further away from the fire were a row of shanty homes, the largest presumably belonging to their leader, Bombasta.

Most of the raiders had already retired for the night, slumping back to their dingy homes or passing out in the sand. Only Abe seemed intent on keeping the party going as he cracked open another bottle of beer, tipping it back to fill his mouth before he swallowed loudly, smacking his lips. I made a face. Jesse tugged on his waistband, his back dark with shadows as he turned away from my position, "I gotta piss," he said. I watched as Abe laughed, cramming a strip of meat into his mouth and muttering around the food, "Go see if the lawman back there needs another drink," he laughed, nearly choking on his food. I narrowed my eyes, *fucker*, and then realised that we were about to get caught and all hell was going to break loose.

[Kato, how are things looking?] I asked, feeling the seconds tick by. [Samantha is nearly in position] he said. [Good, things are about to get dicey] I replied. Abe was alone but was still dangerous.

In times like these, I wished I'd dished out the extra cash and upgraded my commlink for multi-communications. I could speak with Samantha but only if I disconnected from Kato first. It was slow and shoddy, not at all efficient for coordinated attacks like what we were trying to do. I'd just have to trust that Sam knew her role and that Kato could guide us both. [She's ready,] Kato said. I watched as a shadow crept closer to the fire. Abe staggered to his feet, his eyes blinking "Whose there? You're not one of my – oh," he said, the words slurred together. Samantha stepped out from the shadows, her shorts riding high against her brown skin, the vest hugging her curves tightly. Abe was reacting precisely the way we wanted him to. "Wait, you're the bitch we found with the lawman, how the hell – " his voice trailed off as Sam approached him, sliding first her vest off, and then pulling the undershirt up over her head to expose her bra. *Come on, Samantha, you ain't gotta go any further*, I thought as I ran a hand over my face to scratch nervously at the dark scruff growing on my chin. But Abe looked like he was still putting up resistance, she reached down and undid her bra as well. Letting it drop around her waist.

I swallowed.

Abe did too.

And then he stepped forward, reached his hands out to run them over her bare skin. I bristled. Tweet and Jimmy hissed; I knew how they felt.

Literally, I knew how they felt.

Tweet swarmed me with her desire to sink her ivory and metallic teeth into the filthy man touching Samantha. *Don't worry girl, you'll get your chance*, I thought, but I wasn't sure if she actually got the message. I wasn't sure how any of it worked really, but she must have received some impression from me because both raptors whistled amongst their selves and settled back on their haunches. I watched silently, biting my tongue, as Abe began to squeeze a breast between his fingers, stepping in closer, he grinned.

It didn't last long.

Abe's eyes bulged in shock as Sam stepped back and cracked a fist down into his elbow, bringing the heel of her other hand up into his nose.

I winced.

Blood gushed down his face, dripping off his chin. Eyes bulging with shock before fluttering up into his skull. He didn't even make a noise as he fell to the ground with a *thump*. Sam knelt down, grabbing at her discarded clothes and pressed two fingers to the raiders thick neck before beginning to paw through his clothing, searching for the keys to the raptor cage. Finding a keyring, she immediately dashed over to the waiting skaali.

A voice stopped Sam in her tracks. "What the hell are you doing? Hands up where I can see 'em," it was Jesse, back from his piss. He held a revolver squeezed in both hands and looked terrified. The barrel was shaking almost as much as his knees were.

Now that he was facing Sam, I could see this Jesse clearly. He was young, probably not much older than I was when I'd left home. Fifteen, maybe sixteen, and his hands were shaking. A sheen of sweat made his sun-tanned skin glow in the firelight. Blue eyes flashed with uncertainty. He didn't belong here. You could just tell. I knew that story like it was written on my heart. A poor kid from the islands falls into the wrong crowd. Before he knows it, it's too late. He can't go back. They'd hit hard on his family. Or cut off his trigger finger. But he can't keep going either because he doesn't want blood on his hands. Not any more than he's already got.

I held a hand out as I rose from my hiding place, "Easy there, we don't want any trouble. We'll just take our skaali and leave, alright?" I said, inching my way closer to him, "It's Jesse, right? I overheard ya'll talking. Look, no one else has to get hurt. You don't look like you want to –" a bullet whizzed past my face.

Sam ducked down, spread across the sand, still half-naked as she dug for the keys and slid over the sand on her stomach to unlock the cage. I ran for cover, dodging behind a crate. Jesse pulled himself out of his uncertainty and sought shelter for himself.

I could see at least four guns glittering in the firelight. They were all aimed at me.

Sam screamed, drawing my eyes to her, but it was too late. A large man, his head bald and covered in tattoos that trailed down his muscled chest, stood with Sam's neck wrapped in one arm and a gun wrapped in the other.

The arm not holding Sam gripped between thick fingers was made up of a series of wires and rotating pistons that spun in circles. A gun magazine, no doubt fully loaded, jutted from beneath where his elbow should be. He lifted Samantha off her feet, and Tweet hissed from the confines of her cage, clawing through the bars and racking her claws across the sand.

Everyone was quiet.

Scrawled across the man's chest in dark ink, I was able to make out a word, *Bombasta.*

So, this was their leader.

He was as ugly as I imagined he would be.

Sloshing through the sand, Bombasta toed Abe's body and, with a thick accent, said, "You've killed my right-hand man. He was a hard worker. A goodman. You'll pay for this in the pits." He growled. I lifted my gun, finger already on the trigger. He pressed his gun arm to Sam's temple, "You try she dies, it's your choice," Bombasta rumbled. My breath hitched as my finger hovered against the metal.

Dammit, all.

I stood, letting the rifle fall to the ground, arms up in the air. "And the belt," Bombasta demanded. I unbuckled the ammo belt, tossing it aside. Bombasta dropped Sam to the dust. She rolled over and spat, trying to catch her breath as she scrambled away from him. Tweet and Jimmy sat in silence as Bombasta turned to the skaali pair, "You will also fight," he grinned, "I have something special in mind for you all. It will be fun, I think. For me, anyway."

The fighting pit had been reinforced with slabs of salvaged ship metal, welded into place with braces of metal rods all along the sides. The wall itself was roughly fourteen feet tall and sloped towards the ground covered in rust-red sand. Only it wasn't rust. Flies swarmed across the sandy field in buzzing clouds.

Sam and I stood, back to back, as a crowd of misanthropes jeered at us. Waving their arms in the air as they waited for Bombasta's entertainment to begin. The large man stood up in his throne-like chair at one end of the oval-shaped arena. On his head, he wore a helmet adorned with a single triceratops horn and a mane of red feathers. His goggles were blackened to keep the sunlight out, but otherwise, he wore only a ratty shirt tucked into what looked like a kilt. Bombasta leered at us, his gap-toothed mouth working a wad of tobacco.

He raised a hand.

The crowd went silent, the only noises were the flies and the startled shrieks of Tweet and Jimmy as they were led into the centre of the ring alongside us. The two raptors rubbed their muzzles against Sam, nipping at her hair and tugging at the strings on her shorts. Sam glanced over her shoulder at me as she rubbed their snouts, "Grey. What's going on?" she asked.

"I dunno, a dance party maybe?" I quipped. Sam curled her lip at me, "Fuck you. Besides, I don't dance," she answered. I laughed, "Well, I'm sure your about to learn how."

"I didn't say I couldn't, just that I wouldn't. There's a difference."

"Roger that," I said. She snickered at me and then flicked her head to the other end of the arena. The raptors began to snarl as a gate began to crank upwards. An ominous roar echoed from between the sheets of metal.

With large claws splayed out to hold its weight and half its body ravaged by flames, a tyrant stepped onto the playing field. I recognised this tyrant. It was the beast we met in the wastes. And it smelt as awful as it looked. The scent of death played across its shape as it walked with a distinct limp. Its face was the worst. One entire side of its head was missing, exposing bone, teeth, and metal alike. The eye on that side was gone, and the empty socket was smooth and dark, but sparks of light glowed in the hollow. Its gruesome visage made it appear all the more deadly. I found myself feeling bad for the beast as it limped towards us. It paused, lifting its snout to sniff at the fence that lined the top of the wall that was just high enough to keep the tyrant from nipping at its audience.

And then the tyrant lowered its head and roared.

"Are you fucking kidding me!" Sam growled.

From above us Bombasta burst into tumultuous laughter, slapping his hands on the sides of his round stomach. "This will be fun, yes?" he smirked, spitting a wad of chaw to the ground near our feet. He waved at the two men that stood on either side of him, "Here are your toys, have fun!" he said with a smile and laughed again as he settled back into his throne. His men stretched their arms through the bars lining Bombasta's cage and dropped our weapons. The rifle and ammo belt but with three rounds and Sams pistol, also with only three rounds. And no rune-gun. But I already knew there was a fat chance we'd ever see that again.

Screw that bastard.

The tyrant pounded towards us. Sand spraying beneath its feet. Tooth and claws flashing.

In the confines of the arena, its tail whipped against the metal sides, making them rattle and setting the audience alive with cheering. The raptors wasted no time attacking. Jimmy went left while Tweet went right. Muscled bunched. Bodies low. They leapt at the tyrant. Claws flashed, and sparks of metal scattered across the ground along with bits of flesh and a pus-filled mixture of blood and nanofluids as Jimmy hung onto the tryants' damaged brow with his clawed hands. Back feet kicking, like a cat, repeatedly against the tyrants' destroyed face. Jimmy opened his slender jaw, and a series of loud bangs followed as his nostril cannons fired in rapid succession. Doing little damage to the armoured tyrant.

The tyrant shook its head in irritation, it's large hind feet churning as Sam and I dodged out of its way. The tyrant began to rage and shake its body, attempting to dislodge its unwanted guests as Tweet started to claw her way up its backside. She misjudged the tyrants' reach, and its jaws clamped into her thigh and threw her across the arena. The raptor slammed into the wall, sliding to the ground in a heap.

All around us, the raiders stood and clapped in ovation. "Tweet!" Sam yelled, I gripped her elbow and nodded, "Go check Tweet. I'll help Jimmy." She didn't need me to say it twice.

[K, you still out there buddy?]

[I'm here Grey, I'm procuring supplies. You focus on staying alive.]

I dodged another clawed foot. Jaws snapped in the air above my head, barely missing me as I threw myself to the sand and rolled away, *fucking hell!*

I leapt up and ran. The tyrants' feet seemed to have a mind of their own as its injured leg began to kick and convulse at an odd angle. Grabbing the rifle from the sand, I looked up to see Bombasta pressing his face to the fence above me and laughing, "Having fun yet?" he roared. I paused only long enough to flip him a finger before I broke the stock open and crammed the four rounds into the rifle. I chased down the tyrant as it began to circle the arena. Its tail lashed back and forth above my head as the tyrant rammed its head into the ground. Jimmy lost his grip and fell onto his back, feet kicking at the air as he shrieked.

"No!" I screamed as the tyrant's teeth sank into Jimmy. He was small, even for a raptor, and the jaws of the giant made short work of him. Jimmy didn't make a noise as its teeth wrapped around him and squeezed shut, cracking bone, crushing metal, and tearing flesh. Samantha screamed as she stood with Tweet, her hands pressed to the largest of the raptors wounds as blood and fluids dripped down her hide. The skaali flicked her claws, and her jaws clicked in agitation as Sam did her best to hold our last skaali back.

I took my chance.

As the tyrant was busy working on Jimmy, I leapt up and grabbed the tyrants tail, hanging on to it as I was lifted up into the air. The tyrant turned to snap at me, it's jaws covered in gore. But as it turned, the movement whipped me against the fence of the arena, and I clung to it. The tyrant lunged at me, jaws snapping. But, with one eye gone, it misjudged its bite and crashed its muzzle into the wall.

The entire arena cheered.

And then screamed as the tyrant began to tear at the metal and chicken-wire.

Bombasta rose from his throne and disappeared among the screaming crowds trying to rush the exit, but this only made the tyrant more excitable. Snapping and clawing at the edge of the walls it began to ram them. The sheet-metal buckled. The arena shuddered again as bits of the walls started to fall away, and an entire side of the stands crashed to the ground, along with its terrified spectators.

I waved to Sam, "Come on. This is our chance," I said, joining Tweet and Sam as the tyrant gorged itself on fallen raiders. Sliding around the edge, we entered the space where the tyrant had been kept.

Animals of all shapes, sizes, and species sat in cages. Their blank eyes were hungry and scared. But some were just angry and growled as we passed by, reaching claws out to snatch at us. "Hey, you. Human. Free me, and I'll help you escape!" we paused as Tweet hissed.

It was a Yrmian soldier. His tall form was slender like the rest of his ilk, but his muscles were toned, and his four arms bulged with muscle. I looked at Sam, and she nodded, "How do I know we can trust you?" I asked. The Yrmian looked at me, narrowing his purple eyes as he pressed his face to the bars, "I swear to you, I will not harm you. I'm here for Bomtasta. Let's just say I owe him," Sam and I exchanged looks before we both nodded again. An Yrmian would not swear on anything lightly, their honour rested on the truth of their words. I rolled my shoulders, "Okay. Were in a hurry. Bombasta is –" the Yrmian cut in. "You don't worry about Bombasta, he's wanted in two star systems and my home planet. I'll take care of him. I swear this," he said.

I looked the Yrmian up and down as Sam worked the lock, "Like you clearly did before?"

"Very funny. I like your humour, human. I like it so much I'll let you live for that slight against my honour. Don't question it again," the Yrmian said, pressing his face to the bars again and grinning, his eyes shone in the darkness and sharp teeth flashed.

The Yrmian had a custom of filing down all their teeth to sharp points when they earned the right to bear arms. It added to their already fearful prowess with weapons, especially bladed ones.

As Sam swung the cage door open, the Yrmian stepped out and stretched, popping the joints in all his limbs. "Excellent, let's move. We must go this way," he said and guided us through the maze of underground caverns. They seemed to be mainly used for storage of the items they had acquired over the years, but just as many held what looked like beds and a massive butchering room. I didn't want to think what had been murdered and chopped down here. As we explored the underground network, we could hear the screams as the tyrant tore the arena part, it caused Tweet to claw at the ground nervously. Her wounds were no longer bleeding, but she moved stiffly. The tyrant was a problem if we didn't hurry it would enter the compound at large and we needed our supplies if we had any chance of surviving the dunes.

[Kato, were almost out. Be on standby.]

[Excellent, I found your things, Grey,] he said and sent me a blip marked on the map he had previously made. We came to a rickety metal staircase that wound upwards in a spiral. "Here, this is the way out," the Yrmian said, "It leads up into a warehouse, you're on your own now. I must go find that *forsheeth* Bombasta," he said, pounding his four fists together. As he turned, Sam grabbed one of his slender arms, "Wait. I'm Samantha Cowell, and this is Chris Grey. What's your name?" she asked. He seemed confused and then bowed his head, "I am called T'ikkos. But you may call me Tick. That is what my human friends call me. Now I must go," he said and turned heel to run into the dark tunnels, "Thank you. We owe you!" she yelled after him, but he was already gone.

We quickly took the steps up and out, but with Tweet, it took us far longer than I would have liked. She had a hard time climbing with claws and an injured leg. Finally, we found ourselves in a cramped warehouse, the doors were ajar, and we stepped outside; finding ourselves face to face with young Jesse. His surprised face quickly contorted in anger. Gritting my teeth I balled my fist and raised them, ready to fight. He was wearing my duster and my godsdammed hat. I mentioned for the boy to return my items and he did so, stepping aside to let us go we quickly realised why. The place was in chaos. Many of the raiders, seeing that things were going to hell, began to help themselves to the loot. Piling their claimed goods high on the few vehicles they had and joining together in small cliques that fought over weapons and supplies.

[Grey. Hurry, they haven't found me yet,] Kato said. I turned to Samantha, "Kato found some supplies. We need to move quickly though, come on," I said. She nodded, keeping close to me along with Tweet. We made our way towards Kato, keeping low and staying out of peoples way as they tore the place apart. I spotted the skyeye sitting on the metal railings of a buggy missing its tires. I nodded to him as I reached up and settled him onto my shoulders, [In there, Grey. I found some things you might want.]

I slid open the crate and smiled. The rest of my ammunition rested in the container. I quickly pushed the rounds into place along the belt on my waist. I dug around and found a few other useful items, a knife, some rounds for another gun we didn't have, but that might come in handy later, and some half-eaten rations that I threw out. I dug around deeper and grinned, "Fuck yes. Thank my lucky stars," I hissed between my teeth and leaned down into the crate. The rune-gun with the last spell bullet rest at the bottom of it.

I took the rare weapon, slinging the strap over my head and across my chest, so it rests snugly against my back alongside the rifle. Close by we found a saddle-bag and fixed it over Tweets back. "Wait up," Samantha said as she ran out into the chaos. *What the hell is she thinking?* But within moments she ran back and shoved a few packs of rations and some filled water pouches. It wasn't much, but it would do. "I also found this. It'll help. Tweet, I mean," she said and showed me a small metal box with a single tiny needle in it, "Roids," she breathed. I nodded, "Let's move."

The roar of the tyrant made our skin crawl. It was out. We had to go now.

I leapt into the saddle, helping Sam up behind me, "I know your hurting girl, but I need you to just bear with us a little longer," I said, stabbing the needle into her neck. She hissed, reaching a claw up to scratch at the puncture wound. I grimaced at the amount of blood and purple nanofluids rolling down her flank as our weight bore down on her. I hated to do this, but we needed to get away. Patting her neck for the encouragement I urged Tweet into a gallop, jolting across the sand at first but quickly gaining momentum as the Roid pumping through her skaali veins masked the pain and forced the muscles to move beyond their standard capacity. Within minutes we blazed across the desert, clouds of dust unrolling like a cape behind us.

CHAPTER 11

The sun was long gone and the quick relief of the cold night air soon reminded us that, despite surviving the tyrant attack, despite escaping the raiders, and despite managing to keep at least one skaali, in all other regards, we were pretty much shit out of luck. There was enough water for another day or two at most, and our food was nearly gone. Our two-day dash through the desert was going to quickly come to an end if we didn't make it out of the sands. The fire I'd managed to build with the remaining supplies sputtered whenever the wind blew. Tweet couldn't carry two people for long and being overburdened was wearing the injured raptor down. She rested, curled up and half-buried under the sun-warmed sands to keep the chilly night air at bay. The raptor snored lightly with deep breaths, chest rising and falling rapidly. The cuts from the tyrant's teeth were bright pink against the brown scale and feathers. We were lucky the wound wasn't worse; another inch or so and the cyber-filaments would have been torn wide open, making the raptor incapable of movement.

Resting on my duster in the sand, I leaned against a boulder. Sitting in my undershirt, I examined the cuts on my arms. Wrapping them as best I could in strips of bandage salvaged from the remainders of the first aid kit we'd recovered. Scratching the stubble on my chin, I slid a hand up through my hair and ruffled it. Sand fell from my scalp, and I winced when the tips of my fingers brushed against the gash on my temple, it'd probably leave a scar. Sam sat opposite of me, chewing a chunk of jerky. She had her back against the sleeping raptor. Unconsciously she rubbed a hand across the flat scales of Tweets muzzle and into the feathers around her eyes and jaw. Comforting the wounded beast as Sam stared off into the night sky. Stars were brushed across the deep blue like specks of white and yellow paint. Spiralling across the inky ocean like sea-foam. Or so I'd been told.

Other than pictures I'd never actually seen the sea.

I took a bite of my own jerk and nodded with my chin, "What's with you and skaali?" I asked, "I just don't get it, what's the appeal?"

Sam blinked out of her stupid and glanced at Tweet. Her chest expanded as she sucked in a breath, let it out in a drawn-out sigh. She tilted her head to one side and tucked her hair behind one ear, "I don't know. I guess they are just more honest, really. I mean, when they are hungry, they eat. When they are tired, they sleep. And when they are in love, they make love," she said, the corners of her lips twitched into a smile. Averting my gaze, I stabbed at the fire again, stoking the flames and avoided looking at her. My face burned, and my mouth went dry. It caused my voice to come out rough, "Really now?" I mused. She looked right at me, catching my eye, and the light of the fire turned the emerald green of her eyes into molten jade as the reflection of the flames danced across their surface. There was something wild there. Something I didn't recognise that was fascinating but also caused a spark of terror to race up my spine. It was primal. My skin prickled.

Samantha nodded slowly, her fingers gently combing the sleeping raptors feathers back into place, "Plus, they are loyal as hell, they'd never leave you behind,"

The smile dropped from my face, "Listen, Samantha, I have no excuses for your brother or why we left. I won't try to make any. I wish I had come back sooner. When did you become a doctor anyway?" I mused.

Samantha gave a lop-sided grin, "I had some time on my hands and a knack for tools. Seemed like a good waste of my time."

She didn't offer any other details, and I got the feeling she wouldn't tell me more if I asked. We both sat in silence, keeping our thoughts our own. I fell back on the sand, stretching out and folding my arms beneath my head. Gazing up at the stars I said wistfully, "If I had come back sooner maybe things wouldn't be the way they are right now. Maybe I would have realised a bit sooner what you and Jack should have meant to me if I wasn't too busy chasing a girl that had zero intentions of –"

I didn't get to finish my words. Sam was on top of me in a flash, forcing me further down into the sand and settling her body over mine. With one forearm pressed into my neck, she leaned in so close I could feel her breath on my face.

She leaned down to my ear and whispered menacingly, "Don't you dare. You're not allowed to say that, Chris. I don't know about you, but I like my life. I enjoy building my machines. Sometimes life sucks, sure, but you get over it, and you move on. Eyes to the future or die with the past right?" she snarled, leaned down, and pressed her lips to my ear, "What about you, Christopher, where are *your* eyes?" she demanded, her voice harsh as her small frame trembled with fury. I was painfully aware of her body pressed against mine.

I ground my jaw.

My emotions were confusing me.

I couldn't afford that.

I was pissed while at the same time, I felt my body responding to her in ways I was trying to ignore. Body and mind conflicted over my duty to ICO and my growing desire for this woman that both confused and compelled me. I was probably going to regret this.

Staring up into her face, I narrowed my eyes, searching for the source of that fire and reaching out to touch it regardless of if I got burned. I wrapped my arms around Sam, pulled her into my chest and rolled, forcing her beneath me. The shocked look on her face made me smile as I propped myself up on one elbow, gripping both of her slender wrists in my free hand. She gave little resistance as I forced her arms up over her head, "My eyes are right here," I murmured, my voice rough with desire, before lowering my lips to hers.

Again, I thought she'd fight.

Again, I thought she'd get up, grab her skaali and run. Leave my sorry ass behind in the sand.

But she didn't.

I was surprised at first and almost didn't know how to respond. A low moan reverberated deep down in the back of my throat as my mouth and body naturally began to react to her. When we pulled away from each other, I sat there in frozen confusion for a few moments as she stared up at me, her lips pursed together.

"I'm sorry," I said, pulling away further still. Sam shook her head, casting her gaze to the side. She seemed to be rooted in thought. Maybe she was already regretting it as well. I mean, I still had a job to do. This was bad.

Shit, I fucked up.

When we were kids, she was the tag-a-long sister, the one that always followed along even when you didn't want her to. Plus, she was Jack's little sister and had been untouchable in that regard. But then, Jack wasn't here, and I wasn't going to let his ghost continue to get in the way of something awesome. Something about the way that her lips looked, her eyes, her hair, the curve of her hips and breasts— her entire body and that brilliant mind of hers ignited something in me. I felt the heat rising rapidly in my body as we gazed intently at each other; my heart ricocheted between my ears. I wanted every inch of her, and I wanted it right now.

Finally, her voice broke my thoughts, "Don't be sorry. I wanted to kiss you too, Chris. And honestly, I wouldn't mind another."

A smile broke out across my face. I reached out to Sam a second time, pulling her into another embrace. Another long kiss.

I thought for sure she'd fight it despite her words.

Instead, she sank into the kiss with a furious passion, making damn sure I forgot the past.

My face was wet. Something warm, moist, and rough was sliding across my neck and forehead. Its abrasive surface making my skin itch. I slid an arm over my face and opened my eyes. Blinking, I sat up. It was still early morning, and the suns' rays were just coming up over the rust-red dunes setting them ablaze with crimson and orange waves of warm air. It was early, but it was getting hot fast.

Pushing aside the warm snout I sat up, "Tweet, come on," I began but looking up I was startled to see it wasn't Tweet. The head of a giant cat hid the sky from my view. Its pupils were tiny black dots as it ran its tongue once more up my face, licking away the salty sweat before rising up on its hind legs and shoving a gun into my face. Flinching I kicked back in the sand, reaching for Samantha with my heart pounding in my chest. The silver-haired lady with her Kit'th guards loomed above me, and Sam's still sleeping form. Pulling on my jacket and hat, I narrowed my eyes at the stranger, "Do I know you? You're not a Dune Buster…not one I know of anyway. You're not a raider. I saw you back there in Shady Plateau. Which means you've been following us. So, who in the blazing hells are you?"

My voice was laced with irritation as my eyes flicked between the lady and her two feline companions. The woman smiled and flashed her badge, hidden beneath the folds of her cape. I nodded in recognition. Of course, an ICO Reaper. Only the cream of the crop became special bureau agents known as Reapers. She looked too well kept to be a ruffian like myself. The fact that she had the money to keep Kit'th around said something extra about her status.

I tilted my head to one side, uncomfortable beneath the golden-eyed watch of the Kit'th. When the lady opened her mouth, her voice wasn't what I expected. She sounded old. Much older than she looked. It was highly likely she'd had some work done to keep her pretty face intact. Her silver hair had been plaited and hung over one shoulder, her fingers toyed with the end of it as she spoke, "My name is Olivia Cilia Malkovich, you may call me Cilia. Like you, I work with ICO, but unlike you, my job completion rate is one-hundred and ten per cent," she said.

The Kit'th guards knelt down and began to awaken Sam by shaking her shoulders roughly. Protesting Sam leapt up in confusion and quickly grabbed her discarded vest and shorts, "Chris, what's going on?" she asked with a voice filled with panic. Cilia smiled, "Ah, I see. You've been distracted," she said as her eyes roved up and down Samantha's body as a light smile played on her lips.

Cilia stepped forward and grasped Sam by the chin, turning her head left and right roughly before releasing her face with a slap on the cheek. Samantha narrowed her eyes but kept her jaw clamped firmly shut. The older woman circled her like a stalking feline. Stopping to touch Sam on the ass, her breasts, trailing fingers down her smooth stomach, "Now wait a minute you –" pain raced up my leg, and my knees buckled as a swift kick to the calf set me to kneeling on the ground. One of the Kit'th leered at me, his sharp canines exposed and wicked sharp as he curled his lips and snarled.

"Seir Malkovich, we've no time for this. Let me put this fool down," he growled. *Or is it a she?* I really couldn't tell with the Kit'th and I wasn't planning on flipping its loincloth to find out. Cilia shook her head, "No, Raja. ICO might still need him and, unfortunately, he isn't a criminal. At least not yet," she smiled and turned to me, pointing to Sam with an incline of her sharp chin, "I can see the attraction. But still, the job should always come first Agent Grey," she chided, raising a finger and wagging it in the air. I reached out to Kato, why hadn't he alerted me to their presence? He should have known immediately that they were within range.

[Kato, where the hell are you, we've got company,] there was no answer. Something was wrong.

Cilia left Sam to finish dressing and paced towards me, her boots kicking the sand into swirls as the morning wind began to pick up, it would probably storm again and we'd all be better off moving on.

"Why are you here?" I finally asked, ignoring the snarling face of the second Kit'th that approached from behind the boulder with Tweets reigns firmly wrapped in one clawed hand, Kato was in the other, and he wasn't moving. The Kit'th held him by the legs, upside down with wings spread open and eyes wide open, unblinking. I bit the inside of my cheek, trying to keep from saying anything. The Kit'th could be unnecessarily cruel when they wanted to be, and if they'd harmed Kato, I didn't want anything worse happening. Right now, he seemed to be in one piece, and that'd have to be good enough. Cilia crossed her arms and rest her weight on one leg, flipping her braid to the other shoulder, "I'm here to make sure you finish the job. Our employers are…concerned," she said and flicked her eyes to Sam, "For good reason obviously. But they need her alive, and you're barely keeping her in one piece," she shook her head and kicked at a small stone that rolled by on the rising wind, "There has been another death, Agent Grey. They need her now, she could be the key to solving everything."

My brow furrowed, "Another? Who was it this time?" I asked. Sam looked from Cilia to me, confused, and shrugged, "Another what?" she asked.

Cilia twisted the silver band that graced one wrist and tapped a few of the cleverly hidden keys made to look like gemstones. A small holographic projection floated in the air, and a haggard-looking newscaster spoke in tones of muted dismay. I couldn't tell for sure, though. His face was like concrete, displaying no emotion, but then that could be an effect of the shoddy display. Sam crept in closer and rest one arm over my shoulder as she squeezed her eyes to slits trying to read the tiny words that floated across the screen, not that she needed to. The newscaster was basically reading it word for word,

"It's a sad day indeed for those of us here in our glorious capital city of Centrum. This morning at approximately 5:45am High Commissioner Jerome Alfonzo was found unresponsive in his home. High Commissioner Alfonzo was one of the lead commissioners in Project New Eden, a plan meant to reinvigorate the terraforming of Terrafirma V. His financial support, as well as his brilliant ideas, were key in this program, he leaves behind his wife and –"

Cilia cut off the display. Twisting the bangle back into place. "As you can see, we need to get this girl to Centrum, and you've already wasted your eight days. I'm officially taking over. You're excused Agent Grey, go where you will. Raja, Tegra, stop playing with your food and let's go," I raised my hands in protest and stepped towards Cilia, "Whoa wait a minute," I began but the Kit'th, Raja stepped between us and snarled. Wrapping his hands around the scimitar swords at his waist, he eyed me, sizing me up. The

Kit'th weren't afraid of guns. Most of the time, their fur and hide were so thick the bullets barely affected them, but a rune-gun, on the other hand, was deadly to just about everything and everyone. The big cat was wary, his nose twitching and whiskers stiff as he sniffed the air.

The Kit'ths' eyes matched the sandy brown fur of his body; black spots trailed its powerfully muscled hind legs that ended in massive paws and talons more vicious-looking than any Tyrant. Even Tweet wouldn't stand a chance against a Kit'th.

Or maybe she would.

I didn't know if Tweet understood the situation. She stood there looking placid and tired, with her eye's half-lidded and most of her body weight was carried on the uninjured hind leg. For this to work, I needed her to understand the grave danger we were in or really, I needed to impress on her the danger that Samantha was in.

Stepping back, I feigned surrender and bowed my head, using that split second to open a commlink I sent a series of images to Tweet. Pictures of her siblings being torn to shreds all over again, pictures of Samantha and myself facing the same fate.

I felt her agitation, her anger stirring.

Tweets jaws opened wide, and a roar erupted from her toothy maw. The Kit'th holding Tweets reigns let out a surprised hiss that turned into a snarl as Tweet jerked the reigns out of its hand and lowered her head, snarling. The crescent-shaped and wicked sharp rear claws tapped the sand as her tail snapped back and forth, feathers flashing. The skaali didn't hesitate. All four paws were in the air as the Kit'th was crushed beneath the weight of a six hundred pound pissed off raptor. There was clicking, and a flash of sparks as Tweet snapped her metallic teeth together and flared her nostrils.

She began slashing. Her head darted in for bite after bite. Blood splashed across the sand as Tweet made quick work of the Kit'th, cutting across its exposed stomach and tearing at its face and arms. The Kit'th barely had time to let out a gurgling scream before Tweets jaws snapped around its neck, cutting off the cry. She held on until the Kit'ths' tail stopped moving and its chest ceased its rise and fall.

"Tegra!" Cilia screamed, pressing her hands on either side of her face in shock, she watched in abject horror as her guard was torn to shreds. The hot rusty sands turned all the rustier for the buckets of Kit'th blood seeping into the sands. Cilia dropped her fists, curling her hands into claws as her face turned several shades of red. Tweet continued to ravage the alien feline's body, growling in pleasure as she did so.

Cilia whirled on me, pointing at the dead Kit'th, "That just cost me a fortune, Grey! You *will* pay for this later, even if I have to wring it out of you in the dungeons of Watchtower Plateau!" she growled, her body trembling with rage.

The other Kit'th, Raja, stepped towards Tweet and brandished his scimitars. His entire body rippled with excitement as his hair stood on end and his face contorted into a snarl. Without a word, he leapt into action. Tweet met the Kit'th head-on. Teeth and claws and shinning copper and silver metal flashed in the early sunlight as their bodies crashed together. A ball of scale and fur and fury.

Cilia dug through her robes, withdrawing a handgun but she couldn't take aim without hitting her other Kit'th. Taking advantage of the distraction I ran past the twitching body of Tegra, dropping down on a knee long enough to snatch up Kato and loop an arm through one of Sams, "We gotta get the hell out of here," I frowned. Samantha nodded, snatched her bag and began shoving what was left of our supplies into it along with Kato. I stood and began to creep towards Tweet. If we could get her to disengage maybe – a rumbling growl vibrated up through my body and forced my feet to stop.

Cilia bowed her legs and lowered her gun. Tweet bounced away from the Kit'th and scurried far enough away that the scimitars were useless as the Kit'th too suddenly went still, his fur standing on end. No one moved for a long moment. And then, slowly the feline bent his knees and lowered his head to the ground, sniffing, black nose twitching as his jowls parted and let out a hiss. Another rumbling noise reverberated from beneath. It was all too similar to what had happened back on the plateau, but this was no viper.

"What was that?" Samantha asked, her brow furrowing in confusion.

The ground shook again.

"Oh, fuck me sideways," I said quietly as the ground sunk inwards beneath the Kit'th, and he was sucked below the sands.

Not a sound was made.

No one moved, Sam and I stared at each other.

A moment later the cat was sent spiralling up into the air, straight up in a spray of blood and entrails that landed on the ground with a sickening *plop, crunch, gush.*

Cilia turned her head and looked slowly at us from over her shoulder and quietly, carefully, slid her gun back into the holster at her hip. I reached out a hand, urging her to make her way towards as us as the sand around her dead bodyguards began to ripple. Thousands of worms pushed up from the sand, their three-foot-long bodies writhing across the bloody remains, sinking their toothy maws into the torn flesh. Hundreds of them scooped up mouthfuls of the blood-stained sand to filter through their bodies and leaving trails of clean sand castings behind them, having filtered out all traces of blood and other fluids, as they slid over the surface.

Cilia began to back towards us. Tweet stood very still, her entire body like a marble statue as her nostrils flared and pupils so wide her eyes looked black. Her mane of feathers pinned down tightly against the scales of her neck.

Samantha squeezed my arm so tightly I felt my hand starting to tingle with numbness, and I gently pushed her away, nodding in reassurance. I reached into my coat and found my trusty revolver. I began to slide the weapon free of the holster when Sam whispered, "What *are* those?"

I made a face, narrowing my eyes as I watched the worms finish off the last of the Kit'th, leaving only piles of sand and patches of fur behind, "Sandworms," I whispered and pulled a handful of ammunition, quietly as I could manage, from my inner pocket, sliding each round into the chambers of the cylinder. "I thought they were bigger?" she whispered back. I nodded, "They are. Those are the hatchlings. Mama's underground somewhere."

CHAPTER 12

The ground vibrated beneath our feet. Sand shifting like a living thing. Rippling in ways solid ground couldn't. Beside me, Tweet chirped in irritation as worms slid over her claws, smelling the blood from her previous kill. They began to wrap around her ankles, their mouths latching onto her scales. Snapping her jaws, Tweet bit a handful of sandworms in two, their mangled bodies dropping into the sand and writhing beneath the sand. But sandworms weren't that easy to kill. The halves would grow new parts. Multiply. The sand began to boil.

Samantha's eyes met mine. "Run," I barely managed to choke out before the ground began to boil.

Grabbing Sam's arm, I turned on my heel, but the shifting sand gave out under me, and I slipped, bringing her down with me. *Shit!*

The earth shuddered, and with an explosive spray of sand, the mama earthworm emerged, rearing her sightless head. Her body was the width of two men, and at least ten times that length, from what I could tell from the partially exposed sandworm writhing above me. The worms face was ringed with tentacles that writhed through the air above us. In the centre of the fleshy appendages, there was a beak that opened to reveal a circle of teeth. Sharp and black. They were worth a fortune on the black market, but I didn't know what for.

Didn't care.

We needed to get the hell out of here.

Cilia spluttered a stream of curses, most of them directed at me as her usually composed demeanour shattered, she fumbled for her gun, pointing it at the monster.

The worm's great jaws clicked and grated as its teeth rotated in its gaping mouth. Long, sharp spikes lined its body, flailing in the open air like an agitated centipede's legs. Tweet whistled and chirped, jumping from side to side to get a better grip on the shifting sand. The sandworm sensed Tweet's movements and plunged downwards; its gaping mouth aimed at the skaali.

Sam cried out, but Tweet jumped out of reach. Her tail lashing the sand in a spray of rust. The sandworm dove into the ground, burrowing. Sand buckled and pitched as the worm shot back up into the open air a few feet away, emitting a high-pitched squeal.

"Shit," I croaked, helping Sam to her feet. We clutched each other, trying to regain our balance.

Bang! Bang!

Cilia had her gun trained on the agitated worm, firing round after round. The bullets glanced off the worm's thick skin, barely making a mark. The spiny-demon, however, coiled and turned towards the noise of the gun. It reared up to spring.

Cilia had time to fire one last round into its gaping maw before it sprang, spikes bristling, tentacles writhing. A burst of sand showered the air, and I blinked it away, sure Cilia was done for. But I caught sight of her rolling away, narrowly escaping the worm's jaws. The worm dove into the sand and re-emerged again. Opening its beak, it screeched a challenge.

It was pissed.

Before it could take another dive at Cilia, Tweet leapt onto its head, digging her claws into the worm's flesh. The sun glinted off her metal teeth and nails as she tore into the worm, shredding and slicing. The worm snapped its head back, letting out a shrill shriek, tentacles undulating. The rest of its lengthy body wound out of the sand, revealing its twisting bulk, the tapered tail ended in another set of lacey limbs, smaller but still just as nasty to look at.

"What the hell are these worms made of?" Sam yelled, watching as Tweet was thrown off the worms. The raptor rolled in the sand, then leapt back to her feet with a hiss, unharmed but angry as all hell.

Furious, the worm lunged for Tweet again, tentacles writhing towards her but Tweet was ready with a new tactic. Opening her jaws wide, she released her nostril mini-cannons. They streaked right to their target.

Smoke and fire trailed through the air, smashing into the worm's face. The creature whipped back and coiled its body in defence, but it was far from immobilised.

Now it was really pissed.

A piercing shriek emitted from its undulating body as it swung its head around, tying itself into a knot like an earthworm. Uncoiling, it lunged at Tweet, its tentacles twitching and beak clicking as it rotated in deadly circles.

Tweet managed to limp away, but when the worm lashed its head back, it caught her in the side and sent her flying. Gunshots rang out once again as Cilia gave her weapon another go on the creature. I grit my teeth, stabilising myself as the sand once again shifted beneath my feet, threatening to pitch Sam and me forward. *What the fuck is she thinking? If a skaali couldn't take the worm down with its cannons, did she really believe fucking bullets made any difference?*

Sam clutched my hand, shouting in my ear, "Quick, let's grab Tweet and get out of here while it's distracted!"

We raced across the sand, swaying on our feet as we tried to keep our balance. Tweet shook her head, trying to steady herself as she flipped back onto her belly and hopped to her feet, lids clicking over her eyes to clear the sand. Sam leapt up onto Tweet's back and looked expectantly at me, reaching a hand out.

The worm roared.

Cilia screamed.

Twisting to look back, I saw Cilia's body go flying as the enormous worm charged into her, sending her body through the air to roll across the ground. She collapsed in a heap, her gun out of reach.

She was out cold.

The worm arched its back, staring down its prey as the tentacles peeling back to reveal the sharp beak that clicked open and closed in anticipation.

Cilia would become worm shit, and we'd be next if we didn't get the hell out of there.

I stood deliberating.

I couldn't do it.

"Ah, fuck. Give me a minute," I said, slapping my hat onto Sam's head; I rolled my shoulders and bolted back towards the worm and the unconscious woman. I hoped I didn't regret this. But I was already pretty sure I would. *Damn conscious.*

"Christopher!" Sam screamed.

I grabbed the rune-gun from my back, painfully aware of the last bullet sitting inside my pocket. Fishing it out I loaded the rune-gun and hastily dropped to one knee. Gritting my teeth, I aimed at the worms head. Breathed in, breathed out, and squeezed the trigger, ignoring Sam's protests.

An explosion of ice hurtled towards the worm. I looked away as a flash of blinding light obliterated the creature, the sound ear-splitting. My shoulder already aching from the recoil. For a moment everything went white. My ears were ringing. Blinking, I stared at the spot where the worm had been. The back half of its body twitched. The sand in front of my position was coated in a thick sheet of ice that was already starting to melt. Flakes of snow gently fell to the ground, instantly melting against the hot sand.

I frowned when a block of ice pelted me in the shoulder. I jumped, startled and squinted at it and grinned when I realised it was a chunk of worm flesh. More frozen tissue rained down on us. I tossed my arms over my head to protect myself from the onslaught, but none of the pieces was big enough to do any damage beyond general disgust.

When everything had settled, I let out a breath and stood. Slinging the gun over my shoulder, I turned to Sam as she rode Tweet to meet me, "Well, that outta do it," I said with a smile of satisfaction on my face as I sauntered over to Sam. She scowled at me, "That was our last spell bullet."

"I'm aware."

Rolling her eyes, she patted the back of Tweet's saddle. "You coming, or what?" I hesitated, looking back at Cilia. She was still lying prone in the sand and even though the mama sandworm was was dead that didn't keep the babies from coming up. The sand was covered in the young wormlings that convulsed across the sand, stopping to devour bits of mama worm. They were non-discriminatory eaters. *Nice.* A few picked up the scent of Cilia and began to inch their way towards her.

"Come on, Chris," Sam groaned, "She was going to arrest us or worse. We don't owe her anything. *You*, don't owe her anything," she emphasised.

She was right.

I know.

But still. I couldn't leave someone behind like that.

The stench of the worm's flesh defrosting in the intense heat reached my nostrils. The back of my throat was itching as bile threatened to come up.

I fished my bandana out of my shirt and pulled it higher up on my nose to block out the stench, but it did little to help.

"We can ditch her in town," I said. Without waiting for Sam's protests, I picked my way past the chunks of thawing worm flesh until I stood beside Cilia. Her arm was slung out, her legs twisted under her. The baby worms squealed in protest as I kicked them aside, sending one flying through the air. With mamma out of the way, the babies weren't a concern. Or at least they wouldn't be for a few more seasons.

Flipping Cilia over, I quickly examined her, assessing for injuries. Not seeing anything visibly wrong, I fished inside the first aid kit and found some bandages. I used them to wrap Cilia's wrists and ankles together. Sand kicked into my face as Tweet trotted over, a disgruntled looking down at me. She dismounted, "I hope you don't screw us over with your chivalry," she snapped as she helped me lift the unconscious woman and heave her over Tweet's flanks.

Tweet couldn't carry all three of us, not with an injured leg and having run through half the night to escape the raiders. We were forced to continue our journey on foot. Sam remained silent, but I felt her disapproval as we trudged through the sand. There wasn't a speck of a cloud in the sky, there never was in all the years I'd lived here, and there was no sign of shade. Digging in my pack, I pulled out Kato, looking him over. He was still unresponsive, his wings flapping loosely at his sides, eyes closed. I silently cursed

Cilia. *What had she done to you, Kato?* I couldn't see any physical damage. *So why isn't he responding?*

Sam glanced over at me. "Cilia must have hit him with an EMP. An Electro-Magnetic Pulse. Some weapons can do that, it disables electronics. He just needs to be recharged," she said. Sam reached out a hand to brush his feathers with her fingers, rolling him over as she examined him as I had, "He looks intact; otherwise, I can probably fix him."

Some relief washed over me, "I'll just recharge him at our next stop, then. Nearest cyborg repair should do,"

Samantha shook her head. "There'll be more to it than that. It's not like Kato's taking a nap. He needs to be resuscitated. Jump started. You have the cables for that? Or the equipment? Do you even know what or how to do it?"

I scowled at Kato's still form, "No."

Samantha shrugged," I'll see what I can do," she said and faced the high dunes in front of us.

A few moments of silence passed by, "Where are we, anyway? Are we still on track for Centrum?" she asked. She walked with one hand against Tweets side, keeping track of her gait and making sure the skaali took sips of our water supply. I held her reigns in a fist on the other side. The raptor sent me a wave of relief. She was enjoying this. Just a stroll through the desert.

Nice day. No danger.

Full stomach. Happy.

I, on the other hand, wasn't feeling any of those things. I put Kato back into the satchel, feeling exposed without my navigator. I glanced at Cilia, still unconscious on Tweet, and noticed her ICO bracelet. Removing it, I turned it over in my fingers, "It's not Kato, but this might work," I said, activating it with my own ICO employee code. I found the GPS system and pulled it up, watching as a holograph lit in front of me, mapping out our location.

I groaned. This wasn't good at all. *Fuck.*

"We've been pushed way off track," I said, using my fingers to navigate the hologram's map. I pinched the image in and out again, trying to zoom in on our exact location. And then searched for Centrum. Sam moved beside me for a closer look, and I was suddenly very aware of her exposed stomach slick with sweat, as she pressed up against me, "Here are our options," I said, pointing to the map. "We can either head further northwest towards Tylan or, and this is what I suggest, we keep a northeast track towards Aquaria."

Sam quirked an eyebrow at me and cocked her head, "Aquaria? Really? Why not Tylan? It's practically a direct route back to Centrum," she said as she reached over and began to poke at the hologram.

I made a face, twisting the ends of Tweets reigns between my knotted fists, "Can't go to Tylan, let's just head to Aquaria. I'm already well past my eight-day limit – it won't kill me to take a few extra," I said with a grumble. "Besides, I know a guy. In Aquaria, I mean."

Sam glared at me. "We're adding days onto the trip, facing more raiders, possibly more Tyrant –"

I threw up a finger and wagged it at her, "Nope. Tyrants don't stray this far from Halcyon Road. It's easier pickings up that way with the caravans. Out here there's nothing. We travel at night, sleep by day and we'll be safe. Mostly safe. Maybe."

Sam let out a sigh, rolling her eyes and clenching her fists, "We're risking our lives, again, because you 'know a guy'?"

I turned off the hologram and tucked the bracelet into a pocket. "Trust me, he's worth the trip. He might have those damn jumper cables you were telling me about."

Sam groaned, "Sure, fine. Not like I have a say anyway. I go where you go." She scowled, and we changed course slightly.

Yes, Aquaria was a bit off-track, but we were so far out any way that it wouldn't matter. Besides, if we left Cilia in Aquaria, it would be a long trip for her back to Centrum as well. In her condition, the longer, the better. Besides, I needed to get Kato fixed, and we needed supplies. We'd find what we needed in Aquaria.

We travelled another two hours before finding a small ledge of rocks jutting from the sand. It was late in the afternoon, and if we were going to travel by night, we'd need to get a few hours of sleep. I sipped at what little water I had left in my canteen before settling against a pair of small boulders, hoping they would give me enough protection from the blistering sun.

Sam settled on the sand, coaxing Tweet to lay down so she could use her as a headrest. Tweet glanced around, nostrils flaring, before finally lowering herself down, no doubt confused about the sudden midday rest. Cilia shifted on her back with a low groan and rolled off the raptors back as Tweet settled down. "Uh-oh," Sam said, glaring at the

ICO Reaper. "What are we going to do about this extra problem you dragged along?"

Cilia was an inconvenience, there was no doubt about it, but I couldn't leave her. It'd be wrong to do so. "I guess we'll have to set watches," I said. If Kato were still conscious, he'd have been able to keep an eye on things while we slept. But for now, we'd have to do things the old-fashioned way.

Sam nestled against Tweet's side. "You're taking the first watch," she said, and closed her eyes, curling her knees up to her chest. She was in the sun but didn't seem bothered by it at all. They both lay there, Tweet and Samantha, like a couple of lounge lizards soaking up the sunshine.

I couldn't help but notice how smooth her back looked, her tanned skin peeking through her cropped shirt, sand sticking to it in a light dusting. My fingers itched to brush the sand off, to caress her exposed skin, press my lips to it. My body craved another night with her. I could live that night over again and again, and it'd never be enough. *Preferably without the Reaper showing up.*

I looked to Cilia, who was now acutely conscious and staring at me, her eyes flaming with anger, "You'll pay for what you've done, Grey," she spat.

I rolled my eyes as I knelt to sit her up, "Shut up, Cilia. Be grateful I didn't leave you behind for the worms," I said and crossed my arms and ankles as I leaned back against the rock. Cilia spat again, narrowing her eyes at me. I sighed, crossing my hands behind my head, "You might wanna save your spit. We're out of water rations, just saying."

Her glare hardened, "You're a failure, Grey,"

I laughed, "So I've been told many times and yet, I always come out on top in the end."

"After this, ICO will never give you another chance. You're a laughing stock. You disgust me, Grey."

I narrowed my eyes at her and set my jaw, "Pray, go on and see if I don't leave you here."

Cilia chuckled, her voice full of acid, "No one takes you seriously. You're a miserable little back island boy that got lucky. Nothing more. And when I get my hands on you –"

She continued sporting a slew of curses as I stood, ignoring her threats, and crossed the sand. Kneeling down in front of her, I reached into my pocket. Pulling out the remaining ball of gauze. I wrapped my fingers in her hair and pulled her head back roughly, she cursed again, using words I didn't even know the meaning of. Kit'th most likely. And stuffed the wad in her mouth, "Please, just…shut. The. Fuck. Up," I enunciated, and returned to my spot in the shade beneath the boulders. It was just as hot in the shade as it was in the sun. There was no escaping the goddamned heat.

As I watched Sam drift to sleep, I wondered if I had been wrong in bringing Cilia with us. Samantha was right. Cilia was an additional burden, and Aquaria was still at least two days away at our slow pace.

But now that Cilia was here, we couldn't abandon her in the desert. I'd be cut from the ICO immediately. I couldn't risk that, not after everything I'd been through.

I liked Sam. I liked her a lot.

But I liked my job too.

I owed it to someone.

It was nearly impossible to sleep in the oppressive desert heat, but it made travelling in the cooler nights bearable. We hit the road again, keeping Cilia bound and gagged over Tweets back. Sam and I agreed that there was no telling what she would do to collect Sam as her own bounty after her two Kit'th had been killed.

I was grumpy. I didn't get as much rest as I wanted. Thoughts kept toiling over in my head. It was a blow to my pride that Camelia had decided I was inadequate for the job, especially after I'd been explicitly requested for it. But she was right about one thing – my track record needed improvement. Samantha would be that improvement.

Or so I kept telling myself.

Trudging under the light of the rising moons, I used the light of Cilia's display bracelet sparingly. We didn't want to attract anything out here. I could only assume Sam had some form of night vision because she didn't seem to have problems manoeuvring in the dark. An eye augmentation most likely.

Beside me, Sam stifled a yawn, "Three hours was not enough sleep," she said, breaking the silence that had stretched between us for the past few hours.

"You'll get more when the sun comes up," I reminded her, "Trust me, this is the safest way to travel through the Dune Sea."

"I believe you," Sam gave me a sidelong glance. Her emerald eyes glinted in the moonlight. Travelling in the dark made it hard to keep my distance from her – all I could think about was when we were tangled up together under cover of darkness. My mind often wandered to the feel of her skin against mine, the sound of her hitched breathing, her hands as they dug into my hair.

"Chris," Sam's voice broke me out of the memory, and I swallowed, hoping I didn't look guilty. But Sam's eyes weren't on me – they were trained on Cilia's bracelet wrapped around my wrist. I hadn't even been paying attention to it. She wrapped her fingers around my wrist and held it up, pressing her lips into a thin line, "You might want to take a look at this."

I pulled my arm from her, our fingers brushing, and stared at the notification blinking on the tiny screen. I tapped it, and the projection flickered in the air with a memo blinking across its screen. It announced that Cilia was missing, but that wasn't what made my gut wrench. Samantha was wanted – that was old news too, but scrolling next to her name, flashing in bright red with bold lettering with a photo to match, was me,

Name: Christopher Daniel Grey

Age: 30 years **Gender:** Male.

Height: 5'10" **Weight:** 145lbs

Eyes: Brown **Hair:** Blonde

ID Badge: 00234985-IDB

Status: WANTED, DoA

I scrolled through the rest of the information provided. I was wanted for the kidnapping of a fellow ICO member and for failing to turn Sam in. From the way the notification was worded, it sounded like I'd gone rogue.

Sam was wanted alive.

I was wanted DoA. Dead or alive.

I gritted my teeth, a frustrated growl forming at the base of my throat before spitting on the ground in a fury. "Looks like we're both criminals now," Sam teased.

I didn't answer her. My mind raced, trying to find a way out of the situation. It was all a misunderstanding. Once we arrived in Aquaria, I could talk things over with Cilia, get her to help clear my name. She owed me that. I saved her life. I glanced back at the Reaper, who glared at me through the dark, eyes flashing as she grinned. My stomach churned. It was highly unlikely she'd be any help.

My next best bet was clearing my name directly at the head office in Centrum. If I delivered Sam as initially planned, that would count for something. "I'm no criminal," I told her, "There's a misunderstanding. That's all."

Sam snickered, but her voice was cold when she said, "Grey. The ICO have turned their backs on you. You're just too blind to see it."

I ground my teeth together as I glared at Sam. She was maddening. How could I go from wanting to fuck her to wanting to plant her under the sand so quickly?

Knowing that I was wanted DoA changed things. I'd have to watch my back and tread carefully until I reached Centrum. I glanced back at Cilia, still trussed across Tweet's back and looking livid. Damn Cilia and her superiority complex. I wanted to throttle her, but what good would that do? It'd only work against me.

Samantha strode purposefully in front of me, I couldn't help but feel that she was gloating over my sudden switch from active Imperial Dune Buster to a lowly outlawed citizen. Funny that it put her in such a good mood considering her arrest was my ticket to freedom.

The continent of Oceana finally emerged from the sands early the next morning. The incline from dusty dunes to continental shelf was so steady we hadn't even noticed it until we stood on a ridge of rocks, overgrown with brown moss, and looked down at the expanse of sand behind us. The Dune Sea.

We'd survived.

Bull Newts and Bartering

CHAPTER 13

It was another four days walk around the rim of the Oceana continent before we reached the marshlands on the outskirts of Aquaria. Bugs buzzed around our ears and birds twittered in the trees that were strung with moss and vines. The marshland heat was no less oppressive, but at least there was more water to go around. Tweet was foaming at the mouth from the exertion of the past few days, her scaled jaws were flecked with stains of blood and worm ichor. She needed a well-deserved rest in a cold stable somewhere. Finally, we could see the first signs of the city. Pipes shone under the sun and steam caused the air to shimmer.

My heartbeat picked up pace as we approached Aquaria. Had they started border control? Following Centrum's lead to filter out criminals and bandits? Now that my ID was flagged, I wasn't too keen on handing it over to authorities.

I brought my bandana up over my face, "Make sure you cover up," I reminded Sam, "The last thing we want is to be recognised and arrested. Now that our faces are being flashed all over the godsdamned place."

Sam cocked her head at Cilia, nodding at the scowling woman with her chin, "What about her?"

I wished more and more that I'd just left her to the sandworm. Stepping up next to Tweet, I dug the gag out of Cilia's mouth. She licked her lips, worked her jaw back and forth. It'd been a day since I'd last soaked it with a bit of water to keep her throat from going dry, "Did you soak it in your own piss?" she snapped, "Get me a drink, you haven't given me nearly enough water."

Sam frowned and narrowed her eyes at the woman, "Why'd you ungag her?"

"Because I don't have an extra cloth lying around," I said, "and we need to cover Cilia up, too. No one can recognise her."

Cilia cocked a thin brow, "And what happens when I scream?"

I opened my mouth to say something when Sam pulled her gun from her holster, "I have no problems using this," she said, pressing it against the woman's temple. Cilia wrinkled her nose but didn't say another word. I pulled her upright, so she was sitting properly in Tweet's saddle, and tied the cloth around her nose and mouth, pulling the hood of her jacket up over her hair. We could always knock her out, but walking around town with Cilia slumped over Tweets back would only work to draw more attention.

Content that we wouldn't be recognised on sight, I nodded towards Aquaria, the rusty spires of its capitol building jutting into the purple and blue sunrise. "We'll find a hotel near the outskirts of town," I said, "Freshen up. Get some rest and resupply."

"Eat some real food," Sam said, "And ditch her," she tacked onto the list, jabbing a thumb at Cilia.

I pressed my lips into a hard line. Despite the situation, I was more than ready to get Cilia out of our hair. The longer she was with us, the more chance we had of getting caught. I just wasn't quite sure what I was going to do about her just yet.

The gates to Aquaria didn't have much security at all. There were cameras at the entrance, posted on either side of the road that had widened to pass between them. We waited in line with a series of carriages and skaali drawn carts loaded with goods. Most of them were brought by triceratops, Tryk, who were bred for this kind of work. They were dumb, responding mainly to food, but could be dangerous if angered. They made me nervous. Three times larger than a raptor and nearly half the size of a Tyrant, they could crush a man quick enough. The three horns that protruded from their faces were mainly used for protection, but I'd seen one gore a man once.

As we passed through the gates, I kept my head low and crossed my fingers. So far, so good.

No alarm bells.

No shots being fired.

Sam stood close to Tweet, guiding her through the crowd, gun out and hidden beneath the edge of her leftover scarf, pointed at the middle of Cilias' back. If she wanted to stay alive, she wouldn't make a peep.

Aquaria was the first settlement on Terrafirma V, built right on the coast of what was once a thriving ocean. It grew into a small city whose sole purpose was plumbing and water filtration for the rest of the planet. A series of islands branched out from the mainland, and these were used to expand the plumbing system, giving the colonists access to the deep-ocean water. They relied on hand filtering at that time. Once plumbing networks were installed successfully in each town, the city of Aquaria began using an advanced filtration system at the edge of Last Ocean to create potable water. Through deep beds of tightly packed sand and moss, workers were able to widen a canal to allow water to flow into the filtration tunnels, down to town, and distributed to neighbouring regions through their massive pipe networks. Hydro-electric generators were installed shortly after that to ensure water could be pushed up hills and through winding caverns and passageways without issue.

To keep it running, workers are on duty twenty-four-seven. Water flows through an intense process of desalination after being filtered through the sand and moss; which includes boiling the water through power provided from solar-electric heating before it is cooled again for distribution. This process leaves salt and other impurities behind, allowing the water to be safely consumed.

We owe a lot to Aquaria. The settlers here worked the hardest of all the colonists, past and present, to ensure this planet would be capable of supporting life. The growing city became a popular destination for wealthy private spaceship captains to offer cruises, navigating their cruisers to and from Terrafirma V, for a hefty price. At once time, there were ocean waters all around the main continents and the atolls. But then, the terraforming began to fail, and little by little things started to fall apart. Pipes began to burst, cutting smaller towns off. Earthquakes rattled the continents, and the Dune Sea grew more extensive as the earth split apart. It grew hotter, and the oceans grew smaller, their waters sinking into the sandy depths.

With the Last Ocean receding, Aquaria quickly lost its appeal as a beachside destination. Now, it was more swamp than anything, and those poor suckers were still putting their noses to the grindstone to provide the rest of us with safe drinking water. Thankfully, because the city is made up of mostly labourers and pipe monkeys, I didn't think we'd be running into too much trouble. It wasn't like Centrum where we'd have to watch our every step.

As we made our way through the city, I noticed the homes that had been built nearly on top of one another, conserving space. Each house was a customary bungalow, unique in their own way. It had a sort of charm to it. It was a shame the city had become so devoid of visitors. Some of the homes still held traces of their former grandeur in the gentle arches of the circular windows and the carved railings and balustrade of patio and balcony alike.

We found an inn quickly enough. The large sign that flashed in green neon light blinked, *The Sea Maidens Bounty*, and slipped the inn-keep some extra bills for a stable for Tweet. He didn't give us so much as a glance and a gruff explanation of the rules before sliding a key across the counter, "Check out's at ten, later than that, and you get charged an extra night," he said.

I nodded my thanks. Took the key.

While Sam was getting Tweet settled, I escorted Cilia up the stairs to our room, a hand wrapped around both her wrists. She remained silent. Which was surprising considering how vocal Cilia had been up to this point. I knew she had to be hatching up a plan, turning the wheels in her head as she tried to figure out how to turn this in her favour.

I'd be doing the same thing in her position.

I kicked open the hotel door and guided Cilia inside before yanking down the cloth covering the lower half of her face. Her eyes glinted as they bored into mine.

"I'm sure you've heard there's a bounty on my head," I grunted, forcing her to sit on the bed. I pulled the chair out from the small desk and flipped it around, settling on it and resting my arms across it's back, facing her. I reached up and took my hat off, rolling the rim of it around in my hands as I spoke, "Any idea how that came about?"

Cilia scoffed, rolling her eyes, "You really *are* stupid," she said and laid back across the bed, a soft moan escaping her lips, "Finally, somewhere soft to rest my head. That skaali is as hard as a stone, you know."

I debated whether to press her for more information, then decided against it for now. Flipping the chair back in place, I took a seat on the other bed, pulling Kato out of my sack.

Still lifeless.

Gritting my teeth and glanced over at Cilia. This was her doing. I don't know what she did to Kato, but I'd make her pay if he was hurt in any way.

Sam entered the room, her eyes flicking from a very relaxed Cilia to me. "Really? She's taking a nap?"

I shrugged, "We have errands to run anyway. I've gotta gather some supplies, do a few other things."

Sam gestured to Kato. "Meeting up with your guy?"

Oh, right. I nodded and held up Cilia's bracelet, "He's not here anymore. Going to meet up with us in Gardenia."

Sam quirked an eyebrow, her nostrils flaring, "I thought the whole reason you wanted to come here was to meet with him?"

"It was, but I used Cilia's comm bracelet to reach out to him. He's in Gardenia. We were already nearly here, and besides, we need supplies. There wasn't time to change the course."

Samantha threw herself down on the bed next to me, laying on her back, her shirt riding up her stomach to expose the crescent of her belly button. "I understand now why you suck as a Dune Buster, how'd you even become an Imperial Dune Buster is beyond me."

I bristled, irritation making my tongue free, "Why, because I take into consideration basic needs? Like supplies? Rest? Food? The value of humanoid life?"

"Because you took the hard road when you could have taken the easier one all along. Not a quality the ICO looks kindly on, I'm sure. Gets expensive, I bet."

I narrowed my eyes, staring down at Kato in my hands. I didn't have a response to that. My thickheadedness was well known to ICO. Sam leaned forward, trying to catch my eyes as I tried to look away. Her eyes softened. They weren't as vivid here in the low light of the inn room. They were muted, more forest green, she said, "Sometimes the hard road is the best. I mean…, I'm not complaining."

"I'm not taking the hard road," I argued, "My plans make perfect sense. And you certainly sound a hell of a lot like your complaining right now,"

She sighed, "Okay, Grey. Keep telling yourself that."

I stood and pointed at Cilia, "Watch her. I'm heading out for supplies." I marched for the door, pulling my bandana up my nose and snatching my hat from the desk. As my hand curled around the doorknob, I heard Sam shift on the bed.

"Chris?"

"What is it?"

Turning, I found her leaning forwards at the foot of the bed on her hands and knees, I could see right down her shirt. She crept towards me. Like a predator waiting to spring. I flinched when she reached up and pulled the brim of my hat down, tugging it playfully. I swallowed and fought back the tingling heat that flared through my core, "What?" I asked again, more forcefully as my throat suddenly went dry. I hated that my name from her lips had that effect on me; she so rarely used my first name.

Her lips curled into a smile, "Just be careful out there."

I released the breath I hadn't realised I'd been holding, "I will," I nodded. Tearing my eyes from Sam, I left the room, closing and locking it behind me. I prayed Cilia wouldn't pull anything. But she was still bound, and Sam was quick, smart, she wouldn't let Cilia slip away.

I left the inn. Stepping out onto a paved road for the first time in what felt like forever. Damn, it felt nice not to be trudging through sand anymore. The streets were filled with workers heading to their morning shifts, they seemed to be just going through the motions. Just another morning, just another day of mind-numbing work to look forward to. Tryk drawn carts ambled through the streets, making deliveries or picking them up. There was a constant hum as skaali, humans, and machines hummed.

Cutting around the side of a faded brick building, I found what I was looking for. A small bazaar had been set up, and I spotted a merchant selling travel-friendly food and browsed his items, pleased to see a variety of bars and tablets that would give us the nutrition we needed for the day but wouldn't take up too much space in our packs. They were cheap, also.

After paying for my goods, I took a moment to consider my funds. I didn't have much cash left. The moment that was gone, I would be forced to use my ID card to draw out more, and that would instantly alert the authorities. Maybe I could be sneaky about it and pull out cash just before leaving town. We'd be well on our way before they could track down the location I'd withdrawn the funds from.

We would fill our water canteens at the traveller's post just outside the city. After that, I hoped we could blend in with a departing caravan to Millertown, which would be our last stop before Gardenia. At Gardenia, we could catch a blimp to Centrum. That'd be the quickest, easiest, way to get things done.

As I reviewed my plans in my head, a large, water damaged PDA screen entered my vision. I had reached the city's town square.

On display was Sam's face. And mine.

I swallowed back the sudden anxiety that clutched at my throat. With our faces blown up so large in the centre of a small town, we couldn't risk staying much longer

Still, I slowed to a stop, staring up at the screen. Announcements rolled across the bottom of it. Numbers that gave the heat and humidity.

Sun-rise and sun-set.

The usual.

But I wasn't looking at that. I was looking at my face, displayed in maximum high-deff. Text rolled underneath our pictures, giving me more details than I had seen in the bounty notification.

We'd been pegged as suspects in the deaths of High Commissioner Alfonzo and six other High ICO from across all the major cities: Centrum, Gardenia, Xylia, and even the Watchtower Plateau. A knot formed in my stomach and hot anger welled deep inside that knot. *Why? What gave them the idea that I had any part in that?* They knew full well I had been sent to collect Samantha. I was nowhere near High Commissioner Alfonzo when he was killed.

It didn't make any sense. *Am I being framed?*

The thought lodged into my mind, consuming everything I thought I knew. *Who was framing me? Cilia?* But how? Camelia had to have a part in it somehow. I never trusted that tyrant of a bitch.

But again, why? Did she really despise me that much? Why not merely revoke my IDB license and banish me from Centrum? *What the fuck did I do that warranted this?*

I wandered through Aquaria carefully, gathering the rest of the supplies; food, water pouches, another first aid kit and more ammunition. I eyed a few bedrolls, then decided against it. The lighter we travelled, the better. Besides, we'd been doing fine without them.

On my way back to the inn, I could have sworn eyes watched me. I could feel them roving over my back.

Studying me. Judging me.

I was paranoid, after days in the hot desert; maybe I'd addled my brains more than I thought.

I discreetly looked behind me, but only spotted a few straggling workers returning from the graveyard shift. My paranoia was getting to me. Perhaps the heat was too. But just to be safe, I worked my way through the buildings, cutting across streets and around buildings and making the trip longer than it needed to be.

Finally, I returned with the supplies. Cilia was awake, glaring at Sam as she tinkered with her gun. Sam's face brightened when I walked in, and she set the gun aside. "Glad, you're back. This one's been giving me the creeps." She shot a look at Cilia, whose eyes were still trained on Sam. Calculating and predatory.

I set the supplies on the table, "We'll just need to grab water before we go," I said. "I learned something new today, it isn't good."

"Oh yeah?" Sam cocked her head, intrigued.

"Yep. Turns out we're suspects for the murders of High Commissioner Alfonzo and six other High ICO. All dead in the last month,"

Sam's lips parted, and her eyes grew wide. Her previous amusement snuffed out like a candle in water, replaced with confusion. She shook her head, "Why the hell would they think that?"

Cilia chuckled from the bed. Both Sam and I turned to glare at her. "Spill it," Sam said. "What do you know?"

Reclining lazily against the headboard, Cilia eyed us like a cat with her prey. "Of course they don't think you're suspects," she remarked, "It's a cover-up, Grey."

I clenched my fists, feeling my nails dig into my palms, "What are you getting as exactly?"

She looked at me with something that was almost pity. Almost. If the desert froze over. "You weren't ever meant to make it back, Grey. You're a shitty Dune Buster, and your license was suspended the moment you left Camelia's office."

Her words were like a punch to the gut. I refused to look at Cilia or Sam, feeling my face heat up.

"The only reason they sent you after Dr Cowell was because they needed someone to draw her out of hiding. She was snug as a fucking bug in the Atolls. We knew she was there, we just weren't sure the exact location. We couldn't identify her right away since she'd scrubbed her DNA signature from the systems. And now she needs our help," she said smugly as her glare passed from Sam to me.

I frowned, and turned to Sam, confused. "What the hell is she talking about, Sam?"

Cilia grinned as we waited for Samantha's answer. Long, tense seconds passed before she finally spoke. "The commissioner's death… it was an ICO assassin. And it was built by me. But then, I knew too much so…"

Cilia burst into laughter, "Frankenstein's monster sent to kill its creator."

Sam stepped forward, her eyes flashing. Anger radiated around her, palpable in the air. Raising a hand, Samantha slapped it across Cilia's face, "Shut up, just shut up! I wanted to leave. I had to leave. But they wouldn't let me. What else was I supposed to do?" she yelled, thumping a hand against her chest emphatically. Her eyes were wild. Her breathing rapid.

My mind spun, trying to grasp the information being thrown at me. "What is going on, Sam? What do you mean you scrubbed your DNA? And you *worked* for ICO? You said you just did some odd jobs for them…what sort of jobs?"

She whirled on me, "Yes, I worked for them, okay? Don't you get it? I was the lead synthetic-bio engineer. And I knew they'd be able to track me down if I left DNA traces all over the place so I…" she paused and frowned, eyes still wild and nostrils flaring as she struggled to decide what to say next. Moments passed. She took a shuddering breath, looking away from me. "So I augmented myself. I changed my DNA. And I ran."

I narrowed my eyes, trying to keep up. "So, what the fuck exactly does that mean? In layman's terms,"

Samantha shrugged. She refused to look at me as she spoke, "Ruff was my biological brother, more or less. I used his DNA and combined it with my own. I was meticulous in the sequencing; it was only supposed to replace a few select genes, just enough to change my basic biology. Just enough to change the recognition systems from locating me after I escaped. But, even I'm not perfect. There were some other side-effects that I didn't expect."

My stomach lurched as the weight of her words fully hit home, my gaze ran up and down her body. I looked at her, really looked at her and suddenly she just wasn't Samanth Cowell.

I shuddered. I couldn't help it. My skin prickled with the realisation. So many things started to click into place with Sam.

"Okay, that was…not the answer I was expecting. I mean, holy *shit.* What side-effects are we talking about exactly?" I lifted my arms, lacing my hands behind my head, and began pacing the small room. I did not see that coming.

Not for all the water in the Last Ocean. Not for all the sand in the Dune Sea.

Not for all the stars.

Samantha let out a sigh and sunk down onto the small, creaky bed. "I don't need a commlink to speak with Tweet or any of the others for that matter. Raptors, I mean. It's like we're connected. And my eyes have changed," she said slowly, turning her head to gaze out the window.

I was right. They used to be brown. Like her brother's.

"Ok, that's not so bad," I said with relief. She shook her head slowly. "There's more. I'm still changing." She hesitated then, carefully unbuckled her vest to pull the hem of her shirt up, revealing fine scales of blue-green that glimmered across the undersides her breasts, graced her ribcage. I hadn't noticed them before in the dark, in the desert. I thought it was just the sand and salt on our skin.

I shook my head, setting my jaw. I wasn't angry, not really. But I was scared. Terrified actually. And maybe a little sickened by it if I was going to be honest.

"How many more changes are we talking about here?" I asked quietly, settling on the bed next to her. I spread my legs and leaned over, crushing the heels of my hands into my eyes.

"I don't know," she admitted. "I don't have the equipment necessary to check it…or even stop it. I have to get back into the labs at the Centrum branch of genetic laboratories." I turned my head and looked at her, my eyes flicked over her face.

She already knew what was happening to her.

That's why she gave in so quickly to the arrest.

That initial protest was just fun and games once she realised how she could use me to help her. And I'd fallen for it hook, line, and sinker.

I really was a shitty Dune Buster.

Samantha, I could understand. But Cilia? I whirled back on Cilia. "You used me," I snarled, "And now you're trying to get rid of me? Why not just revoke my damn license and kick me out of ICO in the first place? It'd have been easy enough."

Cilia rolled her eyes. "You would have pieced things together eventually. You're stupid, but not *that* stupid. And now you know too much. Keep me tied up all you want, leave me here while you go on your suicidal mission. But no matter what you do…It's over for you, Grey," she snickered, "Dead man walking."

My mind raced with questions and insults to spit back at her. "You were sent to dispose of me and collect Sam as bounty?"

"Correct. Since Samantha changed up her DNA, we couldn't find her. Thanks to you, we know all about her now. I guess you were useful in some aspects," she said. Her eyes fluttered condescendingly over me. I wanted to throw a fist into her sharp cheekbones, see if they'd shatter.

But my thoughts ripped back to Samantha. "You willingly built an assassin? Knowing what it was for?" I demanded, turning to her, angrily, "You really are a common criminal."

Sam's emerald eyes blazed, "My back was against a wall. I had no choice. I was trapped under the thumb of a power-hungry commissioner. I wanted out. As soon as the deed was done, I booked it out of Centrum, changing my DNA and identity just to get away from that blood-thirsty monster."

"Who is it?" I demanded to know. I had to know.

Before Sam could answer, Cilia interjected in a low voice. "I'd be careful what you say, Dr Cowell. They want you alive after all…for now. That could quickly change."

Sam closed her mouth, making my agitation spike. I kicked a bedframe, the pain shooting up my foot. "*Shit!*" I yelled. "Fuck you, Cilia. And fuck you, Sam. I've had enough of this shit."

Samantha shot to her feet. "It doesn't change the plan. I'm going to Centrum, whether you're escorting me or not."

"And I'm still going to rip out your throat the first chance I get," Cilia said sweetly, blinking slowly at me as smile slid across her face viler than Camelia ever was. I whirled, punching her square in the jaw. She collapsed back on the bed silently, blinking in shock. I just wanted her to shut the hell up. Clamping my hands around her throat, I blocked her windpipe, staring with hatred at the fellow Imperial Dune Buster who had tried to bust my ass. Cilia squirmed underneath me for a moment, turning red as her startled eyes widened. Her bound hands weakly trying to wrap around my wrist only succeeded in scratching her nails over the tops of my hands, leaving bloodied trails across the tops of my knuckles.

"Chris, what are you doing?" Sam snapped, "You'll kill her at this rate!"

"I'm not trying to kill her," I growled, watching as Cilias' eyes fluttered, consciousness leaving her. I felt her body go limp beneath me, "Though I'm sorely tempted to." As soon as I was sure she was knocked out, I let her go, standing I dusted my hands off. Just touching her made me feel dirty.

"We're leaving. Now."

"To Centrum?"

I stared down at Cilia, clenching my teeth, I was tempted to punch her again, just for the hell of it but she was unconscious, and I wasn't that debased, "To Centrum."

We quietly left the room with our supplies, leaving the key on the counter along with the last of my cash, and grabbed Tweet from the stables. Her saddle hung on the wall, but next to it was another, more comfortable looking one with saddlebags left attached on each side. I reached out and took it, Sam crossed her arms and looked at me, confused. "I'm already a criminal. Might as well," I muttered. Tweet whistled happily at us, and Sam gave her a quick rub down, pulling away loose down feathers before we slung her new saddle over her back. Double-checking the buckles and sliding the reigns into place behind the teeth farthest back into her jaws, we wasted no time loading our supplies into the bags. Kato's still form resting gently at the top. With Tweet in tack and ready to go, we both mounted, Sam in front, and headed for the watering hole to fill up.

"There's a skaali caravan that makes the trek from Millertown and back every three days when they come to bring Aquaria supplies," I said as Sam filled the water pouches, twisting each one shut and sliding it into one of Tweets saddlebags, "I doubt they'd have a problem letting us tag along." I said, pulling my bandana up over my nose again and reached over to tug on Sams, "Keep covered, remember?"

After we approached the caravan at the edge of town, I quickly discovered how wrong I was. The caravan master, a burly man with a dark goatee, shook his head repeatedly. "No. You pay like everyone else."

"We don't have any money," I insisted. "We just want to travel alongside you. We can keep you safe from bandits. You won't even notice us. You have our own supplies. We won't bother you; I swear by it."

He glared at me, his black eyes narrowing as he crossed his thick arms over his broad chest, "You pay."

Sam stepped in, batting her emerald eyes at him as she gently reached out and rest her fingers on his. "We have a raptor skaali. We can help defend the caravan in exchange for free passage with you. Certainly, another guard wouldn't be a bad thing? What do you say?"

The goateed man looked over her, still suspicious of our covered faces, then looked up at Tweet, who opened her jaws wide, revealing her glittering dagger-like teeth and the bore of the gun mounted in her throat. The man grunted, "An augmentee," he seemed to appreciate the work that went into the skaali and asked a few more questions about Tweets specs, her weaponry, how much ammunition she could carry. I wondered now if Sam had sent a mental message to the skaali, encouraging her to look intimidating. The man scratched at his chin, closing one eye as he sized Tweet up one last time and then finally threw up his hands. "Fine. Stay in the back. And I better not hear a word that you've been asking for handouts."

Sam's gaze turned to me, a smug look crossing over her face. "See? Just a bit of bartering does the trick."

"You were batting your eyelashes and played the pretty victim. Obviously, he wasn't going to say no to you."

"Oh yeah?" Sam fluttered her eyelids at me and put a hand on her hip. "Is that what you think of me, Grey?"

I clenched my jaw in annoyance. She was poking fun at me. "Only sometimes. Most of the time, you're an asshole."

"Oh, *I'm* the asshole?"

"Taking advantage of men like me – yeah, I would say that makes you an asshole. Come on, let's get in the back before he realises your true colours and changes his mind."

Sam laughed, and for a moment, my irritation was lifted. Her laugh had always been a charming one when it wasn't sarcastic. We settled in the back of the caravan, filled with carriages pulled by Tryk, who stared us down with heavy-lidded eyes as we passed. Sneezing as flies buzzed around their nostrils. They were trained to ignore the raptors, but no amount of training could dampen down thousands of years' worth of instinct.

Tryks were the prey, and they always would be.

Raptors trotted on either side of the carriages, snapping their jaws and digging their claws into the earth, creating large gouges. Tweet whistled, tossing her head in response. The men who mounted them were armed to the teeth, with rifles on their backs and belts of ammo around their waist. Several of had swords strapped to their hips for additional protection, not to mention the raptors. I didn't know how many of them were weaponised, but it was safe to assume they all were. We led her to the back and prepared for the long journey to Millertown.

"How long will it take?" Sam asked.

"About a day and a half, maybe two," I answered, "But I believe we'll be passing by some dense swampland. Be ready for mosquitoes."

The caravan began to move, and we took up the rear, making sure to stay out of the way of the working raptors. Tweet was still injured and needed more time to heal, so we decided to walk until we couldn't. I quickly realised the rear was the most unsavoury place to be in the caravan. We had to manoeuvre over steaming piles of Tryk dung but fell freely every twenty minutes or so. The smell was terrible, and the bandana did little to filter out the stench, "Fuck me," I growled between gritted teeth. As we walked, I kept catching myself watching Sam. She didn't seem fazed by the smell. But then, she worked with skaali all the time.

Sam turned her head to me and grinned, "You're staring."

I blinked, "Am I?"

"Yes," A muscle in her neck fluttered as she swallowed, "You're scared of me, aren't you? Now that you know?"

"Can you blame me?"

She settled into silence. This wasn't the place to talk. Everything I thought I knew about Sam had been a lie. And I wasn't even sure I could consider her as human anymore. That was beyond bizarre. What kind of creature would she end up becoming if she didn't stop the effects of her DNA alteration? Would she morph into some kind of absurd skaali-human hybrid with claws and pointed teeth?

Would she grow a fucking tail?

I shuddered, cursing myself. She'd managed to make me fall for her, knowing that our shared past would influence me. That the guilt of Jack's death would still sway me. Even after everything, she was again using me, coaxing me along to Centrum. I was okay with that for now. I'd already decided I'd play along.

But I'd be damned if she stood between me and freedom.

Evening descended on us like a warm, wet blanket. The desert had that scratchy dry heat, but here in the swamps, the air was so humid it was like breathing underwater. Giant insects, the size of my fists, and with shells of blue and green, zoomed around my eyes and ears, pinching and biting. My irritation skyrocketed as I swatted and slapped, trying to keep them off me.

Sam didn't seem to have my problems. She remained calm, occasionally glancing back at me with an eyebrow quirked when I got particularly frustrated and started to punch the larger ones out of the air, "Goddammed insects!" I complained.

"Here, come up here by this Tryk," Sam said, gesturing in front of her. She reached forward and touched one of their bridles. They were laced with rows of strings of beads that clicked together as the Tryk walked. The same beads had been laced into their saddle blankets and hung down their flanks. They smelt strange, it wasn't bad but not pleasant either, "These keep the bugs away," Sam said. *She couldn't have mentioned that sooner?*

"If one of these things shits on me, I swear…"

"Shit or bugs, pick your poison," She smirked at me, but the humour was lost in her eyes after our last words. She was offended that I looked at her differently now. I don't know what she was expecting. How was I supposed to react to the information she finally decided to divulge to me?

I trusted Sam, even if she was a criminal, I thought that maybe ICO was wrong somehow, that I could figure out how to get her out of this situation. Today, she'd broken that trust on more than one account.

Grumbling, I inched closer to her, our arms brushing, and I set a hand on one of the Tryks bridles. The beasts smelled awful, like socks drenched in dung and mouldy cheese. But the bugs weren't flying in my face like before. I breathed out a quick sigh of relief, then held my breath and sucked air in from my mouth to avoid inhaling the stench.

The sun was beginning to set when the caravan pushed its way through a particularly dense part of the swamp, foliage and trees covered in spongy moss pressing in on all sides. I spotted a stagnant marsh to the right of us, a film of green slime resting on top of the water. If I hadn't been travelling so close to the caravan, I might have thought it was a grassy field and fallen right in.

The buzz of insects grew louder as we inched closer to the water, and the Tryk began to slow down. Sam shouted up ahead at lead escort, "We're not staying the night in this swamp, are we?"

He barely glanced at us, and I expected him to ride ahead without answering the question. But he surprised me, "No. We have to pass through this part of the swamp before we can stop. There is a clearing a few miles further where we'll be safe. Should reach it before dark if all goes well," he said.

"Thank you," Sam managed to say before he coaxed his skaali forward, leaving us to continue taking up the rear.

"Thank the stars," I breathed, "This place is crawling with who knows what." As I spoke, the swamp water rippled, the green algae on top swirling as something moved under the surface. I tilted my head to the side and watched.

More bubbles. Sam followed my gaze, and we both watched as the water and algae settled back down, the smooth surface one again.

A bird swooped low over the water. Something shot out from the surface in a spray of green water. Grabbing it and pulling it under without so much as a struggle. Sam startled next to me, her hand squeezing my bicep.

"As long as we don't get any closer, we'll be fine," I said, "Looks like it prefers to hunt submerged."

I took two steps forward before one of the skaali escorts cried out, pointing at the water. The movement continued to inch towards dry land if you could call it that with the thick mud and moss everywhere.

"Lock and load, ladies and gents," the caravan master shouted from ahead, "Looks like trouble is headed for us."

Sam cocked an eyebrow at me, "Looks like you were wrong about whatever that thing is." I rolled my eyes in irritation. *Always have to be right, don't you, Sam?*

The caravan continued to move away, the Tryk lumbering steadily away, but the escorts lingered behind, surrounding the muddy water where the creature was lurking, guns loaded and cocked. A few leaned over their skaali, the long-barrelled rifles resting on top of the raptors head ridge for support. I was more than happy to pass them by with the caravan, but Sam settled a hand on my arm.

"We agreed to be an escort in exchange for free travel," she reminded me, "We should stay behind or risk the wrath of the caravan master."

Groaning, I veered my course, following Samantha and Tweet, to line up around the edge of the water with the other escorts. The water stirred with only the barest of ripples. "What do you reckon it is?" Sam asked the nearest guard. He spat out a wad of chew and adjusted his hat, tilting it back to he could see better, "If we're lucky? Just a swamp croc. They're mean and nasty, but a few bullets to the head will do 'em in."

"If we're not?" I asked.

He didn't get a chance to answer. The tongue shot out of the water, thick and purple, and with a splash, the escort was gone. Sam yelped in surprise, and I yanked her back, away from the edge of the slimy pool. "Shit!" I breathed. All guns swivelled to our side of the water, waiting.

As we stared at the rippling water, a lumpy mass slowly parted the green algae, then two eyes the size of dinner plates, blinking once, twice, to clear away the watery debris. It continued to rise, a thick, slick behemoth of a creature with skin the colour of tar. It slithered right up onto the muddy shore, its mouth gaping open.

"A bull newt!" someone yelled, "Fire at will!"

Shots rang out at the creature, which indeed looked like a giant, deformed newt with a mouth like a bullfrog. It gurgled, eyes narrowing as bullets glanced off its skin. Empty shells scattered across the ground around us.

"The hell?" I cried out. "What's that thing made of?"

"It has a protective, bulletproof membrane around it," Sam shouted, aiming her own gun and firing, "Aim for the belly!"

"It's fucking sliding around on it!"

With a hiss, the bull newt shot out its tongue, faster than my eye could follow, and pulled an entire man into its mouth. Only his legs, kicking wildly, stuck out of its mouth at odd angles. Its toothless maw rolled him around a few times before he stopped kicking and it swallowed him down. Tweet skittered beside me, eager to leap into action, but I suspected Samantha was holding her back to keep her from being swallowed alive.

The tongue darted out again. A raptor disappeared, claws flashing, down its gullet no problem at all. It was able to elicit one screech that echoed from within its mouth before it went silent. The bull newt was entirely on land now, and faster than it looked. Sliding on its belly, it raced between man and skaali alike.

I kept my eyes trained on its belly, which it slid protectively across the mud until I realised that it was heading straight for me. "Shit!" I lifted my rifle and pumped my arm, firing a few rounds at its eyes, its gaping mouth, but the thing was too fast, and it was impervious to my bullets, it was nearly on top of me. I dove out of the way just as its tongue glanced my shoulder, narrowly avoiding becoming newt meat. Thick slime trailed down my arm.

As the creature scuttled past me, I noticed the bulges on its back heaving, wriggling. Training my gun, I shot at its retreating back, imagining one of them would pop, and yellow puss would ooze out. It spun, whipping its long tail so fast it knocked a handful of skaali and men off their feet. Samantha's fingers curled around my forearm.

"Stop! You're just wasting bullets."

With another guttural hiss, the bull newt scraped its talons across a man, gutting him. But the spilling innards weren't what made my skin crawl. The lumps on the bull newt's back had begun to rupture, revealing small, sharp-clawed hands and feet and prying noses wriggling from the dozens of now-exposed cavities. Sam cursed next to me. "Are you fucking kidding me?"

"What are they?" I asked, watching as one of the small creatures crawled out of the bull newt's back, shaking mucus from itself before launching into a man's face. It tore at him savagely.

"The babies. Holy shit. She uses them as a backup."

"In her *back?*" I watched in horror as more of the little bull newts wriggled their way out of the mother's back, leaving pockmarks all along her spine, spawning out of her body like maggots. Maggots with clawed feet.

Despite their smaller size, they could still do some damage. A man ripped one off his face, marked with deep gouges, only to have the creature cling on to his fingers and scuttle up his arm, biting at his neck. Blood spurted as it hit an artery. He fell. Three more crowded over him.

"This is madness," I said, backing up as a little bull newt flew past me. "We should just leave, run while we still can."

In reply, Sam shot at one of the baby bull newts. It flew, twitching on the ground before going still. "They haven't developed their protective membranes," she said. "These guys we can shoot."

I set my sights on the little critters, squeezing the trigger I aimed and pumped, repeatedly, counting my kills as I went.

But mama bull newt was getting pissed.

She hissed and sputtered, foam rolling out of her mouth in vast swaths. She began swinging the thick tail, aiming to knock over as many of us as she could. Her tongue darting out to take anyone within reach.

Dart.

Whap!

Gulp!

Once. Twice. The tongue took them.

I took my eye off her for one second to shoot at an incoming baby newt, and that was all the time it took for her tail to hit me square in the chest, sending me flying against one of the carriages in the caravan. The force was enough to topple it over, spilling its contents onto the marshy ground. The Tryk jolted to one side its carriage flipped over. It bellowed in annoyance.

I sat up, dazed, and Sam ran over to me.

"Are you okay?" she asked as she lent me a hand.

I groaned. "That's one whip of a tail," I said, grabbing her proffered hand. But she had frozen and dropped it before even attempting to lift me up. Instead, she fell to her knees beside me, her eyes running over the spilt contents of the caravan. Small crates and sacks of goods lay scattered across the ground. She picked up a box of what looked like spare parts that had split open and carefully turned each piece over.

I hauled myself up, looking around for more rogue bull newts. The mother was busy taking down a Tryk, and the babies continued to terrorise the men and raptors. I looked back at Sam, her face serious, "What is all this?" I asked, scanning the metal parts – and the not-so-metal parts. Mounds of what appeared to be sheets of flesh spread out of the carriage like an intestine across the mossy ground. My gaze landed on a barrel that lay on its side, spilling out what looked like eyeballs. *Fucking hell.*

She ran her hands over bundles of wire, capsules filled with microchips and sinews. There was a padded crate filled with sealed containers of purple fluid. What looked like individual pieces of skeletal frames.

“Parts,” Sam muttered. She sprang to her feet. “For augmented cyborgs. Like the ones I built.”

She didn’t need to elaborate. The one she built as an assassin. I stared at the parts sprawled in front of us, then looked up at the other carriages. “They’re hauling parts for more assassins,” I said.

She nodded and glared at the bull newt, which had successfully taken down the Tryk, embedding its talons in its flesh with a triumphant hiss. The babies crawled across over it, tearing and biting, their throats expanding as they struggled to swallow bites too big for them to chew.

“I’ve got to burn them,” Samantha said, springing suddenly into action. “All of them.” She scoured the parts, presumably looking for something flammable.

“What, the carriages?” I asked, “The caravan master wouldn’t take kindly to that. This is valuable cargo.”

“I don’t care,” she snapped, “We need to dispose of it.”

She held up a bagged liquid of some type and peered at its label, “This’ll do.” She ripped it open and began pouring it over the carriage, the cyborg parts, the crates, and whatever else was left inside. Calming the Tryk down she undid his harness and pushed on his flank, slapping the flat of her hand on him, encouraging him to move on with the others far ahead.

"Gods," I groaned, but I pulled out the box of matches I had picked up with the supplies and stuck one. I looked at her, raising my brows, the flame quivering between my fingers, "Are you sure?"

She grabbed the matches from me and pulled out three more, striking them all and tossing them onto the flammable pile without hesitation. With a flurry of green flames, they caught fire instantly. The scent of burning meat and plastic met my nose. Tweet screeched in surprise next to Sam, she never wandered far.

The flames drew attention. The bull newt looked up from its spoils, blood dripping down her maw; eyes rotating towards the fire. With a high-pitched scream, it darted for us, mouth gaping open. The babies followed close behind in a slimy swarm.

"Shit!" I lifted my gun, aiming despite knowing it was useless against the mother bull newt. But when she reached the flames, they surged, hotter and brighter than before, startling her. The bull newt reared back in surprise, and that was our moment.

Sam and I fired simultaneously, the bullets shooting right into her soft underbelly. The bull newt jerked to the side, writhing, but the damage was done. A low gurgle escaped her as she collapsed on the ground, curling in on herself. The babies, mistaking their mother's sudden immobility as an invitation to return home, began nuzzling into her back, returning to their bizarre little homes and leaving behind the carnage.

Sam didn't wait another second before she tossed match after match at the newt, who screamed when she caught fire.

A few of her young tumbled out of her back, shrieking, their tails on fire, but I shot them dead.

Not stopping to revel in the victory, Sam spun on the carriage and threw the last of the liquid onto it. Smoke, thick and acrid, billowed up into the sky. Shouts of protest came from the men still standing as they urged their steeds after Sam, demanding she stop what she was doing. I held up my gun, training it on the caravan master, whose dark eyes glittered with disdain. "What the *hell* are you doing?" he demanded, cocking his gun with one pump and aiming it at us. He kept his sights on us.

"Taking care of business," Samantha said, and gave the carriage a shove, "How many more of those carriages are filled with that shit? I'll burn them all," she hissed between her teeth and turned to follow the retreating Tryk.

"Bitch," the caravan master spat. He raised his gun to her.

I didn't think twice.

I fired, *bang, bang*. The noise echoed; birds flew.

The man slipped off his raptor's back.

The six other men stared at me in shock, their confusion evident on their faces, before lifting their own guns and taking aim. Tweet leapt into action, rounding behind one of the escorts and biting his head nearly clean off and dragging him from his raptor's back. Bullets sprayed at Tweet, but her hide was thick. If a Tyrant couldn't bring her down, then neither could simple bullets.

I used Tweet's distraction as an opportunity to run. I grabbed Sam by the arm, hauling her away from the burning carriage, sprinting towards the denser part of the forest. I didn't want to do it, but we'd have to risk it. "Wait, I can't leave Tweet!" she cried, ripping her arm from me.

She must have called her because Tweet came barrelling at us, the bullets still flying at her backside. Sam swung herself onto Tweet's back, and I followed suit, turning myself around and squeezing with my thighs, so I was facing the onslaught of bullets and returned fire. Tweet took off, scampering through the dense, tangled roots of mangrove trees.

By the time the sun had fully set, we were alone, the sudden silence of gunfire as eerie as the reek of burnt flesh and chemicals still sharp in my nose.

CHAPTER 14

The mosquitos had eaten me alive. The rest of our journey, I scratched and swatted, cursing their very existence. Why the hell had they been introduced to this planet? Neither Tweet nor Samantha seemed bothered by them, but Tweets bridle kept most of them away. As soon as we thought it was safe again, we had turned back towards the road, coming out far ahead of the caravan. Tweet seemed to be recovering nicely and wasn't objecting to carrying the two of us. At some point, Sam fell asleep, and she rested now, her back against my chest, as we ambled along the path.

When Millertown appeared in front of us, I almost wept. Almost.

I felt the absence of Kato more keenly as we made our way into town. He would have been useful in scouting out our surroundings, making sure we were safe. Bringing me the news. Now, it felt like nowhere was safe and that we'd be taken unawarés at any moment. There was no telling if Cilia had broken from her bonds and tracked us yet. She had to assume we would be passing through Millertown, as it was a crucial step on the way to Centrum.

Where Tylan was a small refuelling station, carrying only the most basic of needs before the crossing into the Dune Sea along the Halcyon Road, Millertown was something else.

Millertown was the first trading post on Oceana that hosted imported and exported goods from neighbouring towns, and from across the Dune Sea. It was the last stop most people made for proper supplies before the long trek across Halcyon Road. Because of that, the place is a buzzing hub of commerce. From roots carved from Gardenia's trees to sulphur from the Yellow Plateau's Sulfur Flats, there is almost nothing that can't be found in Millertown's markets. Everything has a price, and everything can be haggled, traded, or negotiated for. No limits. The thriving black market was rumoured to hold more exotic fare. Rumours said they received a steady supply of Roids, rune-guns, and spell bullets. How they got them?

No one was sure.

No one cared.

As we walked, I took in the mix of human, Kit'th, and others. There were aliens here I didn't know the name of. My eyes grew wide at the sight of a rare Yrmian. She looked human in all regards except that she had an extra pair of arms and her stick-thin form and long neck towered above me. At her back trailed a mix of Yrmian and Kit'th guards. Realising I was staring, I tore my eyes away when her purple ones met my own. I flinched when something bumped into me. Every shadow was suspicious, every stray movement in my peripherals made my head snap towards it. Hypervigilance was getting to me. I knew I was paranoid, but without my skyeye, I felt I was walking blind. I could almost get Sams' feelings towards her skaali.

Before entering the town, I'd woken Sam, and we double-checked our gear, slid the bandanas back over our faces and had jumped down from Tweet to give her a break. But this place was claustrophobic, and I wished more than anything I could climb up on Tweet and run.

"So, where's this guy, you know?" Samantha asked.

"Huh?" We walked on either side of Tweet, guiding her through the throngs of people.

Samantha rolled her eyes, "Your guy," she said, making air quotes with her crooked fingers, "We're meeting him here, right?"

"Right," I rubbed at my eyes. Sleep deprivation was taking its toll. "He works as a bilge rat in the water pipes. He's got a bungalow on the other side of town."

"Can we trust him?" Sam asked. I couldn't see the frown she was making, but I read the doubt in her eyes.

"Yeah. We've worked together dozens of times," I said.

She raised her brows sceptically at me. "*Before* I worked for the ICO," I clarified. "We're pals. Practically brothers."

"Okay, so what's his name?" she asked. I shrugged, "P'tato Sack Tennessee," it rolled off my tongue as smooth as butter. Sam laughed, "The fuck was that?"

"His name, though generally he just goes by Tate,"

She didn't look convinced, and I didn't blame her. But Tate was a loyal friend. I didn't know if it was his real name, pretty sure it was some nickname he'd earned during his time in the Imperial Military long before he migrated to Terrafirma V. You wouldn't think it from the name, but he was smart. I trusted him with my life.

We passed a line of PDA screens mounted on a wall in the town square, they broadcasted our faces and names for all to see, marking us as murderous outlaws. Again, I had to fight down the rage that twisted like a snake inside my gut. The ICO had no right to peg me as a murderer.

Not after years of service. Not after all I'd given up for them. I might not be the best Dune Buster they had, but I was the most loyal one. *Until now, that is.* I kept going, not stopping to see what else they'd probably added to our list of supposed crimes.

Eventually, the suffocation of rusty buildings, overcrowded streets, and noisy vendors gave way to rows of patched up bungalows crammed together along a stream of runoff. It smelt like sewage.

Piss. Shit.

And who knew what else.

I wrinkled my nose. After trailing that caravan, it wasn't the worse smell I'd encountered that week. I led Sam and Tweet down to the end of the bungalow line-up, until we reached a shack of a place, barely standing. Samantha ran her eyes up and down the rotting wood, pieced metal, and peeling paint. "*This* is where your friend lives?"

"Give him a break, he's single," I replied, stepping up the creaking steps to his front porch. "I apologise in advance for the mess."

Sam frowned, "What about Tweet?"

"There's a tethering post across the street, just tie her up. I'm pretty sure if someone tried to steal her, they'd regret it. Plus, it might be a good idea to have her as a lookout since Kato –"

I didn't need to say anything else. Sam squeezed my shoulder and nodded in agreeance. Securing Tweet to a ring of metal, she removed Kato from the saddlebag and cradled him in her arm as she crossed the street. I waited until she joined my side before knocking at the door. We waited and waited some more. I wondered for a moment if he was still at work until we heard shuffling inside. "Imma comin', hang on," a gruff voice said from inside. There was a pop, a click, another pop, and the sliding of a latch. Seconds later, the door opened, and a balding man with a full beard, braided neatly down his chest, standing a whole head shorter than myself stared up at us. He was wiry but muscled, and his blue eyes lit with recognition when they landed on my barely concealed face as I tugged down the bandana.

"I'll be damned, it really was you. I was iffy when you called me using some random comm," he said grinning. A gold tooth glinted under his curved lip. "Tie me to a tyrant and call me dinner! Christopher Grey, come on get yer ass in here,"

"Hullo, Taters," I greeted, stepping into his dimly lit bungalow. Samantha made to follow me, but Tate blocked her path, crossing his arms, he looked her up and down, "Who you got here, Grey?" he asked, narrowing his eyes.

"She's good," I said over my shoulder as I began to peel off my duster, "I'm escorting her to Centrum."

"Ah. ICO business, then?"

"You could say that."

Tate grunted and moved out of the way, but he didn't invite Sam inside. She peered her head around the doorframe, scowling at me. I bit back a laugh and gestured for her to hurry inside. Sam strode through the door like she owned the place, raising her head high as she examined the mess, "Now I'm seeing why you're wary of guests," she said. The place was a mess.

Tate was a hoarder, but not everything was junk. Tech, old and new, littered the few pieces of furniture in the room. Comm devices and scrap parts. Tools and tinkering gadgets. Crates of salvaged equipment from all across Terrafirma V. It was a treasure trove. His work desk was set up with various lights and magnifying glasses. A magnetic board holding tools hung directly above it.

"I just don't like to get mixed up with the wrong people," he said, giving her a wary glance, "I've seen you two on the news, you know," he said. Tapping the side of his nose with one finger.

"I'm sure you did," I scooted some parts aside and sat on the cracked couch, tossing my hat onto the slab of splitting wood that acted as a coffee table. I looked around the room as Tate shuffled further away from Samantha.

"You said you were needing help with something?" P'tato prompted. "Ah, yeah. Do you have anything for my little guy?" I pointed to Kato, still resting in Sams embrace. I was frustrated that he'd been unresponsive for so long. I felt irresponsible for not working to bring him back sooner, but then again, I had been running for my life the past few days.

P'tato walked over to Sam and held his hands out, she handed Kato to him. P'tato frowned as he turned Kato over in his hands, "What'd you do to him?" he asked.

"Nothing. But someone shot an EMP at him. At least, that's our theory," I nodded at Sam. "She's telling me he needs a hard reboot."

"Hmm," P'tato turned Kato over carefully in his hands again. His fingers, on one hand, glinted in the dim light – his whole right arm had been upgraded years ago to an artificial one after a work accident took it from him. His cyborg's arm proved more useful than his old flesh and blood one. He constantly upgraded it himself with new tools and tricks to improve his abilities. He'd installed some visual and audio upgrades as well.

You couldn't slip much past P'tato Tennessee.

He dropped Kato onto my lap and shook his head, "You'd need a program for that kind of reboot. Something made to recover previous data without damaging it. One I, unfortunately, don't have. I just build things. I leave the programming half of things to professionals,"

My stomach sank.

P'tato stroked his beard, tugging on the braid. "But there's a market I like to frequent that might have what you need. And if you can't find it there," he shrugged. "I hear

ICO has been packaging special little nick-knacks and hiding them for their people to pick up. If you found anything like that, something you could use is bound to be in there."

This caught Sam's attention, "What kind of special little nick-knacks?" she asked, her voice low. I could see her jaw trembling. I wondered how much her emotional control was being affected by the changes to her DNA.

He shrugged. "I assume they're looking for more cyborg parts. I hear they're beefing up their agents so they'll be more efficient." He tossed a wink at me, "Look out, son. You'll be more cyborg than me one day if you ain't careful."

"If I can manage to clear my name," I said.

P'tato cocked his head to one side and quirked a sarcastic brow, "What, you're telling me you *didn't* murder all those high-ranking commissioners? The nerve."

I chuckled, "You know me too well."

"Or not enough. One day you might surprise me."

Sam cut in. "Where are the ICO hiding these parts? They could be dangerous."

"If I had to guess," he paused and yanked on his braid a few more times, "I would bet somewhere in the moss gardens. No one goes there but an occasional worker or two, and it's not a monitored area. Agents could slip in and out with considerable ease."

Samantha balled her hands into fists, growing angrier by the minute, "I have to find it." She looked at me. "If anything, we might find something for Kato. But if there are more augmented parts –"

P'tato frowned, "Augmented? I doubt that. Didn't think they were into that tech anymore."

"Oh, you'd be surprised," I grumbled. With a sigh, I stood. My feet felt numb from all the walking and running we'd been doing.

All I wanted was to take a nap and have a good meal.

Dammit. I grabbed my duster, slapped on my hat and retied the bandana. Sam did the same.

"I guess we're heading out. You okay if we crash here tonight? We're absolutely beat."

"Certainly. But just the one night. I don't want no Imperial Dune Busters busting down my door. You know, besides you, Chris," P'tato clapped me hard on the back with a laugh. I nearly toppled over; I was so fatigued.

We left the messy bungalow, and Sam threw me a look. "*That's* the guy we came all the way out here to see? And he doesn't even have the parts we need!"

"He'll find them. He's a master at it."

"I'm curious about these rumoured secret transactions," Samantha mused, untying Tweet, who twittered with excitement. "If Tate is right, the ICO could have been smuggling goods for years."

"I wouldn't put it past them," I said. We both mounted Tweet and set off for the gardens, located at the eastern end of the city. The bungalows gave way to abandoned shops, and then nothing at all but green, mossy foliage where they filtered water. A few workers could be seen here and there, but the gardens were largely left alone by the Millertown citizens.

We dismounted Tweet and set about searching, looking for anything that might look suspicious or out of place. All I could see were shrubs, trees, and moss. So much moss. It was a pivotal element to Millertown's filtration system.

Samantha walked deeper into the gardens, her emerald eyes matching the greenery around us. "They wouldn't go too far out of their way to collect the items, right?" she mumbled under her breath.

I shrugged. "How the hell should I know? They go through the effort of smuggling them, so they might play it safe and hide them deeper in the gardens. We'll just have to look harder."

Sam slowed. In front of us was a small pond, still and stagnant. Swarms of bugs hovered over it. A frog burped somewhere nearby. I had flashes of the bull newt we'd barely survived, and my spine tingled, but this pond didn't look natural. It looked man-made. "What's this doing here?" Sam wondered aloud.

"It's just overflowing? Backed up pipes maybe? It happens."

Sam didn't seem convinced. She inched closer to the pond. It was only about twenty feet wide. Tweet dipped her head toward it, sniffing the water. She clicked her jaws and backed away, swinging her head in irritation when the biting bugs swarmed her head and crawled up into her nose. Sneezing several times, she shook her head and chirped in anger.

"Sam, there's nothing here," I said. "We're wasting our time. I need to find the booster so Kato can – shit!"

Something shot out of the pond, tall and humanoid. Its eyes were replaced by round black circles, its lips peeling back to reveal inch-long teeth that gnashed together into a terrifying, pointy mess. Its shell was a dark green colour and looked utterly naked. My eyes dropped down to his groin – there was nothing down there but smooth metal plating.

A cyborg.

An old one that was more machine than man.

I slung an arm out to keep Sam from advancing, backing us up. "That's not suspicious at all," she remarked. She pulled out her gun. The swampy cyborg scanned us both, taking in the weapon in her hands, and bared jagged teeth.

"Sam, put that thing away. We need to get out of here. More than likely, this thing is ICO property."

"Which means whatever they're hiding is in that pond," she said. She kept the gun trained on the cyborg.

I clenched my teeth in frustration. "They know we're here now. There's no time, Samantha. We need to leave."

"If they already know we're here, then we might as well finish the job, Christopher1!" Without another word, she fired at the cyborg.

Its chest opened, and two long swords emerged, twirling and spinning threateningly. A blade slid out of both arms, and it gripped them with slimy hands. Too much pointy metal for me. But Sam was right.

We were here already.

Too late to back out now.

Gritting my teeth, I pulled out my own gun and shot. The swords at its chest moved quickly, deflecting the bullets. Impressive. "It must have some kind of advanced motion sensing programmed into it," I said, "No way we'll be able to defeat this thing. Unless we blow it up."

"Like that won't attract attention," Sam said. She frowned at the cyborg. Besides brandishing its blades, it hadn't moved from its spot in the pond. "He's not coming after us. Maybe it's all a scare tactic."

"Or maybe he's just not threatened by you."

Samantha glared at me. I tried and failed to hide a grin. She looked to Tweet, then raised her gun again.

It all happened quickly.

Sam made three shots.

The cyborg deflected them.

Tweet zipped behind the cyborg, latching her jaws around its head and ripping it off. The cyborg stood, sparking at the neck, before dropping the swords and crumpling into the pond water. Tweet tossed its head around like a toy, gnawing at it and pawing at it with her claws.

I holstered my rifle, and Sam smirked at me. "Not threatened by me, huh?"

"I guess he should have known better."

With the cyborg gone, we carefully approached the small pond. My anxieties tugged at the back of my thoughts. The cyborg had scanned us both. ICO had to know we were here. They could arrive at any moment. But Sam didn't seem to care about the danger. Before I could protest, she knelt onto the mossy ground and stuck a hand deep into the pond, scrunching her nose as she felt around the muddy bottom. "Well?" she snapped, "Are you going to stand there or are you going to help me?"

The last thing I wanted to do was stick my hand in that pond water, especially after seeing what came out of it. But Sam's hardened green eyes nailed me down. I couldn't say no. Kneeling beside her, I was struck by her actions.

Sure, she'd helped build cyborg assassins. But she clearly despised her hand in it and was doing everything necessary to keep the ICO from crafting more – even if it meant risking her life.

Her hair dipped into the murky pond water she reached further down, the water up to her shoulder. Swallowing hard, I dropped my own fingers inside the pond water. It was warm from the sun. I searched aimlessly, prepared to have my hand bitten off by some unseen creature, but there was nothing. Just the soft bottom.

A sudden cry burst from Samantha's lips. I pulled my hand from the water so fast, I flicked myself in the face with droplets. "Sam!"

But she was laughing. "You scare easy," she teased and reached back into the rancid waters. There was a clicking sound, followed by a squelching noise. The pond began to drain away. She drew her hand out, and we both watched as the water disappeared, leaving behind an empty pond. In the centre of it, where the cyborg had probably been lying in wait. was an airtight sealed box, "Jackpot."

My irritation for her poor joke quickly dissipated. I watched in silence as Sam dragged the box out of the pond and opened the latches. The lid flipped over and inside it, lined up in neat rows, were dozens of smaller boxes. The size of my palm. Perfect for concealing in a pocket. She lifted out one of the boxes and turned it over in her hands.

It was engraved with the ICO crest. "The rumours were true, then," I said, "They're hiding things out here in the swamps."

Samantha nodded as she tried to open the small box in her hand, "Damn. It's locked."

I frowned, "What could be inside? They're too small for cyborg parts, right?"

"Not at all, could be anything really," she said, "They could be microchips or filament bundles." She examined the box's lock, then pulled out a set of small tools from her vest. "I should be able to unlock this," she muttered. I looked around nervously. "We should go, Sam. You can do that later."

"Hold on."

Tweet tossed the cyborg head up in the air and let it fall. It rolled until it stopped at my knees. Purple liquid dripped in syrupy strings from the severed arteries. Picking it up, I moved to toss it as far as I could, pulling my arm all the way back and preparing to launch it.

"I wouldn't do that if I were you," Sam said lightly as she continued to work on the box.

I froze, "Why not?"

She looked up from her work, cocking a brow. "It probably has the programming and some cables we need for Kato."

I lowered the arm, cradling the grisly but precious cargo against my chest, "We really should go," I said again.

"I almost have it…there!" Sam sat back on her hunches triumphantly as the lock clicked and she pried the lid to the box open. She stared at the contents, her lips parting in shock.

Craning my neck to see, I spotted not microchips or filament bundles as she had suggested. No, it was bullets.

Spell bullets.

There were dozens of them in the box.

There were dozens of boxes in the case.

There were possibly hundreds of bullets here.

Sam's eyes shot up to mine. I tried to wrap my mind around what I was seeing. "Spell bullets are illegal," I said slowly, "What the fuck are they doing with so many goddammed spell bullets? The Kit'th, they don't make them no more. Or at least, that's what they're always saying."

Sam scrambled to her feet, collecting as many of the small boxes as she could carry and shoving them into my duster pockets. I shook my head in disbelief. Spell bullets were rare. Or at least they were supposed to be.

"It's ICO, Chris. Just because they make the laws doesn't mean they follow them," Sam grimaced.

CHAPTER 15

My fingers brushed back the curtains for the thousandth time as I peered out P'tato's window.

"Chris!" Sam snapped. "Get away from that damn window, or I swear I'll toss Kato into the trash and be done with it."

I dropped the curtain, throwing her a scowl. "It'd be the last thing you ever did," I said.

She sat on P'tato's floor, tools scattered around her, her legs crossed as she bent over the inert skyeye, trying to fix him with the cyborg cable she'd found hanging intact from its brain cavity, "Besides, after what happened today, we can't be too careful."

Sam connected the cable to Kato and an electronic recharge device P'tato had in his piles of goods. "You worry too much," she said.

P'tato laughed from the kitchen table. He was halfway through a whiskey, his face already ruddy from the spirits. "She's a keeper, Grey. Handy with a wrench and tells it like it is."

"She's a doctor of bio-engineering. And her carelessness got her into the mess she's in now," I said. Sam froze, her hands still on Kato. I regretted the words instantly. Tension ballooned in the air, suffocating.

"You know what? You can fix your own damn bird," she said, tossing Kato none too gently to the side and standing up.

"Samantha," I started. She'd already stalked to P'tato's stash of alcohol and poured herself a glass, downing it in several quick swallows. I wandered to Kato, still a lifeless mass of metal and feathers, and picked him up, checking to make sure she hadn't damaged him. P'tato raised his brows at me. I sighed, setting Kato on the already cluttered table and approaching Sam. "Look, I didn't mean it that way. It came out wrong. I'm sorry."

Sam turned away from me, her cheeks pink. "I know you think less of me after our conversation with Cilia," she snapped. "But I can take care of myself. Always have. Especially after Jacks' death." Her words punched me in my gut, and I recoiled.

"I'm sorry," I said quietly.

She sniffed, then turned her bright green eyes on me. "Respect me, Grey, or I'll leave your ass trussed up for Cilia to find while I make my own way to Centrum." She stalked past me and picked up Kato, again, mumbling an apology to the inert bird and refocusing on reviving him.

P'tato cleared his throat. "So, spell bullets, huh?"

The boxes of bullets were laid out on the table. "Yeah," I said. "We were surprised, too."

"What do you reckon the ICO needs them for?" P'tato asked. "And do the High commissioners know about it?"

"I'm sure they do," I said slowly, "In fact, I think a few power-hungry commissioners are in on it. Does that sound right, Sam?"

She didn't answer. She'd started the boost on Kato and was busy with her work, jaw set as she peered into the hatch usually hidden by feathers, exposing his inner workings. A small computer monitor was set up next to her. Kato was plugged into it, and occasionally she would reach over, tap a few keys, narrow her eyes as the code output, and then continue working.

"Corrupt politicians," P'tato said with a shake of his head. "Who woulda thunk?" He winked before pouring himself more whiskey. He extended the bottle towards me, raising his brows in question.

I waved my hands in protest and shook my head. "I need to be in full possession of my senses right now."

"Gods, are you going to even sleep tonight?" Sam asked from the floor, she wasn't even looking at me. I made a face at her, curling the edge of my lip in a sneer.

My fatigue wore on me, but I couldn't imagine sleeping. Not when the ICO could be barging in any moment. Not when I was wanted *dead* or alive. "I'll sleep better when Kato's on watch," I said finally.

"He'll be conscious soon enough," Sam said, "I've managed to debug his hard drive. Restored some missing software. Fooled around a bit. He had some weird shit on there, some program I've never seen before was suppressing his archival data. It's old, though so it was easy to by-pass. He should start to remember it when he wakes up."

My chest tightened. "Come again?"

"I said, I debugged his machinery. He had some files locked uptight, but I opened them. He'll be able to access them after this."

"You hacked his original source files?" I said tightly.

Sam glared at me, not liking my tone. "Yes? Isn't that a good thing?"

No. I liked Kato the way he was. I didn't need him remembering his past. It might open all kinds of issues – it could alter the personality he'd developed from our bond together. I bit back my annoyance. Sam wouldn't understand. Or maybe she would. But she clearly didn't view Kato in the same way she saw her raptors. Who knows? Perhaps Kato remembering his past could be useful somehow.

"You never told me," P'tato slurred, setting down another empty glass. "Why exactly are you trying to get to Centrum? To turn her in?" He pointed at Sam.

Sam and I looked at each other, eyes locking. "No," I said quickly. "No, things have changed now. I'm helping her to –"

"He's escorting me there. I have personal business to attend to," she said, cutting me off.

Tate smiled as if he were in on the secret, tilting his glass back and emptied it. He tugged at his braid and grinned. "Right. Personal business." He filled his glass again and raised it to Sam in a tipsy toast. "Well, you should head to the black-market before you leave. Might have some useful items. For sneaking around and the likes, ya' know?" He winked at me, swallowing and pouring himself another glass. At this rate, the bottle would be gone in a matter of minutes.

"That might be a good idea," Sam said briskly. Kato shuddered under her hands – the first sign of life I'd seen from him in days. Relief surged through me. "We should go tonight," she said, "We'll probably leave tomorrow morning. Right?"

My head pounded with the thought of delaying sleep yet again. But Sam and P'tato were right – it could be useful to root around for some supplies.

Kato's eyes flew open, and Sam smiled. "Hey, little buddy." I rolled my eyes with at her saccharine smile, if only he'd witness how she'd treated him a few moments ago. With a ruffle of feathers, Kato lifted himself to his feet, extending his wings as he moved them up and down, checking to see that everything worked.

I could have kissed Sam right then. I opened a commlink and reached out to Kato.

[You with me, K?]

[Of course, Grey. I am at your service. As soon as my re-boot protocols are completed, that is]

The skyeye fluttered from Sam to my outstretched arm. I scratched the short feathers around his face and earholes, "Good to have you back, Kato," I said aloud with a smile. My eyes met Sam's. "Thank you," I said, "Really."

She shrugged. "You're kind of a jackass without your bird."

P'tato barked out a laugh. I didn't crack a smile. I suppose I deserved that, after what I'd said about her earlier. I looked at Kato, who looked back at me, his eyes adjusting to the dim lighting of the bungalow.

[It appears I've missed some things while away]

[Not much] I thought, and continued to scratch around his head and neck, he leaned into it. His skin receptors enjoying the sensation.

[Sam said she uncovered some of your old archives. You remember anything from before we met?]

Kato's thought didn't come right away, that made me nervous; finally, he said [Yes]

Sam had gotten up to grab another drink. P'tato stared at Kato and me like he knew what we were talking about. He couldn't say, but he could undoubtedly guess, I asked Kato directly, [Care to share?]

[No] The answer was quick and final. I frowned as confusion and curiosity conflicted and crashed together in my mind. I could order him to tell me. I was his master and could technically order him to do anything I wanted, but I viewed Kato as a valuable friend, no matter what Samantha or anyone else thought of him.

[Will I ever find out?]

[Yes. When I'm ready] he said. I waited a few moments as Kato shuffled through the memories covering the past few days that I'd uploaded over the commlink, getting him up to speed. [Why am I not surprised you've gotten into so much trouble without me, Grey?]

[Yeah, I know, right?] I laughed and opened the door to let Kato out to stretch his wings and get a good overview of the town. Already I felt much safer with my skyeye up and flying again. My thoughts seemed less empty. I hadn't realised just how lonely I felt inside my head, thoughts bouncing around without an echo, without his constant contact and commentary against my thoughts. The skaali was always there, but it was different with Kato.

"So, are we going to the market or not?" Samantha asked. I nodded, lifting my bandana over my face and pressing my hat down over my head. I turned to P'tato, surprised he could still stand. He always did carry his liquor well, "Tate, lead the way."

The three of us set out, leaving Tweet behind to rest. The sun dipped behind the bungalows in a display of purple fading to dark blue and black. The back of my eyes felt dry and itchy from lack of sleep. I'd be resting well tonight assuming I got to rest in a bed at all and not in a box hauling my dead body to Centrum.

I had the rune-gun in my back holster, previously useless, and I felt much better knowing I had a pocket full of ammunition for it if I needed it. I didn't think we'd come across any spell bullets anytime soon, if at all, but Samantha had insisted we hold on to the rifle, and it was lucky we did.

P'tato led us into a dark, marshy part of town, then down decrepit cement stairs to a cavity under what was once supposed to be a train station. It never saw any use after dune bandits hijacked one too many, killing most of the passengers and stealing all the goods.

The underground area smelled damp and musky. Mould and rats. I couldn't see them, but I felt their beady eyes watching us. And it was wickedly dark. My senses were on high alert, expecting a DB to pop up in front of us at any moment, but the lengthy tunnel was silent.

No, not silent – voices bounced off the walls, quiet at first, but by the time I spotted the orange light pulsing from a bend ahead it had increased in volume. We emerged in a pocket of space with a high, two-story ceiling, making the underground room echo. Dozens of merchants had set up shop here and there. Tables spread out with goods they called out to passerby with prices and recommendations, all while their hawk-like eyes observed as cash passed from palm to palm. We didn't have some money, but I did bring along a few boxes of spell bullets to wet their whistles with in case they weren't interested in the gadgets Tate brought with him.

"This is incredible," I said, as we entered the market, "How have the authorities not caught on?"

"The local ones know about it," Tate said, "But they don't stop us. Helps boost our shitty economy, really and keeps us out of trouble." He led us through the stalls, waving off salesman trying to pitch their goods to us until we approached a thin woman who looked about a hundred and fifty years old, which wasn't even much of an exaggeration. The bags under her eyes were riddled with purple veins and drooped, the skin on her face bunched up around her chin and jaw.

"P'tato Tennessee," she croaked when they approached her. "Thought I'd be seeing you soon."

Tate turned to us. "Guys, meet Maggie. We call her Magpie. If you want something unique and useful, she'll most likely have it."

"Pleasure to meet you, Magpie," Sam said pleasantly. I scanned the items she had laid out on her portable table. Around her, there was more merchandise piled in boxes and spilling onto the floor from a tarp she had pitched up like a tent behind her. I picked up a small black box that rested at the edge of the table and held it up.

"That's a cockblocker," Magpie said.

I made a face; sure I'd misheard her, "Pardon?"

"She means a comm blocker," P'tato said. "Useful when there's security like scanners and cameras. It blocks their comms temporarily so they can't send or receive any alerts. By the time you do, you'll have the chance to get outta there."

Samantha grabbed the comm blocker from me. "We're taking this," she said and rummaged around in her belt for a handful of spell bullets. "We don't have money," she said, "but we'll trade with these." She held out her hand, the shots resting innocently in her palm.

Magpie didn't look too shocked to see them. She lightly picked one up in her knobby fingers, examining it. "Five of 'em," the old woman said.

Sam's eyes narrowed, "Spell bullets are illegal. Even just one would fetch a higher price than this thing," she said, holding up the comm blocker.

"No here they ain't. We see 'em all the time. And do you think that box is legal?" Magpie chuckled, "I'll take four bullets, no less. Take it or leave it, and then you can leave my stall. I don't deal with back hagglers."

My eyes flicked from between Sam and Magpie. *Was she really going to blow four bullets on a stupid little box that would only delay the inevitable?*

"Sam," I started.

"Done," she said, and before I could stop her, she placed four bullets in Magpie's hand. Snatched the comm blocker and shoved it into her satchel. I did a quick calculation in my head. There were six bullets in each box we'd found, and we collected five boxes. Giving up four spell bullets didn't sound like a lot now, but if we kept spending them like this, we wouldn't have any left to defend ourselves with.

Sam wasn't going to need that damn box anyway, I thought irritably. But I kept quiet. After a bit of searching, Sam also found some high-powered suction devices for climbing up walls and a laser crystal to install in Tweet when she had the chance. "Can you imagine how cool she'd be with a laser shooting from her eye?" she nearly squealed.

I reached out to Kato but didn't get a response. I tried not to worry about it. It was probably nothing. I breathed out, calming myself. I doubted a commlink could make a connection down here. Too much interference with layers of concrete, plumbing, cables, and the like.

We left Magpie with six spell bullets and wandered the market a bit more, but dawn was approaching, and many of the stalls were closing up, and none of the remaining items was as useful as Magpie's. I wanted nothing more than to head back to Tates', get some food in my belly, and sleep off the last few days.

"You happy now?" I asked Sam as we left the market and made our way back out of the sewage system.

"Yes," She turned to me, her eyes gleaming as she grinned mischievously, and my chest constricted. She really thought I was going to help her break into a Centrum lab.

As soon as we left the tunnel, Kato broke into my thoughts, [Grey. Bad news. Cilia's here, and she doesn't look pleased about it one bit]

Fuck.

CHAPTER 16

"Dammit," I growled through clenched teeth. Sam, Tate, and I ducked into his bungalow. The early morning sun throwing bars of shadow across the floor.

"Sorry I can't be more help, Grey," Tate said as he watched Sam and I gather our things. "I hope you make it to Centrum." He turned to Sam, considering her, "And I hope you find what you're looking for, Miss."

"You've done plenty, Tate," I said, "You might want to lie low a bit. Cilia's clever. She might know we were with you."

"I can take care of myself right enough," Tate said and spread his arms wide, stepping towards him, "Come here, boy. Bring it in." I hesitated for a second, then walked into Tate's quick embrace. He wasn't a hugger. Not from what I remembered and I felt my suspicions rise. He slapped me on the back. Two hard thumps, "Watch out for that one," he whispered in my ear. "She might not look like a killer, but they never do." I pulled away from him, stamping down my doubt, and he grinned at me like nothing had been said. "Safe travels, Grey," He placed his hand in mine, tucking some money into my palm as he winked, "For the blimp."

We left the bungalow as soon as we had everything we needed, stopping to untie Tweet. "Is it wise for us to leave this late in the morning?" Sam asked, mounting the raptor, "If Cilia is around, we'd be easy to spot."

"Kato has an eye on her," I said, keeping my voice low, "He'll let us know if she gets too close. I imagine she was informed about us in the gardens, but she doesn't know where we are now. The best thing is to get as far away as possible." I mounted Tweet behind her, and we set off, leaving sleepy Millertown behind and making our way to Gardenia, which, thankfully, was a short five-hour journey. Once we arrived, we'd resupply and catch a blimp. As long as we kept ourselves covered and paid with the cash Tate lent us, we shouldn't raise suspicions.

Settled on Tweet's back, the rhythm of her quick but steady gait made my eyelids droop. All I wanted to do was lay my head down and sleep. With each step the skaali took, I hunched forward a bit more until Sam's hair tickled my nose. She smelled of gunpowder and leather.

I wasn't even aware I had started sleeping with my cheek pressed against Samantha's back until I nearly slipped off Tweet. Awaking with a start, I wiped a bit of crusted drool from the corner of my mouth and straightened.

Sam glanced over her shoulder at me, "Finally, you were starting to snore," she said.

"You're the best pillow I've had this entire trip," I muttered, stifling a yawn.

[Kato, how far are we from Gardenia?]

[Fifteen point two miles. Estimated time of arrival is two hours and ten minutes at your current pace] he said, his shadow passing overhead. *Damn, it was good to have him back,* I thought as an overlay of our path flashed across my retina. The road was a straight shot to Gardenia and should be a comfortable trip. Assuming Cilia didn't catch up to us, that is. First, we'd cross through the last remnants of marshland, then pass through a bit of dessert, and then the path would enter thick forests that lined either side of the trail for as far as Kato could see.

"You can go back to sleep if you like," Sam said quietly in front of me, "I can handle the rest of the journey myself. I'll just follow Kato's shadow." She looked up as my skyeye swooped low over our heads.

I hesitated, knowing she must be as tired as I was. "Aren't you tired? You could catch a few winks."

"On Tweet? There's no way. I can't sleep like that. Besides, I don't need much rest. Not since – well, not anymore."

I bit back a comment, sucking air between my teeth even as I stared at Samantha's back. The soft fabric that invited me to once again lay my cheek against it. The roundness of her bare thighs and hips spread between my chaps. Relenting, I leaned forward, looping my arms around Samantha's waist in case I tried to slip out of the saddle again. She didn't react, but my heart beat a little faster with the close proximity. Her scent was wild and wonderful, smelling of the desert and warm leather. Just a few inches up or a few inches down and my hands could be going places they remembered all too well. But I barely finished the thought before succumbing to sleep.

What felt like only a few short minutes later, Kato woke me, [Rise and shine, cowboy. Gardenia is ETA, ten minutes]

Peeling my eyes open, I licked my lips. They'd gone dry in the air grown dense with the heat of the day. I straightened, arching my back and stretched as it popped. My neck ached from the awkward position I had subjected it to for so long, but at least I felt more rested. Two hours was just enough to let the aches and pain settle in, but my head did feel clearer. It was better than nothing.

I looked around. On either side of us were thick trees and greenery. In my sleep, I'd missed our passage from rusty swamp then through the desert to lush forests. A shadow passed overhead, and I tilted my head back, expecting Kato. It was a blimp. And beyond that, Gardenia.

Blimps rose into the sky from the Imperial Blimp Tower, making their slow northern trek across the sky towards Centrum. Tall buildings twinkled with lights in the evening light and vehicles, like the kind you'd see in Centrum, great metallic beasts that hovered and flew through the skies, honked and spluttered over the streets. Despite the noise and lights, Gardenia was a shadow of what it once was. Most of the tall buildings had gone dark and unoccupied. The few citizens that still lived here weaved in and out of streets that were once bustling with energy and lined with shops, bars, restaurants, gambling casinos and more exotic forms of entertainment. Old shops that once sold sunglasses, towels, seashell jewellery, and bikinis stood dark and empty. Gourmet seafood joints were boarded up, leaving only a few grease spoons still in business. Deeper in the wasting city, one began to notice man versus nature battling it out. The further east you went, the more nature conquered. No one really tried to cut back the overgrowth that had occurred in the last eighty years as trees and thick vines fought to take back what was once theirs. Once, the coast was lined with pristine white beaches dotted with luxury hotels. Now, no one wanted to brave the thick foliage to get to them, and the buildings have been left to rot.

Sam tightened her newly purchased scarf, courtesy of two spell bullets from Magpie, "I would have loved to live here when it was flourishing," she said.

"Everything was probably overpriced," I said.

"Better than being trapped in Shady Plateau, surrounded by desert sand and worried about getting Rust Lung."

I shrugged, "Fair enough."

Couldn't argue with her on that.

We picked up a few supplies like food and water, and some sunglasses to replace the bandanas. We weren't going to get away with wearing them out here in the wetlands, and certainly not in Centrum. After we'd picked out our sunglasses, we led Tweet through the streets to the blimp station. Kato circled overhead, taking in the city's layout and sending me images in quick succession as he scanned the Blimp Tower. It was ICO property specifically, and unless we could come up with serious cash, we'd be needing to find another way on board. Sam waited with Tweet while I got into line for tickets, hoping Tate had given me enough. Usually, I would just flash my badge, but right now, that wasn't a possibility. This was the one area of Gardenia that they had managed to maintain the upkeep. The ticket booth windows were scrubbed free of grime, and the doors leading into the station shone with polished brass.

I fingered the money in my pockets until I reached a ticket booth, the woman behind the counter smiled at me, her eyes hard.

"Two tickets to Centrum, please," I said.

"Round trip or one way?"

I hesitated, "One way. We have a skaali that needs transporting, as well."

"We have an area for the animals and skaali," she assured me. When she told me the price, I just about keeled over. I had no idea it cost that much. Damn, didn't I feel privileged knowing ICO had paid for multiple trips in the past. I dug into my pocket as she asked if I planned to pay in cash or credits. I was shocked to see Tate had given me just enough, and a little more, to cover the cost. *He must have already looked up the prices. I owe that blessed fucker*, I laughed. Smiling I paid the tickets, then strode over to Sam and Tweet.

"Our blimp leaves in twenty minutes," I told her, "Tweet will need to be with the rest of the skaali. Her ticket was twice the price of ours. Imagine that."

"I mean, would *you* want to handle a bunch of creatures with sharp teeth and guns were hidden inside them while miles up in the air?"

"They give them a sedative to help them relax and cooperate, EMP claspers keep the weapons disabled, but it's temporary. Not like Kato," I said, and eyed Tweet, "Sorry, girl."

She clicked her jaws and whistled at me, oblivious but sending tumbling thoughts.

Fish. Sunny day. Back itches.

Inside the large station was a cafe with a few old photos mounted on the walls. They were of Gardenia in its glory days. Families making their way to the beach, blimps filling the sky like balloons on a birthday, long lines in front of the famous ice cream parlour. A pang of nostalgia hit me, even though it was a time I wasn't alive for. When I came into the world, Gardenia had already begun to crumble a long time before.

In front of us was a set of steps, and near that, an elevator, gleaming with gold leaf. We took the elevator because I didn't think I could brave the stairs, and there weren't many people around anyway.

Tweet was checked in with a handler, who sedated her before our eyes and led her away, assuring Sam that she'd be fine and if there were any issues we'd be notified immediately. We shuffled into line with about twenty other people who all looked like they needed a nap.

The ticket master barely looked at us as we handed him our tickets. Everything was going surprisingly smoothly. I expected Cilia to crash through a window and tackle us before we could board. But Kato, perched on my shoulder, didn't say anything, and we were let through. We walked down the runway and entered the blimp, which had an antiquated feel to it, and found our seats. Nestled into the plush furnishings, I was finally able to breathe.

"Almost there," I murmured.

"We haven't even taken off," Sam reminded me. She blinked sleepily as she stared out the small window she was seated next to. From our perch, we could get a better view of the crumbling city – I even spotted a wall of vines crushing the brick of an old auto shop and a ship on its side half-buried in the sand with trees bursting out of its side.

It was the first time I was able to relax in a long time, but I knew it'd be short-lived. Once we got into Centrum, we'd have to go through a security checkpoint. I had no idea how we'd get past that. The sunglasses would do little to obscure our wanted asses. Thoughts began tumbling over each other as I tried to come up with a plan ahead of time.

I was calculating our chances in my head when Sam's head settled on my shoulder. I froze. She sighed deeply; she'd been up the whole night and day. At least I'd managed a couple of hours of sleep. A warmth filled my core, and I wrapped an arm around her shoulders, holding her protectively against me. She wriggled closer, "Wake me when we get there, Chris," she mumbled, half asleep.

I savoured the pressure of her weight against me. My fingers trailed up and down her arm, soft and free of scales.

For now.

I pushed the thought out of my head. She would get help; reverse the effects her DNA scrub had caused and get better. No more changes. No more skaali. Her breathing slowed as she fell asleep, and I had to wrench my thoughts away from pressing her closer. Memories of that night, making it hard to breathe as my pants grew tighter. We'd already been intimate, and she was more than flirty enough. Did she view me as a one-night stand, or would she mind a few more rounds?

My mind came to a screeching halt. I wasn't here to get distracted. I still had a mission to complete, wanted or not.

I had a job to do.

A reputation to repair.

A reward for securing.

Samantha was beautiful, intelligent, strong, brave, all the things I'd ever want in a woman. But she was also manipulative, deceitful. And not human.

The journey wasn't long – two and a half hours by blimp. It would have been another four days on skaali thanks to all the overgrowth. I stared out Sam's window as we descended, my heart leaping into my throat. Kato stirred on my other shoulder. His eyes clicked as he scanned the city below.

[They don't check all IDs] he reminded me. I nodded silently.

It was true. Centrum had an enforced security system, but it was lazy. Occasionally you'd get a new guy. Some hotshot fresh out of the academy that felt he still had something to prove. He'd stir up trouble by taking his job too serious. Pull aside someone he shouldn't. Next day he'd find he either didn't have a job or he wished he didn't. Many an unsuspecting newbie found themselves shipped off to fulfil their duty at the Watchtower, changing the bedpans of criminals held there. Or worse, he might find himself in drug-riddled Spurtown. No one envied the poor sap assigned to Spurtown.

I know.

I've been there. It sucked.

Visitors were to filter in from checkpoints, but only about half of them were stopped for an ID check. The chances we were stopped were fifty-fifty. Not the best odds, but I'd seen worse. I snorted, *my record was worse.*

I just didn't know what to do if we were pulled aside for ID check. Nervously I thumbed the spell bullets resting in my duster pocket. I was surprised I managed to keep them on me, but then they didn't really do much of anything security-wise back in Gardenia. They probably assumed Centrum would take care of anything nasty, leaving their hands free of it.

As the blimp drifted towards the tower landing pads, I could see the magnetic claspers waiting to grasp the keel to hold the blimp in place. A sting of regret buried itself in my cut, twisting. Not quite sixteen years ago I'd managed to sneak my way onto a blimp with Sam's brother, Jack. And not quite sixteen years ago, Jack died. I pushed the thoughts down. I didn't have time to dwell on the past. Reaching a hand out, I tapped Sam's shoulder, her skin warm beneath my hand, her eyes fluttered open. The emerald green of her eyes flashing, they were threaded through with gold, *that is new*, I pressed my lips together, "Welcome to Centrum."

Sam rubbed at her eyes and blinked out the window, taking in the tall, cramped buildings. "It's as much of a shit hole as the other places we've been to," she remarked.

I laughed at that. What was she expecting? Most of Centrum was shitty. It got its reputation as a glamorous city from its centre, where the wealthy still lived in luxury and ignorance to the rest of Terrafirma V. I doubted their blissful days would be endless. But for now, that was all they cared about. The moment things got really bad they'd just launch themselves back into space and search for a new place to start their debauchery all over again.

"You get enough sleep?" I asked Sam.

"I did."

I smiled, "That's my girl."

She paused, eyes locking with mine as she tilted her head. "You don't like that? Kato was right, my bad." I said by way of an apology.

"Hmm. My girl…no. But, I could get used to it." She flashed me a smile that made me want to lean in and kiss her. Instead, I turned away, watching as passengers stood from their seats, getting ready to leave the blimp and carry on with their mundane lives. "Tweet is upset," Sam said beside me.

I quirked an eyebrow at her, "Oh?"

"The sedative is wearing off, and she doesn't understand where she is. Or where I am," Sam chewed at her bottom lip, "I hope she doesn't get violent."

"I'm sure the handlers deal with skaali all the time," I said, "They'll give her another sedative if they need to."

We disembarked from the blimp. Only a few paces ahead was the checkpoint I had been dreading – narrow gateways everyone had to pass through before entering the capital city at large.

[Kato, keep an eye out for me. If things get dicey, where can we run?]

[If you get stopped, there's a possible escape route at your disposal] Kato said at my shoulder. His feathers brushing against my ear.

[Where?]

[There's a bridge just outside this station with a door beneath it. It leads to an intricate underground system where we could lose anyone following us]

I frowned. If I wasn't in a desert I was underground it seemed. We stepped closer to the checkpoint. Four security guards systematically waved people through and stopped every other passenger for an ID check.

[Are you sure?] I asked as we grew closer to the guards.

[I've accessed the schematics from my archival files]

We were closer now, only a few more people in front of us. Sam's hand slipped into mine. I looked down at her in surprise. Squeezed her hand, interlacing our fingers.

[I have a confidential map in my database that covers Centrum's underground network. I've been down there myself numerous times]

I tried to keep my surprise from my face, it'd make me look suspicious if they knew I was talking to my cyborg privately, [Since when? From your previous owner? Why would they have a map of the underground?]

[That is classified information] Kato hooted softly.

Sam leaned up and pressed her lips to my ear, "If we look like a couple, crazy in love, they'll be less likely to stop us," She whispered. Her lips brushed my cheek. I grew hot all over. She squeezed my hand hard. Time to play along.

"Enjoy the trip, babe?" The pet name felt foreign on my tongue. We were ten people away from a security member.

Sam giggled and clung to me, nuzzling my neck. "As much as I enjoyed our romp last night." She winked at me, and I swallowed hard. *Romp? No one uses that word.* Her acting was terrible. I'd have booed her off the stage if I didn't need her to keep this up. Our lives depended on it.

But mine wasn't much better. I could feel myself getting more irritated the closer we inched toward the checkpoint. "That'll be a distant memory compared to what I have in store for you tonight," I said, wrapping my arm around her waist and pulling her in tight against me. I caught a nearby woman rolling her eyes at us. *She's just jealous*, I snickered to myself.

Sam lifted my hat off my head and combed her fingers through my hair, "Your hair has the most precious golden streaks," she said, her eyes flickering over my hair, my face, my eyes shielded behind the sunglasses, "I do hope you don't go bald one day. You know, from wearing this hat all the time," she said, but her smile had turn acidic. She was enjoying this. A bit too much.

I reached out and took my hat from her, flopping it back on my head, I grinned and leaned over her, pressing a kiss to her forehead. "You'll still love me, even if I'm bald," I teased, feeling my throat go dry. Five people.

"Gods, I love everything about you," she shouted. "I can't wait until you're officially mine. All mine. Just a quick trip to the ICO Headquarters, sign our names on the line, and it's done!"

Her tone had become possessive, almost as if she was serious, and it was kind of a turn on. I nodded, keeping the grin plastered on my face. Trying to make it look friendly. Not serious. Not worried.

"Love you," She planted a kiss on my lips, wrapping her arms around my neck so that Kato fluttered up in the air before settling back down when she released me. I almost forgot about our impending doom four feet away from us.

"I love you so much," she said again and giggled. She actually giggled. Like a teenager.

It was awful.

[I hope you know I am recording this] Kato said.

"Sir, wait."

My adrenaline spiked as a hand blocked my pathway through the door. We had been so close. So goddammed close. *Fuck me.*

"ID card, please," the man held his hand out. His scanner ready in the other.

I swallowed, tried to keep my smile, "Certainly. Just a moment," I muttered, slowly reaching into a pocket and, of course, finding only bullets. I was considering what might happen if I cracked one open when Samantha tapped my shoulder.

"You gave it to me for safekeeping, remember?" Sam said. She smiled at the guard, flipping her hair as she unslung her pack from her shoulders. She made a show of rummaging around, holding the line up. The security guard's annoyance was palpable. "I'm so sorry," she said, zipping and unzipping different compartments. Digging around, shuffling clothes out onto the floor along with her scarf, hairbrushes and clip, a bra tumbled to the guards' feet. *Holy fuck, how did she get all that shit in there?*

"I know it's in here somewhere,"

The guard sighed irritably, "Forget it. Go ahead. Just be ready next time."

Sweet relief filled my lungs, making the world bright again. "I'm so sorry," Sam said again, shoving things back into her back and slinging the pack back over her shoulders.

I didn't let out my breath until we had cleared the checkpoint area. "Quick thinking," I said.

"It was a risk." Sam stepped away from me, and the absence of her warmth was noticeable. "We got lucky."

I steered us towards the animal pick up centre. "So you enjoyed our little *romp* last night?" I teased.

"Shut up. We did romp around last night. On Tweet."

"We going to do more romping anytime soon?"

She rolled her eyes but didn't respond. Tweet waited for us amongst a few other animals and skaali, some cyborg and some not. She was by far the most active, hopping up and down and swinging her tail. She whistled at us as we approached, feathered head dipping up an down in greeting. "That wasn't so bad, was it?" Sam asked Tweet affectionately, scratching her scaley chin and eye ridges.

I caught sight of the many PDA screens surrounding us. They were far more numerous here in the capital than in any of the other cities and town. Most of the technology developed in Xylia or was imported from off-world came to use in Centrum.

Our faces were rolling across the screens. Eventually, not even sunglasses and hats were going to help us. "Let's get out of here," I said. "It's a miracle these sunglasses did the trick, but I'm not betting on any more miracles today."

"Where will we go?" Sam asked as we led Tweet outside onto the city streets. Cars and skaali passed with riders. I spotted a pair of Imperial Dune Busters, their badges out and flashing for all to see, laughing as they entered a restaurant. I swallowed. This place would be crawling with IDBs eager to collect on their bounty. Especially if it was within range of the IDB and ICO Headquarters.

Quick pay off made it all the sweeter. Some IDB only took the inner-city jobs while others, like myself, were willing to travel to the ends of Terrafirma in search of their bounty. Inner-city posts made for a quick payoff, but the jobs that took you out to places like the atolls paid more in the long run. A few good jobs and you'd be set for a year. And sometimes it was just nice to get away from the city.

"Kato has a map of the old underground systems," I said, lowering my voice. "I've heard about them. Some citizens who've been evicted from their homes but can't afford to leave live down there. They're called Grime dwellers."

Sam frowned, "Who built it? What was it for?"

[It was an abandoned project for an underground train system] Kato informed me as he took off from my shoulder, taking to the skies. [With the earthquakes after terraforming failure. The tunnels were left unused. Too risky. So the grime dwellers gave them a purpose]

I relayed the information to Sam and led her and Tweet towards the location Kato had directed we go. "Would we be welcome down there?" Sam asked.

"I don't know," I looked her up and down and then grinned, "I'm surprised they let us on the blimp. You look homeless. You'll blend in." She smacked me on the arm just a bit too hard. We both could use a good shower.

We reached the bridge. And the door was there just as Kato said it would be. Thankfully, it was big enough for Tweet to squeeze through. Though she did protest as her sides scraped across the frame.

It was dark in the tunnel, with little light coming from the small yellow bulbs, most of which had gone out. Those that had remained glowed weakly. My night vision switched on automatically.

"We'll find an area to camp out," I whispered, my voice carrying through the long tunnel. "Lay low until we have a solid plan," I was painfully aware of how close ICO headquarters was. I could barge in there, demand to talk to Camelia, and get my name cleared. But I'd need Sam to get on their good side. I grit my teeth. Turning Sam in was my only out – but was I really that heartless?

[Kato, we need a place to set up camp. Something easy to defend, just in case]

His voice echoed in my head, cracking. The connection was terrible down here, and the more I thought about it, the more I wished he just come in with us. I already went a long week without him, of walking half-blind. I really didn't want to experience that again.

[The central station is just a mile ahead. However, that's where most of the dwellers' lounge]

Tweet growled deep in her throat, lowered her head, and snapped her jaws. Her tail lashing behind. Sam cried out in disgust. A family of rats scurried across the damp ground, narrowly avoiding Tweet's jaws before clamouring up a metal shaft and disappearing in a hole in the ceiling.

"What a nice place to live," I muttered.

"These people down here must be desperate," Samantha said. "Do you think they know about the bounty on us? We can't hide behind sunglasses down here," she said, removing her hat and the glasses, she shoved them into her bag. Dumping half the clothes she had packed. I looked at her, quizzically, "What? I only put them in there in case we needed a distraction. And we did," she said. I reached up and removed my glasses, sliding them into my pocket. Sam looked at me, her eyes flicking up to my hat and then back to my face. I shook my head, "The hat stays. We'll keep our heads low," I said. "Hopefully, no one will recognise us."

Sam shook her head, tapping the brim of my head with a fingertip, "What is it with you and that damn hat?"

"A friend gave it to me, a long time ago," I said gruffly. She twisted her lips to one side, "What kind of friend?" she asked. I was about to answer when Kato sent a warning,

[Dwellers moving up ahead]

I heard the voices a second later. We turned a corner and spotted two men stretched out on cots. I sniffed the air. A whiff of smoke reached my nostrils, something burning. It made my throat dry and itch. Some kind of drug most likely. I felt their gazes as we walked closer to them.

"You lost?" one called out.

"Looking for a place to camp out for the night," I said.

"Aw, you don't want to stay down here," the other man said, sitting up. "Book yourself a nice hotel."

"We don't have money," Sam said.

"Everybody's got something," the man stood, walking towards us, his back hunched. Tweet hissed and snapped her jaws. "Especially ones who've got a skaali."

"Please, let us pass," I said, my voice tinged with a warning. I pulled my duster back, hand resting on my pistol. The rifle wouldn't be practical in this tight space.

"This is our home," the man said, squinting at me. His eyes flicked down to my weapon, but he didn't seem phased, "We require a fee."

For fuck's sake, I was about to shove him out of the way, but Sam put a hand on my arm. "What's the fee?" she asked.

"What have you got?"

"That's not fair."

"Life's not fair, sweetheart."

Samantha scowled and fished in her pockets. I knew what she was grabbing before she spoke. I really wish she'd quit throwing those things around like "I have a spell bullet. It won't work without a rune-gun, but they're valuable to those who have one. You'd fetch a good price for it."

The man snatched it from Sam's palm and examined it. "It'll do," he said with a sniff. He bowed out of the way. "Enjoy your stay," He grinned, revealing missing teeth.

"Bastard," I muttered under my breath.

When we were a safe distance away, Sam spoke. "I know you didn't want to give them anything, but if we put up a fight the moment, we stepped inside. We'd probably never make it out again," she said.

"He swindled you. They're penniless swindlers who have nothing better to do than take money from people."

"Calm down, they're just people trying to make a living," she said. I shook my head, "No. They're exactly the type of swine I'd –"

Sam turned on me, her eyes sharp and bright even in the dim light, "You'd what Chris? Truss them up and throw them in prison? And for what?"

I didn't have an answer. I set my jaw and pushed past Sam, letting the subject drop before I said something I might regret.

We encountered more people on our way into the underground station. Men and women shuffling around as if it was a typical day in any city. There were many with kids running up and down the tunnels, their faces smeared with dirt and soot from the fires interspersed throughout the area. They caught one look at Tweet and veered off course, their eyes bugging out of their heads. It probably wasn't common for a skaali to wander around down here.

Finally, the tunnel funnelled into a large station, just as Kato had said. The Grime dwellers lounged around in every available space. Some did work like washing sheets in steaming bins or sat knitting holes shut in torn clothing. These likely were small things they did to get a few coins or some food. After meeting the two men further back, I expected to feel revulsion for the grime dwellers. A pang stabbed me in the gut. It wasn't much different from the life I lived back in Shady Plateau. I wondered how Centrum had fallen so far. There were too many people crammed in this space, more than I had imagined. No one deserved to have living conditions like these while the wealthy above squandered their money on luxuries no one really needed.

Grime dwellers stared us down as we picked our way past the people, trying to find an unoccupied space. A woman approached us, middle-aged with greasy hair pulled back in a bun. Her face was dark. Wrinkles deeply cut with grime and dirt, but her eyes were bright. Intelligent. "Need help, hun?" she asked me.

"We just need a place to rest for the night," I said. "We don't have money for a hostel."

She nodded, "This isn't exactly bed and breakfast," she said.

"We understand," Sam said, "If there's a place we could tuck away where no one will notice us?"

The woman shrugged, casting her sharp eyes across the walls and ceiling, "There are plenty of tunnels. Stay away from the northern ones," she said, pointing towards a series of dimly lit tunnels. "They belong to our personal local gang of annoying teens with too much time on their hands. They put a stake in their own tunnels," the woman rolled her eyes, "Selfish, the lot of them."

"Thank you," Samantha said. She pointed. "What about those tunnels there?"

"Sparsely occupied due to rats, mostly. You'd have better luck in that tunnel there." She pointed to a tunnel behind us. "Not as many rats and not many people. We like to stay close together. Sometimes soldiers come down to take stock of us, and we'd prefer to be in one big group. Intimidate them, you know."

I blinked in surprise. That was news. But then, I wasn't privy to their inner workings. So ICO did send their military down here once in a while. I hoped we weren't around for the next bout of inspections.

We thanked the lady for her help, handing her a bag of ration tablets, and made our way to the tunnel and dipped inside. It was dim but cold and dry. A few people lingered around the mouth of the tunnel but then died off deeper in. We picked a spot to settle and sat, leaning against the granite wall. Sam sighed next to me, looking up at Tweet, who remained standing and paced around curiously, snapping at things we couldn't see.

"We'll go to the lab tonight," she said quietly.

My stomach flipped uncomfortably.

I wasn't sure I was ready for this.

"What's your plan?" I asked slowly, stretching out as far as I could without my toes tipping in the slimy scum that trickled down the centre of the stone that lined the tunnel.

She rummaged through her bag. "When I worked there, I studied blueprints of the building in preparation for my escape. I've discovered there are large vents leading from the ceiling and out into the air at the top of the building – which is ten stories, by the way."

"I've been to the labs before," I said.

"Good." She pulled out the suctions. "We'll use these to get up to the vents. They should be large enough for you to fit through," she said, looking me up and down. "Assuming you'll infiltrate the lab with me. I suppose you could just walk away at this point."

I shrugged, but my heart rate picked up. "I'm here now, aren't I?" I scooted closer to her. "Besides, I want to help in any way I can."

But I also knew I couldn't sacrifice everything I'd worked for, for just one person. It just didn't make sense.

She smiled at me, "You're not such a bad guy, after all. I guess."

I didn't acknowledge her comment. Instead, I pointed at her pack. "I supposed we'll be using the comm blocker."

"Right you are," she pulled out the small box, turning it over in her hands. "This should buy us at least five to ten minutes. It should be enough time for me to go in, read my DNA sequence, and make the proper adjustments. If anything, I can slow the side effects."

"How will you access the equipment?" I wondered. "Isn't their database password protected?"

"I have my own data," she said, flipping a palm-sized PDA device out of her pocket. "I just need to use their DNA sequencer to alter what I can. Undo the damage." She hesitated, then pulled down on her shirt, exposing a large portion of her chest and cleavage. My eyes locked onto her smooth flesh, then stopped at the fine scales that had crawled further up.

"It's getting worse," I stated.

She nodded, "My nails,"

She held out her hand, and I took it cautiously. I hadn't noticed before, but the nails were being replaced with a thicker, harder material that looked dark grey against the pink, "You're growing claws?"

"I think so," She looked to Tweet, and her face looked absent, almost whimsical.

"I can hear and feel everything she does. Worse – I've been craving…things. Meat. When she went for that rat earlier, I freaked out because I wanted it, too." She dropped her head back against the wall, her eyes scanned my face, waiting for my reaction, "Am I grossing you out?"

I shook my head, "Nah, I get it. We've been living off bars and meal replacement pills for nearly two weeks. I could really go for a steak right now."

She laughed, "Maybe we can trade a spell bullet or two for a fancy meal here."

I cocked my head, a slow smile spreading across my face as I reached out and pushed loose strands of hair out of her eyes, "Like, go on a real date?"

She slapped my hand away, "No. Just two people going to a restaurant."

"A fancy restaurant," I smirked. "With steak. Old-world style with all the sauce smeared all over it. We ought to go out on a proper date. I don't think fighting tyrants and sandworms counts."

"It was a bonding exercise," she smirked.

Damn, I wanted to kiss those soft lips.

I wanted her moaning in my arms when I touched her in the right places.

I wanted her asking for more when I pulled away, willing to beg for me. I wanted all of it. And I could have it.

That's what hurt more than anything.

I stood quickly, trying to squash my feelings. Damp down the urges that pulled at my heartstrings.

"I'll be back. I want to get a better sense of our surroundings with Kato."

She blinked up at me, surprised that I had ruined the moment, "Okay. Bring me back a steak, will you?"

"I wouldn't get your hopes up." I hesitated, then swooped down and placed a quick kiss on top of her head. Lingering only a moment as I breathed in her scent, "Stay low. Stay safe. I'll be back."

I made my way up to the surface, going back the way we'd come. Kato was waiting for me before I'd even thrown the massive bridge door open. I leaned against the stone and metal frame beside the door and tore off my hat, wringing it between my fingers. *Dammit, dammit all to hell.* I flipped the hat over, attempting to straighten it back out as my eyes fell on the name embroidered on the tag, *L. Carlson.* I stared at the name for a while and then sucked in a breath, tucking the hat back on my head; I tied my bandana around my face and reached out to Kato waiting nearby.

[We're not really scouting, are we, Grey?]

I shook my head, [I still have a job to do]

[Are you sure you okay with that? You and Samantha have become close]

[Are you trying to be my conscious now?] I snapped at Kato.

[Of course not, Grey. I'll always be on your side. Please remember that if it ever comes into question]

I stepped out from the shadows of the bridge, welcoming the fresh air and what little sunlight peeked through the dense clouds. People walked by, stopping to window shop. I was at the south side of the marketplace, which had shrunk significantly over the years, but where the middle class still liked to frequent. I turned a few corners, finding a location that was private where no one could see me or overhear my conversation without being right next to me.

[Keep an eye out for trouble] I told Kato, then opened a commlink. I hesitated before dialling out. Was I really going to do this? *Am I really going to just go through with this? Just like that? Cut and dry?*

I scoffed at myself. Of course. What other choice did I have? Jail?

I wasn't going to jail for a criminal who'd built a cyborg assassin, no matter what her intentions or how I felt about her. It just didn't make sense.

Sucking in a deep breath, I dialled Camelia's number.

Her amused voice answered almost immediately, "Grey. Where are you hiding?" she asked. Straight to the point.

I clenched a fist, trying to calm the rage I felt towards her for letting me be placed on ICO's naughty list.

"I don't understand," I said, "I was doing my job. Bringing in Samantha Cowell. Why do you have a bounty on my head?"

"Oh, you adorable but ugly little duckling," she laughed, "You're more useful dead than alive, I'm afraid. Can't be leaving a track to follow."

"Am I? Any luck capturing your misplaced Doctor? How's that going for you now?"

"There have been a few hiccups, thanks to you, but someone's working on it for me,"

"Lemme guess, Cilia Malkovich?" I asked. There was only a slight hitch in Camelia's breathing. Did she really think we hadn't figured that out by now? Cilia was pretty free with the information, but then, she thought I'd be dead by now.

"I have Samantha Cowell. I can bring her in."

That irritating laugh rang through my ears. "Really, now? You're clutching onto the hope that, what, you'll be reinstated and your name cleared?"

"No," I said. "I'll turn Samantha in exchange for clearing my name. I haven't assassinated anyone. We both know this."

Camelia didn't reply.

I half expected her to hang up.

I could hear her taking a draw of the cigarette she no doubt had hanging on her lip.

"If you don't agree to my terms," she said quickly, her voice clipped with a hint of strain, "I will spend the rest of my life making sure you never see that girl again. You might catch us eventually. But not before I've –we've – spread the information she carries far and wide and reveals just how corrupt the High Commissioners are. She can name names, and she will. I'll make sure of it."

That last part was a bluff – Sam hadn't even revealed names to me yet. She didn't seem to know anything. *Or she was really good at pretending she didn't. Which ones more likely, now?*

Camelia laughed again, but it wasn't as high-pitched. It had a dark, nervous tone to it. She was on edge. "Can you have her to us by tomorrow?"

"By tonight," I said, "But only if you clear my name."

"That's really all you want?" Her voice was smooth, sultry. She was waiting for it.

I hesitated, "Is there any way I can be reinstated as a Dune Buster?" I asked. "You can demote me from Imperial, I know I've fallen below those standards. But I want, need, this position…I owe it to Carlson. You know that."

"Hmm," I waited, keeping my eyes peeled for any trouble. "If you were to arrange a certain sum of money to fall into my hands, I believe I can get you reinstated, *and* your name cleared. Provided you deliver Dr Cowell, of course."

My heartbeat hard against my chest. This was a dangerous game I was playing. Dangerous for both of us. "What sum are we talking about here?"

"Fifty thousand," she purred.

My jaw dropped, "I don't have that kind of money."

"Find a way to get it. Dr Cowell and the money will purchase you your freedom, guaranteed. The money will help grease some palms so you can continue work as a DB. Even I'm not that good, Grey. I can't bribe anyone without the funds."

My mind worked overtime, trying to fathom how I could get that much money. The spell bullets were valuable, but not worth *that* much. I'd get maybe forty thousand, tops, if I sold each shell for two thousand. Tweet flickered into my mind. Guilt instantly riddled through me.

But if Sam was being turned in, where would Tweet go? I could find her a good home and get at least ten thousand for her. *Unless they sent her to the pits in Watchtower Plateau or dismantled her for parts.* The equipment she was carrying alone could fetch a small fortune.

It would be hard, but doable. "I turn in Sam; you clear my name. It'll take me some time to collect the money, but once I do, I get reinstated as a Dune Buster."

"You'll have one week to get me the money," Camelia said, "If you fail to do so, our verbal contract is void, and you will once again be a regular citizen."

My throat became sandpaper dry. I tried to think of another solution, but knowing Camelia, it was the best I'd get. I could be a free man tomorrow morning.

"Deal," the word fell heavy from my mouth, "I'll deliver her to the ICO lab around midnight."

"Good man," Camelia laughed. "You're lucky I'm a compassionate woman. I appreciate your hard work."

I clenched my teeth, swallowing down my sarcastic reply. Camelia cut off the commlink, and I stood in broad daylight, my heart hammering.

I had traded Samantha for my freedom.

It made sense. It had to happen.

I was going to turn her even before I became an outlaw. *Why do I feel like such shit then?*

CHAPTER 17

Sam was playing fetch with Tweet when I returned with Kato in tow, throwing a steel bar she had found. Tweet liked the noise of it clattering to the ground and snatched it into her jaws happily each time, trotting back to Sam and dropping it in her lap for another round. The raptors thoughts touched mine as she tried to share her pure joy, but shrank back when I refused to let her in.

Samantha beamed at me. "No steak?"

"Fresh out," I said, taking a seat next to her. I reached into a paper bag, "But they had these."

I extracted a box of chicken wings, covered in spicy seasonings, I'd nabbed from a street vendor. Sam's green eyes dilated, and she grabbed them from me, tearing open the box. "Oh, my gods," she groaned and set to work tearing into them. I couldn't help watching her as her fingers grew sticky with spicy sauce and she sucked the meat off the bones. Her teeth flashed, sharper than before.

Sam threw her bones at Tweet, who caught them in the air and swallowed them whole as a small treat. Sam knocked my shoulders with hers. "Thought we didn't have any money?"

"Just enough in change."

I felt like I was feeding Sam her last meal.

They wouldn't hurt her, though – imprisonment at worse, make her work for them at best. She didn't have a death sentence.

Not like I did.

We finished our food and Sam leaned against me, her stomach content. "That was the best meal I've ever had."

"You haven't had many good meals, then," I chuckled. I wanted to put my arm around her, but it felt wrong.

She nuzzled into me. "I can't stop thinking about one of the first nights we began this adventure," she said quietly, "That pent up aggression. The hot sand, the cool night air…"

I swallowed, my mind remembering the one night I'd allowed my emotions to take over. Sam's lips pressed against my neck. I sucked in a breath. It was nice. She reached up and playfully tugged on the hair of my chin. It'd grown long since I hadn't been able to shave. Wordlessly, her hand reached under my shirt, trailing along my stomach and fingering the buckle of my belt. With a click, it was undone before I'd even noticed. Her fingers slipped to my zipper.

Kiss her back, you fool, I shouted at myself.

My gut clenched and my hands froze.

I couldn't move.

I was paralysed. My stomach flipped, threatening to empty itself.

"I forgive you," she said, her lips against my ear.

I swallowed, my mind trying to make sense of her words. *Did she know? Fuck, how'd she find out?*

No, she couldn't know. If she did, she would have left already. "For what?" I asked, my voice tight.

"For my brother." She pulled back, levelling me with an emerald stare. "I blamed you for so long. But I know he was your friend. You didn't mean for it to happen."

My panic deflated, she didn't know. I nodded my head at her words, "But it did," I said softly.

"And I forgive you. We all do crappy things sometimes, to make sure we can survive. I've done my share of fucked up shit." Samantha raked her hands through my hair, and her steady gaze wavered. "You're sweating."

"Probably cause your hands on some very sensitive parts of my body, and your nails are very sharp,"

It wasn't a lie. My nerves were as tight as they could be. Nothing made sense, my whole world stank of shit.

Her gaze softened, and she leaned forward for a kiss. Her lips met mine, and I nearly gagged on the guilt riding inside me. I gently pushed her away. "Sam…"

"Chris, it's okay. We can have a little fun before tonight," Sam said, her look seductive as she pushed her lower lip out in a pout. She lifted one of my hands and placed it against a supple breast. "Chris, I want you more than ever. Don't make me wait," she whispered.

I slipped my hand away from her. "I'm sorry, Sam. Not tonight. I'm exhausted."

Her eyes narrowed, and her jaw set. "You haven't been able to tear your eyes off me this whole trip. I'm giving you an opportunity here, Chris."

"I know," I kissed her softly on the cheek. "Rain check?"

The hurt shone in her eyes. She shrugged, acting nonchalant.

"Okay, sure," her brows arched. "This isn't because I'm growing scales and claws, is it?"

"What? No." But my reaction had been a fraction of a second too late.

Sam moved away from me, her eyes going cold. "I thought we had something deeper than physical affection, Grey," she said. "I guess I was wrong."

"It's not that, Sam. Really. Why would it be? You're fixing it tonight anyway."

She turned to me; eyes luminescent and wild. "Then why don't you want me?"

I had deeply offended her. I could tell. Her body was still and pulled away from mine. Her warmth withdrawing like I'd thrown water on a fire. A fine repayment after she'd forgiven me for her brother's death just moments ago. Something I'd been regretting for over a decade.

I was a complete and utter asshole.

But I thought fast.

"The last time I slept was for two hours last night on Tweet's back," I shot back, "Trust me, I want nothing more than to push you up to this wall and fuck you from dawn to dusk. But what I really need right now…is a nap. Can you at least give me that?"

She settled into silence. "Fine. Take your dammed nap." Getting to her feet, she stood. "Come on, Tweet. Let's see what else this dreary tunnel has to offer."

She began to stalk away. "Be careful," I called out to her. She ignored me.

Feeling like a dumb fuck, I rolled onto my side on the floor and closed my eyes. There was no chance in hell I was falling asleep, not with everything running through my mind. I was left in misery for nearly two hours before Sam returned. I heard her and Tweet trot back down the tunnel, and I closed my eyes, pretending to sleep. I heard her curl up on the ground next to me, Tweet whistling through her nostrils. After a while, Sam fell asleep. I could hear her steady breathing.

I rolled over to face her. She was curled up, facing the wall, using her pack as a pillow. Tweet was resting right next to her, her body acting as a shield to the open space of the station outside the tunnel. I hesitated, then scooted closer to Sam, lightly running my fingers through her hair. Unable to resist her, I wrapped an arm around her waist and curled against her, closing my eyes and breathing in her scent for what would probably be the last time.

I needed to remember this.

I hated myself.

It wasn't right to turn her in, I knew that.

But it was my job, even if I technically didn't have it right now. I heard Kato and his soft hoot from above my head somewhere, hidden by the darkness.

[Are you sure we can trust Camelia?] Kato asked.

[No, but what choice do I have? I have to try to get my life back together. Without Samantha.]

I drifted to an uneasy sleep, nestling my cheek against Sam's neck. My chest to her back, I could feel her body mould against mine. It felt nice. It felt right. Too bad it wouldn't last.

I woke when Sam did. She lightly pushed me off her and sat up, stretching and checking the time. "It's nearly midnight," she said. "We should get going."

Sitting up, my stomach lurched, and I could feel the bile backing up my windpipe. Keeping my nausea in check, I stood. Duster the grime off my duster and slapped my hat on my head.

"We'll keep Tweet here," Sam said, "The people down here are afraid of her and won't come near. She won't make us a target on the city streets."

I nodded. "In and out," I said, hoping my voice didn't betray my nerves. I could already feel my body shaking from the inside out. Teeth grinding. Bones threatened to crush beneath the weight of the guilt I was carrying. If she noticed how nervous I was, she must have assumed it was because of our plans to break into the labs.

We left, heading down the tunnel and finding the exit. The night air was cold, the city quiet. It had once been bustling with nightlife, and it still was in the city's centre, but the surrounding areas kept to a strict sun-down, in-house schedule. It was safer that way with all the dangerous vagrants and ruffians and ladies of the night that were just as likely to stab you as they were to take you to bed.

The lab was located near ICO headquarters, so we'd need to keep an eye out for roaming security guards. There might be an IDB or two looking for an easy job if some protestor showed up to egg the place. Thankfully, the lab's security was the traditional camera scan. If someone entered the premises without keying in some specific codes, the cameras would scan their face and send them directly to ICO personnel, who'd arrive on the scene within two minutes. It was an effective system, but we had the comm blocker, so the camera wouldn't be able to send out an alert right away.

Not that it mattered.

We wouldn't get that far.

But Sam didn't know that yet, and the plan was going along fine for now.

Sam led the way, not speaking to me. We weaved through some buildings, taking a route I was unfamiliar with. I wondered what Sam's life had been like while she worked here. She used to be so close to me when we were kids. I'd mostly ignored her as we got older and my attention went elsewhere. Perhaps things could have been different if we'd ran into each other before she abandoned her life here and returned to Shady Plateau. I'd been in this building hundreds of times to check in bounties and yet, I'd never seen her. I didn't exactly have access to the inner knowledge the higher-ups had but, I wonder if she had ever seen me coming in. If she knew who I was at the time. *Who commissioned me for this job? Who knew that I knew Samantha Cowell and could coax her out?*

There were only two people I could think of. *Samantha Cowell herself and Camelia.*

My heart hammered in my chest at this realisation. We were less than a mile from the lab. If I wanted to turn back, it was now. I'd tell Sam to stop, explain to her what I did, and face her wrath. She'd ditch me, and I'd be found and shot – by Cilia, most likely.

No, I can't back out now.

Sam took a right turn and began walking down an alleyway. I figured she was trying to take a non-traditional route to throw off whoever might be following us but didn't think that was necessary. Kato entered my head, his soft voice dismayed,

[She's no longer heading for the lab, Grey.]

He was right. She was blatantly going a different direction, leaving the lab well behind us. "Sam," I called. "The lab's back that – *oof!*"

She'd spun, slamming a fist into my jaw. Her bony knuckles cuffing my cheekbone and making my eye water. I stumbled back against the alley wall, putting a hand to my burning skin. "What the hell, Sam?" I hissed.

She leaned back, and the heel of her feet caught me in the gut. Strong. Powerful. Pain exploded through my body, and I wretched. I slid down the wall, back pressed into the cool marble.

Unable to move.

Tears stinging my eyes as I vomited up the last bit of food I had left in my belly.

"I've gotta hand it to you, Grey. You really had me going," Sam said. She knelt down and punched me; straight into my nose. I felt the bones shift and hot blood washed over my lips. Dripped off my chin.

"I can't believe I was naive enough to think you'd help me. Of course, you were going to look out for yourself over anyone else. That's how you've *always* been! It's always been about what you want,"

Another blow hit me on the side of my face, reopening the cut on my temple. It was definitely going to scar.

"What are you talking about, Sam?" I gasped.

"Do you think I'm stupid? I saw the way you were sweating like a pig earlier – after you'd gone to scope out the place, you've got Kato to do all your dirty work. And then I really knew something was up when I could smell your anxiety spike worse than when we faced the damn bull newt. A guy like you – an operation like this shouldn't have bothered you at all. All in a day's work, with your profession. But you were too agitated. Too nervous. I could hear your heartbeat racing a mile-a-minute. It was easy to figure out. I know you only came here to turn me in," her voice had grown thick, heavy.

[You can always change your mind, Grey]

She hit me again, and I didn't even try to resist. Her words cut me; the pain almost as bad as the physical blows.

"I trusted you, Chris," she wailed. "I trusted you, and now. You've ruined my chance to fix myself." She kicked me in the stomach, and I double over, wheezing in pain.

"You're not even gonna try to deny it, are you?" she demanded, "Well? Are you? Tell me, I'm wrong!"

I gritted my teeth. The world spun, the pain searing through me. She dropped down to my level, catching my face in her fingers, her nails digging into my skin. "Answer me! Do you deny alerting the ICO that you were bringing me in?"

I stared into her flaming eyes, greener than I'd ever seen them. For a moment, she looked more raptor than woman. "No," I croaked.

[Grey, be careful now]

There had been a sliver of hope behind those eyes – something that longed for me to deny it, to prove my innocence. To tell her she was wrong. But the hope extinguished, replaced by cruel disdain. She slammed my head back against the wall.

"You made a deal with them, didn't you? Trade me in for your own stinking hide. Makes sense, I guess, for someone with no regard for anyone but himself. I should have known you'd betray me. Cilia was right. You *are* a shitty Dune Buster, and I hope they never let you back in. I hope you find yourself falling with a short drop and a sudden stop,"

She gave me one last kick to the side, sending me flat to the ground. I groaned, my face and ribs aching.

"Enjoy the last moments of your miserable existence," she spat. I heard the crunch of gravel as she spun on her heel and ran.

Double Crossed

CHAPTER 18

Camelia narrowed her dark eyes at me as I approached, alone and blood-smeared. She and two other ICO agents stood near the entrance of ICO's main laboratory gate, guns in hand. I was surprised that she was there herself to make sure the job was done.

"You look like shit, Grey," she said, her voice tight and sing-song as she tapped her cigarette. The ash trailed a spark of red through the air before tumbling, and dying, on the ground at her feet.

"I feel like it, too," I mumbled.

She stared at me, blinking slowly. "Well?"

"Well, she got away," I swiped an arm across my nose, trying to clear up the drying blood.

Camelia's laugh grated on my nerves. "I should have known you couldn't finish the job," she said. She gestured to the agents with the fag between her fingers, "Arrest him."

"Wait, I –"

They didn't.

Grabbing my arms and forcing them behind me, the steady pressure forced me to my knees before Camelia. "Sam's in the wind. You can't find her without me."

The shrill laugh pierced the night air, and I winced. "You're overdue on your assignment by over a *week*, more than a week if I recounted," she scoffed. "You had Dr Cowell in containment only hours ago and lost her before you had the chance to turn her in. Lost her. In Centrum, no less." She laughed again, making the hair on my arms stand up. I heard the clink of metal. The click and shift of a lock dropping into place. The slight tingling as the blood flow was cut off from my wrists. The agents had successfully cuffed me.

"I know where to find her," I insisted. "I've spent the last few weeks with her – I know her strengths, weaknesses, methods. You might find her eventually, but I can help you find her much sooner. Don't let the trail go cold. You need me, Camelia."

Camelia eyed me; her pale skin ethereal in the darkness of the night. "I've already given you a second chance, and you failed," she quipped.

"I won't this time. I swear it." I glanced at the silent agents at my side, then lowered my voice. "And I can still meet the monetary requirements of our deal. But only if you let me finish what I started."

Camelia stared at me, still as a marble statue. Then she barked out a laugh that ended in a deep but resigned sigh. She needed me, and she clearly needed the money.

"Alright, fine. But I'm assigning you a partner. Zander, get out here. I'd send Cilia, but…she has issues with you that I'd rather not get in the way at this point,"

Cilia glared at me, her jaw working as a figure stepped from the shadows. He was slim and draped in black. He'd shaved his head, revealing tattoos all over his skull and dripping down the back of his neck. His right eye was a round silver orb that glowed with a red light, the scarring around the socket gave no doubt to the augmentations he'd gone through. The light flickered when he looked at me, taking in my face. No doubt he had pulled up all of my information with just one scan. He looked about my age, maybe a little younger. Though he wasn't built with muscle, his silent stealth looked deadly.

"Zander will be your partner in the search for Dr Cowell," Camelia said, "He is a special project of mine," she purred, pacing around the black-clothed man, she reached up and cradled his face in her hands, "An IDB of exceptional promise. He could certainly do the job single-handed, but," a smile crept up her face, "He's a little unstable. His body is still working on integrating his new augmentations, and his mind is still adjusting from the traumas. Plus, he doesn't know what you know, Grey." She smiled and released his face, "You two will play nicely together, right, Zander?"

Zander looked from me to Camelia and gave a single nod. Somehow, that nod felt like a death sentence.

Camelia waved her hands, and the agents removed my cuffs. "The trail is still warm, yes? Go get her."

Zander strode up to me, staring me down with his flashing red eye. He was a full two inches taller than me and moved with a grace I had only seen with Kit'th. *Was he some sort of new hybrid? Or from a different planet altogether?* He brushed past me, expecting me to follow. I gave Camelia a slight bow before turning.

"Grey," she called. I froze, hoping she hadn't already changed her mind. She chuckled. "Don't fail me again. Or you'll wish you'd never been born."

I believed it.

I nodded and turned away, "Oh and one more thing," her voice sang out. I turned and stared at her. She was fanning herself with my hat. She turned over the worn thing and stared at the name sewn inside. A brief smile played across her lips but was gone before I could really be sure of it, "Don't forget your hat." She laughed and threw it at me. I caught it and settled it down over my head. And with a nod, I turned to follow my new partner.

Kato flew overhead, [You got luck, Grey.]

I watched Zander's back as he stalked into an alley,

[But not lucky enough.]

"What is this information you and nobody else has?" Zander asked, his voice thin and reedy. I was dead tired, and sure my nose was broken, but Zander had made it clear we wouldn't rest until we caught Sam's trail.

"I know she went to the underground tunnels to get her skaali," I said, curving down the alley Sam and I had walked through just half an hour ago. "She's probably secured her already. If we're fast enough, we could apprehend them."

"We're fast enough," he said and broke out in a sprint.

The last thing I wanted to do was run, but I wasn't about to be left in the dust. I chased after Zander as he called back over his shoulder. "Which exit?"

"The one-off Bridge Street," I said, already running out of breath. My muscles screamed at me, and my stomach heaved in protest. I was a fit guy, but even I had my limits. After weeks of nonstop fighting and travelling and next to nothing in sleep, I was already beyond my limit.

We raced to the entrance of the tunnel and Zander wrung the door open, then stared at me, his cyborg eye narrowing in on me. "Well? Is this your mission or not? Ladies first."

Pride stinging, I ducked inside the tunnel and jogged down, expecting to run into Sam and Tweet at any moment. [Kato, see if you can spot them]

The skyeye swooped over my head and disappeared into the darkness of the tunnel. Zander jogged quickly beside me, not even breaking a sweat. The guy was a monster.

"You fuck her?" he asked.

I was taken aback by his question. *Who the hell asks something like that?* It was none of his business. "N-no," I spluttered, "She's a job, not a whore."

His smile was slow and spread to his ears. His teeth shone white and sharp even in the dim light of the tunnels, "I knew it, you fucked her. I would have too."

Nausea crept up my stomach into my throat, making it burn. "What the hell is wrong with you?" I asked under my breath. Zander glanced at me, his good eyes sharp and calculating as it passed over me and his face split into a wide grin, my skin crawled.

Kato's voice entered my head.

[No sign of her, Grey. She must have taken another exit.]

Sam was smart. She had to know we would come after her down here, and she wasn't about to exit the same way she came in. "Shit," I muttered.

"What's that?"

"She's in the tunnels somewhere, but not this one. We'll have to ask the grime dwellers if they've seen which way she went."

We burst into the station area, where most people were sleeping. The woman who had directed Sam and me when we first arrived stared at me in shock. I approached her, "The woman with the skaali. Where'd she go?"

I'd never seen a woman give me such a dirty look before. She seemed offended by Zanders presence as he flashed his ICO badge, "Answer the question lady," he said flatly. The woman turned to me. She narrowed her eyes and bit her lip, looking uncertain, "I thought you two were travelling together?"

"We were. Where is she?"

The woman backed up, "I didn't see her."

She was lying. I was just about to firmly ask her again when Zander snatched her, pulling her against him with one of her arms twisted behind her back. He pressed a blade, the edge sharp but serrated, to her throat. "Answer now, Grime Dweller, or I'll slit your sorry throat."

"Zander," I said as calmly as I could. "There's no need for that."

He ignored me, pressing the blade deeper against her skin. A prick of blood welled up from between the folds of her neck, "*Speak*" he commanded. His voice low and dangerous.

The woman's eyes were wide as they rolled around to stare at me. With a shaking finger, she pointed. To the rat-infested tunnels. The ones she warned us to stay out of. Great.

Zander tossed her aside and gave me a nod. "You. Lead the way."

I wanted to apologise to the woman, but she had scampered away already. Gritting my teeth, I made for the rat tunnels. Several people had woken with the skirmish, and they stared with bleary eyes as we ran past them. Zander didn't even make an effort to avoid stepping on hands and feet splayed around him.

The rat tunnels were dark. I let my eyes adjust with their night vision and goaded Kato ahead to scout Sam out. There, unless she was riding Tweet, which was most likely. I would.

I cursed myself. Once Samantha exited these tunnels, there was no telling where she'd go. There were entire neighbourhoods of abandoned buildings in Centrum. Her challenge would be getting past any wandering IDBs or other ICO agents and soldiers.

[She's no longer in the tunnels] Kato informed me. [There's an open manhole. I will take to the skies and find her whereabouts.]

[Thanks. Let me know as soon as you spot her.]

"She's escaped the tunnels," I told Zander, our feet pounding across the wet stone surface. It made my teeth rattle with each jolting impact as I tried not to slip. "My skyeye is going to scan the city. She'll be easy to spot – either riding a raptor skaali or sneaking around close by."

"I can't believe you didn't fuck her when you had the chance," Zander said again. He jogged backwards so he could throw a nasty smile my way.

"I won't make the same mistake, a tight package like that." He let out a crude whoop and spun back around, sprinting ahead of me. I wanted to tear his limbs right from his body. I knew the ICO could recruit some shady figures, but this guy was a whole new level of dangerous. Not for the first time, I wondered if I'd survive the night. If he touched Sam, I'd carve him into pieces.

A rat scurried across my path, but I ignored it. I'm sure we'd be seeing plenty more if what we'd heard about these tunnels was true. We burst from the tubes into the open air. [Any sign of her?] I asked Kato.

[Not yet. IDBs are roaming the streets, she's careful.]

I slowed to a walk and Zander cast an annoyed glance back at me. "Giving up already?"

"No. I doubt she's running anymore. She's hiding."

Zander's grin made my skin crawl. He rubbed his palms together like a greedy kid asking for candy, "I love me a bit of hide and seek," he said breathily as his augmented eye rotated in its socket, zoomed in and out like an old-world camera, adjusting to some new setting he switched on. The red light turned to a dull blue that pulsed. "Heat vision," he said, noticing my look. He swept his gaze around him, shaking his head. "Not here. Where are you my sly little pretty."

"Perhaps we should split up," I suggested.

"No," he said, "I want to keep you close."

"It'd be more efficient if we split up."

"It'd be more efficient if I put a bullet in your brain right now and saved myself the trouble later, wouldn't it?"

I shut up. Clearly, Zander wasn't going to let me out of his sight. Which confirmed it for me – he wasn't my partner. He was my babysitter, making sure I got the job done.

But no Imperial Dune Buster would agree to a babysitting job, especially not one of Zander's calibre or Cilia for that matter.

There was something else going on here.

When this was all over, Zander would kill me. I felt confident of that now. He'd collect the bounty money and split it with Camelia. My throat went dry. I really was a shitty Dune Buster to not see this one coming.

We crawled along the streets, peering down alleyways and into abandoned shops. I listened for Tweet's tell-tale whistles.

Kato interrupted my thoughts. [Found her. Two blocks north. Making her way slowly so as not to attract attention.]

[Kato, where would I be without you?]

[Dead in the streets somewhere, I'd presume.]

I chuckled at his dark humour but remembered with a chill that Kato didn't use to crack dark jokes. I wondered if his archival memories brought out that characteristic.

"Two blocks that way," I told Zander, pointing north.

"You have a damn good skyeye, I think I'll keep it after your gone," Zander said, sprinting in the direction I'd pointed. *Fuck, even his running is eerily silent.* I sounded like a tyrant thundering after him. I heard him suck in a breath next to me. "Got her."

He pulled out his dagger, slowing.

"Remember she's wanted alive," I whispered, eyeing the blade.

"Alive, certainly, but not all in one piece," he said with a grin. For the first time, I noticed his teeth had been filed into points. I shuddered.

"This is my job," I insisted. "I'm bringing her in. Not you. You're just here to make sure it's done if things get dicey."

He paused and bowed, gesturing I go ahead. "You're right. My bad."

I stepped in front of him, trying to focus on jumping Sam and Tweet around the next corner, but I couldn't shake the feeling I was about to get a dagger wedged between my shoulder blades.

[You're about to cross paths. Twenty feet. Fifteen. Ten. Five. Zero.]

I whipped out my pistol and rounded the corner, coming eye to eye with Tweet. She startled, snarling as she reared back. She flashed her claws with a hiss, and then recognised me and whistled. Sam stood beside her skaali, the shock plain on her face.

"Grey," she said with a cough, halting in her tracks. She glared at the gun pointed her way. "You bastard. Tweet, take him out," she commanded. The words dropped so smoothly and quickly from her mouth that I was taken aback.

Tweet blinked slowly and cocked her head, no doubt getting mixed signals. I felt the raptor's presence in my head. She was scared. Hungry. Confused.

Samantha didn't really want to kill me, did she?

I didn't have the chance to find out. A shot rang out, and a tranquiliser designed explicitly for augmented skaali embedded in Tweet's neck. She jerked back in surprise, her jaws snapping in anger as he clawed at the dart, trying to dislodge it. Zander stood behind me, lowering the tranq-gun. He shot a look at Sam, his eyes running up and down her body, his lopsided smile was pure evil. "Hello, gorgeous."

Tweet swayed, then collapsed to the ground, her breathing heavy. Eyelids drooping shut. I whirled on him. "You didn't tell me you had a tranq!"

He shrugged. "How else do you expect to take down a skaali?"

Sam's eyes lit with fury. She took one glance at Tweet, then she spun on her heel and sprinted down the nearest alleyway.

"Shit," I muttered, kicking off after her. Zander zipped down another street, presumably to intercept her.

"Sam!" I yelled. "Don't make this hard on yourself."

I caught her making a hard right, then spotted Zander fly down the opposite street. My sides ached from all the running, and I desperately needed a drink. But I couldn't stop now. Not when I was so close.

I followed Sam, gaining on her. "Fuck you, Chris!" she screamed, and whirled around, pointing a gun straight at my chest. With one eye closed, she sucked in a breath.

Held it.

Squeezed.

The shell arched through the air, glittering in the street lights. I threw myself behind a trash bin, hearing the bullet whizz past. I thanked the heavens that, even though she had most of the spell bullets in her possession, I had the rune-gun in mine. Otherwise, this could have gotten really messy, really fast.

I heard Sam run off, followed by a gasp and squeal. I jumped up from behind the trash bin and raced after the sound, rounding a corner to find Zander wrestling Sam's gun from her grip, making her drop it by applying pressure to her wrists. He pressed her back to his chest, wrapping an arm around her throat, his dagger pressed against her side. Sam struggled, but he pushed the blade harder against her ribs, and she sucked in a gasp of pain.

"Stop!" I yelled, running up to them. "Zander put the knife down. We have her."

He made a face. "You're no fun." Instead of dropping the dagger, he slid it up, letting it snag on her shirt as he rested the tip against the underside of one of her breasts. "Have you ever felt them squirm under your grip, Grey?"

My vision went red. "Don't you dare hurt her," I growled, rage edging into my voice.

"Or what?" he scoffed, "You'll shoot me? Report me? Grey, you don't even have an active license in your possession. You've already murdered so many people, what's one more?"

Sam's eyes were wide, staring straight at me, the anger sharpening into fear as she gasped again. My chest constricted. Zander pressed his lips against her ear, his tongue sliding up the space behind her ear, "Why don't you show me how wild you are?" he purred.

A growl ripped through her throat, and she twisted under his grip, but Zander tightened his hold around her neck, lifting her off her feet. Sam kicked, trying to find ground, her hands flying to his arm, trying to pry it off her neck. Sharp nails leaving trails that shone with blood behind as she scratched at the pale skin.

I didn't even second guess. I rushed at Zander, pressing my gun against his temple. "I'll shoot you; I swear I will," I snapped. In one quick moment, Zander had thrown Sam to the ground and knocked the gun up and of my hand with a flick of his wrist. He shoved his knee into my stomach, making me double over. A kick to my back so hard I went flying into a brick wall, my head cracking against it.

My vision blurred. I heard Sam gasping, trying to fill her lungs with air. Zander stalked toward her, predatory. "I can't decide which game to play first – kill Grey or fuck Dr Cowell. Both are equally enjoyable. Too bad I can't too both," A strangled sound, what I assumed was supposed to be a giggle escaped his throat.

I staggered to my feet, rage coursing through my body. "Don't you fucking touch her again," I warned.

Before Zander could crack back a reply, Kato scooped out of the darkness, slashing his talons across Zander's face, temporarily distracting him. Sam lunged, grabbing the gun Zander had knocked out of my hands and pointing straight at him. She didn't hesitate to pull the trigger.

The shot echoed through the alley, and Zander jerked back. She'd caught him on the shoulder, but the bullet had glanced off. He grinned. "Gotta do better than that, beautiful."

She shot again, and it bounced off his chest, his stomach, his groin.

"Trying to shoot off my balls?" he laughed.

Either he was more cyborg than he appeared or his black uniform was bulletproof. Sam screamed in irritation. Zander reached for her, and I sprinted, knocking my body into his, shoulder first. We toppled to the ground together, and I threw punch after punch into his face. I felt the crack in my knuckles and ignored it. The pain numbed by rage.

[Grey, incoming]

[Not now. Busy]

[Cilia, Grey!]

My face stung, ears ringing. Stars flashed across my field of vision as a kick to my face left my groaning. I rolled off Zander, my hands and knees scraping against the cold asphalt. Looking up, I saw the bitter smirk of Cilia, a gun in her hand. Silver hair shining.

Sam had her gun trained on Cilia. "One more step and you're dead," she shouted.

Cilia scowled at Sam, "I've made it my mission to hunt the two of you down," she growled. Her gaze turned to me. "After the trouble you've put me through. I'll enjoy killing you, Grey."

"You can't kill him," Zander got to his feet, wiping the blood from his face, "I was just about to."

Cilia took in his current state, "Clearly."

Zander spat a wad of blood and saliva on the ground. "Fine. You take Grey, I'll get the good doctor."

They turned to look at Samantha and me. I stood protectively at her side, one arm out to hold her back from doing anything stupid.

Cilia sniffed and turned her steely eyes on me,

"Alright, deal."

CHAPTER 19

Samantha released a flurry of bullets. Cilia ducked out of the way. Zander twirled his dagger in his hand, lunging for her. I gripped Sam's arm and tugged her away. "We have to run!" I shouted.

We streaked down the streets. [Kato. What's our best route to the city's centre?]

[The centre? Why do you want to go there?]

[Just trust me. How can we get there quickly?]

[Turn left.]

I tugged Sam left with me. "Where are we going?" she shouted.

"Away from here!"

A shower of bullets rushed at us, and I dragged Sam down another street. "We need cover!" Sam yelled. "Zander is bulletproof, but if we use the rune-gun, we might have a chance."

"If we get to the city's centre, we'll have an even better chance. We need a clear shot," I said. "The streets aren't as cramped. This time of night it should be empty, I hope."

"We're not going to survive that long."

Another three shots echoed down the street, and we ducked. I sucked in a breath as a bullet grazed my arm. The sting of it making my skin itch.

[Zander on your right] Kato warned.

I shoved a trash bin into the cross-section of the street and heard a satisfying thump as Zander ran smack into it. We kept running. I could see the lights of the city's centre up ahead. My lungs and legs burned, but I pushed forward, sticking close to Sam.

"This doesn't mean I forgive you," she panted next to me. "You're still a grade-A jackass."

"I deserve that," We dove down another street as another shot rang out. [Kato, where are Zander and Cilia?]

[Zander is tracking you on the left; Cilia is falling behind you. If you're going to make your move, make it before Zander reaches you. He's the more dangerous of the two. Don't tell Cilia I said that] Kato finished. I chuckled.

We burst into a wide-open street, empty at three in the morning. "Give me a bullet," I said. Sam didn't hesitate. I unholstered the rune-gun and loaded it. Sam put a hand on it.

"It's my gun," she said with a smirk. I let her take it.

[Zander is coming up out of 32nd Street.]

I clutched Sam's shoulders, spun her in Zander's direction, and she squeezed the trigger the instant he sprinted into our street. The bullet exploded. Light flashed. Ice scattered, sharp ends climbing up walls and across the street. Windows shattered. Street lights flickered and died. Dogs barked. The air was frigid, and I felt ice on my eyelashes. My skin was damp with sweat, and melted droplets of ice Snow swirled in a gust around us.

Zander was completely engulfed.

He didn't even have time to scream.

When the deadly blizzard subsided, he stood frozen like some morbid statue.

Sam spun, trying to find Cilia.

[Cilia is retreating, Grey, but staying close. She doesn't want to be in the path of a rune-gun.]

[Wise, but disappointing.]

"Cilia isn't barging after us anymore," I told Sam. "But she's lurking. We need to find a hideout."

"No, we need to find Tweet and get the hell out of here," she snapped.

I shook my head, another idea forming, "No. We need to get you to the lab and get you fixed." I said.

Sam grinned. Her teeth looking sharper than usual in the dim light. Eyes glowing green and gold. She reached up and touched my face, her nails were sharp. Her palms rough with scale. Sam's eyes dipped to my lips and then my throat before flicking back up to meet mine. "I was going to kill you," she said.

"I know," I swallowed.

"How do I know you won't turn against me again? I can't trust you anymore," she said. I frowned. I couldn't blame her hesitation. I wasn't sure I'd ever able to trust myself again either. I shook my head and took the rune-gun from her. Slinging it over my shoulder. "I know," I said again. It was the only thing I could do. Reaching down a hand, I helped her keep steady on her feet as we left the ice behind. Cilia was still out there. We had to move fast.

The lab was easy to get into.

In fact, it was suspiciously easy. There was no sign of Cilia nearby though we knew she was lurking in the shadows. Kato gave regular updates on her location. She was on the move, but she wasn't close to us. I wasn't sure what she was up to, but I didn't like it.

Sam was right, Kato confirmed that the air vents that lead into the lab at large were directly connected to the outlets on the roof. The problem was going to be getting back out again.

We scuttled on hands and knees through the slick network of chutes, pressed between steel pipes and tubes of wire and cable. Outside, Kato continued to keep track of Cilia. The remains of Zander and the damage caused by the rune-gun had been discovered, and now the authorities were on high alert. Kato flooded my thoughts with images of newscasters wondering if this was related to other incidents when it was revealed that Zander was a Spec-Ops IDB being developed by High ICO as bodyguards using a new type of augmentation. I relayed the news to Sam.

Sam scowled and slammed a fist onto the metal flooring beneath us. There was only enough room for us to crawl with one behind the other, "Those assholes," she growled, "I knew it. As soon as I found the capsule in the desert viper, I knew it. Fuck!" she spat. I reached out and grasped her ankle, trying to calm her down, "What is it, Sam?" I asked. Not sure if she'd divulge her secrets.

"Fucks sake, Chris. Haven't you figured it out yet? The desert viper, Zander, Cilia…me? Where all the same," she said with a cry. I shook my head, "I'm sorry Sam, I'm not getting where you're going with this. Care to clear the air?" I asked.

She sucked in a breath.

She shook her head.

Kept moving forward.

"I only need a few minutes," she said, "The serums I need should be exactly where I left them in my old lab. No one would have messed with it. I have the entire room keyed to my DNA." Sam explained. "Except your DNA isn't yours anymore," I said slowly. She turned her head to look at me and grinned. She sat up as far as she could, her knees up to her ears and dug around in the satchel she'd insisted on taking with us to carry the comm blocker. Digging around, she pulled out a small cylinder in a protective case. It was a vial of blood. "I'll be damned, you've had this the entire time?"

She grinned, and we continued onwards.

The grate over her lab office was tight, but after a few minutes, I was able to wrench it free. "Wait," Sam held up her hand and dug the comm blocker out of her bag along with what looked like a small portable computer. She sat, typing for what felt like forever before snapping the computer shut and activating the little black box that would keep our hides safe for a short ten minutes. "Ok, I set the cameras on a feed-back loop. The comm blocker will give us added protection. With that, we slipped into the room.

The office was more extensive than I thought it was going to be. It was set up similar to the one she had had back in Shady Plateau only more prominent, and shinier, with black and chrome fixings. Several refrigerators lined one wall; the centre of the room held two gurneys outfitted for surgery. The padded straps bolted into the floor around them made me shiver. I didn't want to think about what she did here. There was a line of windows on one wall, and thankfully the blinds had been drawn shut and the city beyond was dark.

[Grey, it's Cilia. She's moving in your direction again. Others have joined her]

[Shit. Who is it?]

[Camelia and several IDB and ICO soldiers. A small army at least.]

I relayed the information to Samantha as her fingers fluttered over keyboards and equipment alike. Using drops of her blood from the vial to activate the machines she needed to synthesise a cure. Or at least something to stop the changes.

"Sam, the comm blocker won't last much longer," I said, "We've got to go. I'm sorry."

She shook her head, "It's okay. They already know where here. Just give me some time. I'm almost done…*fuck*," she breathed. I whirled, moving to stand behind her; I looked down at the display screen on the PDA she held. I couldn't make sense of it, but Sam confirmed what I thought I was seeing, "I'm changing faster than I thought I was. I thought I had figured it out, slowed it down. The Evanescent Destroyers, they weren't supposed to – it happened so fast, but with Zander and Cilia it was perfected. I *built* them, Chris. I *made* those monsters! It was my experiments that created them. But *what* did *I* do wrong when it came to me?" she muttered more to herself than me as she turned back to her work, lost in thought. Sam continued to grumble and type as I readied the rune-gun. Slipping my hand into my pocket.

Just a few spell bullets left. But this tight space wouldn't be ideal. It'd just as soon kill us all if I used it here.

[Grey, they're almost there] Kato said. He sounded urgent. [They are entering the building]

I nodded, [Keep me updated, K]

[They've opened the lobby and are now waiting at the elevator. A few soldiers have taken the stairs. You need to hurry, Grey]

"Samantha, we really need to get outta here!" I emphasised by squeezing her shoulder. She whirled around in her seat and got up, running over to a machine that had come to life behind us. She reached inside and pulled out a long syringe, placing a plunger on it before twisting a needle into place. Staring up at me, her eyes seemed larger and greener than they'd ever been before.

Hair wild.

Teeth flashing.

Her nails were grown sharp and thick. Her fingers were shaking as she worked. It was difficult for her to keep a hold of the needle, "I need your help, Chris," she said, I nodded. "Of course, what do I need to do?"

"I need you to let me test this on you," she said. I cocked an eyebrow, my jaw dropping open. Holding my hands out and waving them, I began to back up away from her, "Whoa now. Wait, I don't know what that shit will do to me. I mean, look at you," I said. She shook her head, approaching me with a thumb on the plunger. "I fixed it. There was a problem with the…I don't know how I missed it. It doesn't matter. You wouldn't understand. I just need to test it. You're unaltered, it wouldn't harm you like it would me," she continued. Her words were beginning to slur, and I swore I could see the scales literally sprouting from the skin around her jaws, her brow, up and down her neck.

Slick and green and shinning like a freshly shed snake.

[Grey, they are here. You have to get out now!] Kato screamed in my thoughts.

I glanced up at our escape route.

I could push Sam through first and then use the chair.

Sam plunged the needle into my bicep, driving it all the way home. Pain exploded through my arm, making it tingle.

"The fuck, Samantha!" I yanked the empty syringe from my skin, throwing it to the floor and kicking it aside. She ran back to her desk, grabbing another sample and placing it into the machine.

She waited.

Made another needle.

Placed a cap over the sharp tip to save for later. I could hear voices now. The sound of heavy boots thundering across the floor. Armed and ready to bust down the door. I was wanted dead or alive.

They didn't give two shits about me.

But I couldn't leave Sam behind.

Not again. Not ever again.

I felt buzzed. My head heavy and my limbs like noodles.

"Ah, shit." I moaned as the room reeled around me.

I heard Samantha yelling my name. Felt her trying to heave me up onto her shoulder, but we had nowhere to go. If I couldn't lift myself into the vent she sure as hell couldn't either.

My heart was racing. My ears ringing as darkness tinged my vision. My body went limp, and I felt Sam, her hands hooked under each arm, guiding me away from the door. I felt the warmth of her lips press against my forehead as she swung the window open. Cold night air rushed in, but I could see the traces of early morning sunlight peeling over the glittering cityscape. I winced, blinking against the absolute brightness of it. "Chris, I'm sorry."

[Grey. Can you hear me?] Kato sounded distant.

"You've got to promise me, you'll find me," Samantha was saying, but I couldn't focus on anything else but her eyes. They were large and green and sucked me into their black centres.

[Grey?]

"You'll be okay, I swear. I made the proper adjustments. It'll happen fast, any minute now and it'll kick in, and you'll be left better than ever," Samantha was saying but the pain exploding behind my eyes, the rapid beating of my heart, the stretch and bulge as my muscled convulsed wracked my body in pain. It would throb one moment and then dissipate only to come back worse than before.

The pain was too much, I felt like I was being ripped apart from the inside out.

I screamed.

If they didn't know which room we were in before they did now.

The door burst open, and dozens of armed men and women stormed through. Camelia and Cilia at their head. With lips, puckered, Camelia stared down her nose at us, "Arrest them. The girl is to be taken into custody. The man, well, we don't need him anymore. He's a failure on all accounts,"

Samantha screamed as hands reached for her, wrapping her arms around my neck she pressed her lips to mine before nuzzling her face against my ear, she whispered, "Trust me. Please, take care, Christopher."

She placed her hands on my chest and shoved me out the window.

Chapter 20

I stared up into Sam's face, watching as hands and arms sheathed in black armour wrapped around her, pulling her back from the window. Wind raced up around me as I plummeted the three stories to the ground.

The impact was softer than it should have been. No pain but then if there were any pain, I wouldn't have been able to felt it over the roar of the headache.

"Samantha," I croaked. My throat was dry. I couldn't think straight; I just knew I had to get back to her.

My hat drifted to the ground beside me, but I didn't care, it was the least of my concerns right now.

I closed my eyes for a moment and felt my body moving as I drifted in and out of consciousness. At some point I thought I had seen a dozen faces peering at me. Hands pulled me up and then down again. Down into darkness.

Voices.

Laughter. Water trickling.

The smell of food cooking over a smokey fire.

Something warm was trickling over my tongue and down my throat. It was good. It tasted like something I'd had before but couldn't place. I needed more of it. My stomach growled.

Wait.

I sat up and snapped open my eyes to find a dozen dirty faces starting at me, "Where am I?" I asked. My voice came out wrong, deeper, rougher than I remembered it. I looked between the faces. The only one I recognised was the lady standing next to me with a bowl and spoon in her hands. She smiled as recognition dawned on me. The Grime Dweller.

"Well, good morning to you too, handsome," she said and sat the bowl on the small table beside her. Looking around, I realised I must be in her home. The bed I was laying on was clean enough, and my clothes had been washed and placed in a neat pile at the foot of the bed. I looked down to find I was naked for all to see, but bandages covered most of my body. We were in one of the tunnels underground, a curtain had been looped through rings bolted to the curved ceiling for privacy.

The woman leaned in and poked and prodded at the cuts on my face, "Ouch," I protested. She shook her head and smirked, "Oh, shut up. You're alive, so you can't complain," she peeled up each eyelid before leaning back and resting her hands on her hips. "Bless my stars, eyes like those would set my heart a flutter when I was younger," she said, "You'll have scars, but I did my best, and they'll heal right with time," the woman finished and handed me a mirror. I blinked at the stranger in the mirror.

The cut on my temple, twice opened, was laced up with black stitches. My lip was swollen and also cut. Black and blue bruises surrounded my nose, but it looked like it had been set and would probably heal well enough. But it was my eyes that pulled the most attention. They weren't dark-brown any longer, now they were green tinged with gold-threaded out to make a ring around the green.

Fools gold if I'd ever seen it.

I looked up at the woman, "Thank you. But…What's your name. And why?"

She rolled her eyes and smiled, "You can call me Gerda. And I only helped you because of the girl. She was kind to us, while you were out gallivanting around she'd gave us enough money to feed us for the next year. Said we'd deserved it more than she did. And she left these for you." Gerda said and placed a box of spell bullets on my blanket-covered lap along with the rune-gun. I pressed my lips into a line and frowned.

They weren't mine.

I didn't have anything.

"How long have I been here?"

"Oh, it's only been about four days, five max, you were out cold when we found you in the street. If it weren't for your skyeye and that skaali we –"

"Kato and Tweet, they're alive?"

As if on cue the whistling noises of the raptor that I'd grown so accustomed to hearing echoed from somewhere outside Gerda's tunnel. Children laughed following another whistle. "She's quite a personality, but she misses her owner," Gerda said, crossing her arms. I missed her owner too. I reached out tentatively to Kato.

[Kato, are you there?]

[Grey! I'm here!] the answer came immediately, and seconds later, the curtains drawn around the bed were stirred as soft wings carried Kato to land at the foot of the bed. [Sorry, I was playing with the children.]

[You? Playing?] I laughed and reached out as Kato hopped across the blankets to me, nuzzling against my chest with his warm cyber-filament feathers. Kato stepped back, his large eyes blinking and his tone suddenly serious. He began to relay what had happened after Sam shoved me out the window.

Dr Samantha Cowell was now in ICO custody. She had been arrested for illegal augmentation and hybrid experimentations leading up to the deaths of four High ICO and planning for the assassinations of many others. Sam was no longer in Centrum. Kato theorised that they had taken her to the Watchtower for forced servitude. She could use their extensive laboratories there to continue her experiments and create more monsters for Camelia and the ICO. No one ever figured out who had hired the hits on the High ICO employees but the assassinations stopped just as suddenly as they had started. Still, many a representative walked with bated breath, and extra guards were added to many ICO homes. Camelia had moved up the ranks and, in the space of days, was now in charge of Centrum. Cilia now worked for Camelia exclusively.

[You've been listed as dead. I'm sure they wholeheartedly believe you were killed and eaten by the grime dwellers] he said.

I snickered; Camelia would relish the thought I was sure. I glanced over at Gerda and held my hand out for the bowl of soup. I'd need my strength if I were going to go after them. I'd been wrong about so many things. It was time to make them right.

CHAPTER 21

Three weeks later and most of the wounds had healed. I yelped like a new-born babe when Gerda pulled the stitches out after a few days, but a swift kick to the ass gave me something to really to cry about. I spent days helping out around the tunnels, scaring off enormous rats and dishing out food for the populace. Just because they had plenty of money didn't mean they wanted to waste it, the Grime Dwellers were a conservative community of people and didn't spend more than they needed to. Though, I was told the quality of the food was much better than it had ever been.

Here I was, alive and well right beneath ICOs feet. It was pretty damn funny when I thought about it.

I was upset at first about my death, but honestly, it would make things a lot easier for me. Gerda knew some people and those people knew other people, and they all worked together to arrange a new identity for me.

It was easy.

After the DNA scrub began to fully take my eyes had completely changed from brown to golden-green, and my skin had taken on a copper sheen as fine scales, barely noticeable unless you rubbed them the wrong way, covered the surface of my back and shoulders, forearms and the tops of my hands. The heat didn't seem to bother me as much, neither did the cold really. But I was hungry, all the time. So long as I had the lion's share of meat though, I was okay. I only hoped that was all the changes would do to me. And, as the days went by, nothing else happened. No nasty surprises.

My bond with Tweet had cemented, her thoughts coming more easily to me. They were still pictures, sure, but I also felt the impressions behind them.

I had no idea about Sam. If she'd managed to fix herself with the last vial before Camelia and her goons had taken her.

It didn't matter. I'd still find Samantha.

I still hoped to fix my mistakes with her. And, even if I couldn't, at least I'd free her.

I was stronger now. Faster.

I'd never work for ICO again. That was a given. I'd have to pay Carlson back in some other way. But there were plenty of independent hunters out there. Mercenaries willing to take on any job for a price and I saw no reason not to keep doing what I did best. Being a shitty Dune Buster meant I was a brilliant criminal apparently.

There was a reckoning to be had. I owed Camelia for my new life, and I'd make sure I got the chance to thank her personally for that. The news reports told me that both Cilia and, regrettably, Zander had recovered and were dubbed hero's, having brought in Dr Cowell and taken down the vile murderer, Christopher D. Grey.

Cilia with her smug smile and Zander frowning. Their faces were all across highrise billboards and flashed across PDA screens throughout the planet, probably even the galaxy.

ONE MONTH LATER

The three of us, Tweet, Kato, and I stood on the edge of the continent, having made a quick and easy exit from Centrum via the underground tunnel system. With my new ID, it'd been easy to catch a ride back to Gardenia to make the trip straight down to Tylan.

[Grey, are we going to not?] Kato asked as he spread his wings and lifted from my shoulder. He soared out over the expanse of sand that was the Dune Sea.

I looked behind us, Tylan was a rust bucket of a town made of salvaged bits of rotting ships and broken warehouses. Old forklifts and heavy cranes creaked and groaned in the hot wind that blew up from the desert.

I'd made sure to fill up on supplies, and my saddlebags bulged with jerky and other necessities. I nodded at Kato, who tugged at my thoughts again.

Pulling the bandana over my face, I jerked the reins. Tweet wheeled around as I urged her into a run, muscular thighs with improved internal hydrolics returning her limp back to a smooth gait,

"Hang on, Sam, I'm coming to save my girl," I said aloud to no one in particular. My skaali ride responded with a rumbling growl and a whistling blast of air through her nostrils, reminding me again why she was named Tweet.

Run fast.

Help friend.

With clawed feet that pounded against the cracked ground, she carried us further from Centrum.

I'd had enough of that shithole. And of ICO. And especially Camelia.

My new plan was to save Sam, settle down on one of the atoll islands, and live happily ever after.

The End.

Kato brushed over my shoulder with the tips of his wings as he glided swiftly overhead, his shadow like an arrow on the ground to lead the way.

[I still don't think Sam would approve of your misogynistic epitaph] Kato said, his voice a whisper in my thoughts as he flew further onwards.

[But I think she'll forgive you just this once]

I could hear the laughter in Kato's voice as the hot winds carried him high above my head to slice through the only cloud I'd ever seen on this gods-forsaken planet.

GLOSSARY

Aquaria – a smaller city, based near the Last Sea that produces potable water. It is also the main framework for all piping systems across Terrafirma V and is vital to survival.

Blimp – flying ships used for large cargo transportation such as water kegs, cloth, certain food goods, etc. Allows for safer travel across the Dune Sea between Mainland and Islands though it does come with its own dangers. Significant cities and some islands have a Blimp Tower for maintaining them.

Bull Newt – a giant amphibious monster that hides in shallow water and attacks with its long, sticky, tongue. Dragging its victims beneath the water to drown. It's ugly as hell and carries its young borrowed in the skin of its back.

Centrum – major city and the location of the ICO headquarters. Jobs for IBDs are an issue and collected from here. It is on the largest mainland.

Comm Link – Communication Link, also referred to as a comm. An internal device implanted into the ear and sometimes includes a visual feed with newer versions. It uses cyber-filaments to attach to the brain to send and receive signals.

Cyber-filaments – filaments of fibre optic cable used to transfer/transform information between electronic elements to biological tissue and back again.

Desert Viper – a giant desert snake. They can sit for days waiting for their victim in absolute silence. Their venom is deadly.

Dune Buster – mercenaries, DBs, hired for various jobs.

Dune Sea – the stretches of space between continents and islands were oceans and seas used to be.

EMbomb – an Electro-Magnetic bomb made of thousands of microscopic particles polarised with magnetic energy. When the bomb erupts, it releases an Electro-Magnetic Pulse with a vast radiance of effect. Often used to stamp down riots.

Eva Defender – A series of automatons called Evanescent Defenders armed with heavy weaponry used for warfare. After the Sydian Wars, many of them were decommissioned and scraped, but a rare few were maintained for personal defence. You can still find the wrecks of them scattered across the Dune Sea.

Eva Destroyer – A series of automatons/augmented cyborgs used for attack and counter defence. Like their smaller cousins, there are still a few in use today. They are often robots, but evolving technology merged with genetic engineering has allowed the creation of customised Destroyers in both size, appearance, and ability.

Forsheeth – a Yrmian word, close in meaning to the English word for 'fuck/fucking'.

Grime Dwellers – the lowliest of the citizens. Grime dwellers have a city all their own in the sewers and abandoned pipe projects of Centrum.

Halcyon Road – An interstate that passes over the main continent of Oceana, through the Dune Sea, and up through the lesser continent of Caludra to Geneva. Originally it was a significant passage route used for transportation and relocation that passed through beautiful stretches of woodland. Now it is mostly a broken relic being reclaimed by the desert.

Herth – abbreviated from Herth Kaddîska, the home planet of the feline aliens called Kit'th.

Imperial Dune Buster – DBs who are contracted by the Imperial Commission Office for specialised jobs. Their license gives them a range of freedoms not afforded to others.

Imperial Blimp System – blimps used for travel by the wealthy Imperials and their families to travel swiftly over the sands.

Imperial Commission Office – a police force of sorts that is controlled by shareholders, the wealthy elite (Imperials) and vote to determine which laws are enforced. Enforces common law, as well as the hiring of Imperial D.B. s The Imperial Commission Office, is also known as ICO (Eye-Koh).

Imperial Military – military maintained by ICO it maintains all division of the police and active militia at both ground and space.

Kit'th – a feline humanoid from the planet Herth Kaddîska. They were first encountered roughly two-hundred years ago and were receptive to peace talks so long as we were willing to provide them with work. They like to feel useful.

Nano Blood – a liquid with plasma-like properties that can be used to shuttle nanomachines and/or chemicals throughout the blood. Acts as a buffer/carrier.

Raptor – a Velociraptor. Usually augmented for essential communication, tameness, and weaponry. A popular mount for traveling. Doubles as a riding mount and bodyguard.

Roid – a mixture of various types of steroids and other drugs popular among fighters in the fighting pits and among recreational drug users.

Rust Lung – a type of tetanus brought on from breathing in the rust from broken down steel relics.

Shady Plateau – a small island. One of a series of 'back-water' islands of little note. If a bayou still existed, these islands would be the equivalent.

Seir – a Kit'th term with a meaning similar to Lord or Master. However, it can also be considered a term of endearment among mated pairs.

Skaali – thanks to genetic experimentation with local wildlife that had survived the initial Terraform Rest and Reset phase, several species of dinosaurs were introduced into the wild. Many of these home-brewed genetic mutants died off within the first few decades, but the raptor family was especially tenacious though their numbers are in steady decline. We call them skaali (scaly) for obvious reasons though many also have feathers. The largest of the skaali, based on Tyrannosaur DNA, are mostly extinct but occasionally one pops up.

Skyeye – a type of cyborg that specialises in aerial surveillance and so are often capable of flight.

Spur Town – the most distant city on the planet. Commission branch office is small and needs some guidance. Known for its cyborg chop-shops and illegal skaali races/fights as well as drug production. Its isolation makes it difficult to regulate despite its large size.

Sydian War of 4506 – A war between Earth Empire, Herth Kaddîska, and the Yrmia Consolidate. After the war treaties were made and trade established between Earth and Herth Kaddîska while the Yrmia retreated back to their colonies.

Terrafirma V – the planet we live on. Terrafirma V is a failed terraformed planet. At some point during the process, the Germination didn't take. The planet has been steadily dying since then. Christopher Grey is 7th generation native-born TF-V and has never been to Earth or Earth II.

Tryk – Triceratops. Used as draft animals for their moderate size, strength, and docile nature. Their thick hides make them resistant to attacks.

Tyrant – Tyrannosaurus. When they were first created, they were used for defence as living tanks, but they quickly lost it and became hard to control. The few that remained escaped their confinements and now roam the Dune Sea. Generally, have a terrible attitude.

Watchtower Plateau – a medium island that works as a military base of operations for ICO while also maintaining a functioning prison.

Yellow Plateau – a small island. A 'back-water' island. Named for the yellow crust that always seems to gather over the sides of buildings from the sulphur mines burrowed into its side.

Yrmian – an alien from the planet Yrrma. They are tall, slender with four arms and purple eyes. Their females act mainly as collectors of rare artefacts while the males often become warriors and seek glory through battle.

TERRAFIRMA V
WORLD INFORMATION FILE

It's been decades since anyone has ever mentioned Earth or Earth II for that matter. The only ones that ever seemed to hold interest were the ICO scientists. They utilised the information from the previous planets, and successful colonisations to establish life on Terrafirma V. Though the world ultimately failed to provide adequate life and growth, a specific section of humanity was forced, or chose, to remain and continue its attempts at colonising the barren planet.

Oceana was the first continent to be settled on Terrafirma V and remains the most populated after the planet's failing due to the success of Aquarius' water treatment facility in the south, and the bustling city of Centrum toward the North.

- **Aquaria** was the first city established on Terrafirma V. This series of small islands serve as the primary developer for the piping framework required for all other regions to hold potable water. Only through the hard, and tireless efforts of the workers stationed there was plumbing successfully installed, and access to water made available to even the furthest cities.

Once plumbing networks were installed successfully in each town, the city of Aquarius began using an advanced filtration system at the edge of the Last Ocean to create potable water. Through deep beds of tightly packed sand and moss, workers were able to widen a canal to allow water to flow into the filtration tunnels, down to town, and distributed to neighbouring regions through their massive pipe networks. Hydro-electric generators were installed shortly after that to the main connectors to ensure water could be pushed up hills and through winding passageways without issue.

Water flows through an intense process of desalination once filtered through the sand and moss filtration system; it includes boiling the water through power provided from solar-electric heating before it is cooled again for distribution. This process leaves salt and other impurities behind, thus allowing the water to be safely consumed by Humans. The process is lengthy and costly, which is the reason why the workers living in Aquarius operate on 24/7 shifts and remain in town to avoid delays or mishaps.

Small cottages were built in tight rows against one another, despite an abundance of space across the shoreline. The only inhabitants are the workers who find the journey to the treatment facility on the coast much easier by foot. Each cottage is modest, with its own decorative touch of paint, chosen by the workers and their family to show some uniqueness of course. They are comfortable, single level bungalows with three medium-sized bedrooms enough to fit a bed, a dresser, and a desk; as well as a living room, bathroom, and eat-in kitchen. There isn't much need for driveways or garages as visitors are few and far between, and the workers are often too busy for travel.

However, roads have been paved through, just as they've done on previous planets, and it was not uncommon for large Skaali to travel the town every weekend to bring visitors to tour the Water Treatment Facility. The facility itself is a large, concrete building that stands out amongst the beige sand and deep brown hues of the cottages. It was built with solar panelling on its roof to ease the stress of the hydro-electric generators during higher influxes of water intake such as in warmer months.

A few small Skaali are utilised to move equipment down the long, narrow, unguarded bridges above the water vaults; this is partially due to their slender forms, as well as their ability to navigate sharp turns without distraction or fear of falling. Workers load the tools, or supplies necessary for the job into packs strapped to the Skaali's backs and send them off to the worksite; it is much easier to do so than having the workers themselves traverse the massive length of the facility themselves. There are 12 separate water vaults holding a hundred gallons of water at any given moment. These serve as reserves just in case of power outages, or water shortages and the more rural communities begin to dry.

- **Centrum** is the largest city on Terrafirma V, and home to the Imperial Commission Office Headquarters. It was built as a central hub, operating like the busiest cities that once spanned the original Earth; like Tokyo, Japan, and New York City. Though many sought to reside within its borders, only the wealthiest, and those employed by the newly founded ICO were permitted to buy the property.

Housing was built sparingly at first, with acres of grassy plots being bought up and two-storey brick homes built on their surface. They were family homes, with up to five bedrooms, two or more bathrooms, a fully finished basement, a formal dining room, and a chef-style kitchen. Even two-car garages were attached to some homes that allowed for hobbyists to turn them into workshops, or for Artists to turn them into personalised studios.

As the city grew, many of the houses began to sell for double their original pricing and condos were built in their place. Single-Skaali travel to and from neighbouring communities became too cluttered for the two-lane roadways to handle so more massive Tyrant Skaali were moved in. The Tyrants were equipped with car extensions similar to trains to manage the increase in civilians moving around the city. The raptors and tryk were moved from single-family ownership to factories and other rural communities where their small frames could be put to better use, such as in Aquarius' Water Treatment Facility.

Deforestation crept into Centrum long before the planet's failing, and the droughts began, as the need for lodging and business far surpassed the need for public parks and recreation. ICO Offices began to expand their services, sprouting up new locations for contracts in each neighbourhood to accommodate both full-time staffs and contracted mercenaries. Buildings began to grow larger, and taller, stretching toward the sky as the city continued to grow and thrive.

The previous rule of residency was abandoned shortly after the city itself began construction to allow for small shop owners to set up businesses, and thus appeal to the wealthy community. Convenience stores were placed on every corner, and a Pizza Parlour was usually only a block or so away. As ICO offices expanded, residents desired to stay closer to home rather than in the city centre, so shopping malls and boutiques also began to put their foot in the door; gown shops began to occupy condo lobbies, while five-star dining was only located next door. The drive to have so many convenient options also rose the demand for more lower-income housing and thus Centrum had to expand itself outward again to allow for cheaper apartment complexes to be built, and older buildings to be moved and occupied by shop owners and restaurant staff.

However, as the planet's life forms began to fail, the climates shifted, and so did the community. Businesses shut their doors, moving away with what little money remained to care for their family. Shopping malls went out of business and were left abandoned, while restaurants simply closed their doors and never opened again.

As the terraforming of the planet continued to fail, the ICO offices continued to grow. Dune busters began to inhabit the broken neighbourhoods, mercenaries willing to take up any job so long as the payoff was worth it. Many communities became militant-like outposts, stored with rations and ammunitions from the Dune Busters, but in the city centre, it seemed like business as usual. With the abandoned areas slowly being sectioned off, the wealthier residents moved closer inward, refusing to take notice of the fewer faces in their offices, and the lack of cafes that dotted the city streets. So long as there were bounties to chase, they'd have paychecks to cash.

The Dune Sea is filled with tattered ships and broken dreams. The hulls of forgotten vessels lay cracked, filled with the dust and sand of years of solitude at the depths of the swollen basin. Once the vast sea that spread its icy veins through the narrow passages of the continents, it was filled with Skaali the size of cargo ships and traversed by both civilians and sailors alike. Ports were scattered all along its shoreline for both business and pleasure, with cities like Xylia harbouring cruise ships for that long-awaited getaway vacation.

But soon, it too began to waste away as the terraforming planet struggled to thrive. Jagged rocks started to expose themselves, tucked just beneath the waves that would then carve themselves along the sides of passing ships, sinking them to the bottom of the blackened sea. As the water evaporated, trade channels began to shrink and disappear, leaving many port towns without tourists or supplies. Docks were left to rot away or be buried beneath the sand, and the vacation getaway towns were abandoned as locals moved away in search of work.

Halcyon Road, however, remained; a broad bridged roadway that floated along the waves, re-enforced with thick and long cement beams now tucked beneath the sand. As the water faded, the sand and rock rose to greet it, but still, it held firm. Beams were built with iron mesh to allow for expansion and contraction to adapt to both harsh and calm weather, thus allowing the road to endure years after the water ran dry. It could withstand rain, wind, and sea, as its engineers long ago decided it would remain, even if Humanity chose to leave. It was initially built as a vital supply run passage to serve the deep woodland nations, and mountainous regions the ships could not access. It stretched over all of Oceana, from Centrum to Aquarius, before spanning across to Caldura, and even up to Geneva. Though still in use, much of its surface has been reclaimed by desert sands, making even veterans of its roadways often rethink their journeys across it.

Few islands still dot the sandy sea, their surface sitting high atop solid sheets of rock like the Shady Plateau and Watchtower Plateau in the North. They are better served by Blimps that navigate the skies above, than that of the few Skaali still capable of enduring the trips across Halcyon road.

From high atop the Blimps, it is easier to see what remains of the once-powerful sea, now filled with forgotten ports, and riddled with the ghosts of a once prosperous past.

- **Shady Plateau** is a small back-water island that was once home to a tiny fishing village. Those wanting to establish a new life on Terrafirma V, but hoping to find the solitude of their own region over the hustle and bustle of the city, chose to take up residency on the small islands scattered across the dune sea. The plateau once sat in a marshy bayou, challenging to navigate by large motorboat, but easy enough to traverse by canoe or paddleboat. A single dock still stretches from its shore, cracked and lop-sided from vicious windstorms. Initially occupied by a band of close-knit fishermen, it is now home to few individuals who remain somewhat self-sufficient, relying only on the water supplied from Aquarius to thrive. Their source of food comes from the deep beds of sandworms that inhabit the still cold trenches around their island, making for long and dangerous dig sites that can collapse at any moment, and swallow up an unsuspecting passer-by if left unguided through the area.

- **Watchtower Plateau** was initially the location of Scientific Research and Operation bases for Terrafirma V's establishment. It has since been remade to serve as an ICO Military base, and Prison Island.

When Terrafirma V began accepting human civilian residency, the Scientists of Watchtower Plateau began to hasten their research and progress on all varieties of life forms that could potentially thrive on the planet. Their priority, of course, was the Skaali; genetic mutations of dinosaurs that had been bred from the successful rest and reset phase from experimentations completed on local wildlife. These creatures were housed in large, acrylic cells while a way to tame, and train them to work with, and for humanity, was completed. As their success continued, their numbers dwindled, and the ICO put a cease to their operations, believing no further advancement or testing was necessary for the ways of the Skaali or local flora.

With Skaali shipped off to designated facilities and communities, the labs were left empty, laying to waste. The ICO was quick to turn them into their primary military base, as it was well-hidden, and well-protected from the public eye. The cells once housing Skaali were altered, becoming prison cells for the unruly, and degenerates of Terrafirma V.

Of course, without further research, and advancement in the local plant-life of the planet, and the newly created Skaali, those who remained of the Scientists watched in horror as life began to wither and die. Scientists who remained were there to serve the military operations, but their hearts grew cold as they watched entire breeds of Skaali die off; large, water-cruising Skaali was left beached and died from suffocation as the water disappeared, while others, unable to adapt to the sandy terrain, became trapped in dunes and holes, left to starve.

- **Yellow Plateau** is similar to its cousin, the Shady Plateau to the South, as it too is a small back-water island that once hid in the wilted trees and thick cattails of a bayou. Its inhabitants were many, dotting the island with a barrage of small apartments and cottages. Individuals here worked deep below the plateau's surface in the sulphur mines, and along the sulphur flats to the island's side. Those not journeying deep below Terrafirma V's crust to work the long, demanding hours of the Sulphur trades held produce stands and small businesses above to adequately supply the workers with food, and services like laundry and housekeeping.

Though the mines are still in operation, the sea that once cleansed the Devil's Gold from the shores has faded, leaving yellow dust to collect on both land and home with its toxic visage. Some buildings have gone into rot, but many are still maintained due to the large workforce that still inhabits the island. Those able to cope with the toxic fumes of the Sulfur flats that encompass their once beautiful island home continue to work. However, they rely much more heavily on their neighbouring communities for sustenance than they had done in the past. They trade sulphur, used for rubber production and gunpowder, for food and water so that they may survive.

- **Gardenia** was the pride of Oceana. Its shoreline spanned for miles with beautiful wind sand beaches and radiant turquoise waters lapping at its edge. It was a thriving market town, a paradise for tourists that was still close to home. Numerous stands were filled with beach necessities like towels and sunglasses; to smaller stands that held local artisan crafts like sea-shell bracelets, and hand-crocheted bikinis. It was a bustling network of entertainment both night and day with beach cabanas for rent, and waterfront condos to own.

Though it resides on the last ocean, one of the last known resources for water, its crowds have died down. Paradise away has since become home for few with condos overtaken by massive tree growth; their vines and branches twisting and stretching through windows and down narrow corridors. Shops are sparse, few remaining open to selling only the necessities required by the small community that remains. Stands have disappeared, leaving the streets barren, and the shoreline is devoid of all laughter and life.

Without tourism, the town shrank with only a few locals to remain, allowing the well-fed land on the waterfront to flourish and grow beyond all control. Still beautiful on the way by, the ferocity of the forest now deters many visitors from making their way through its numerous passages to see the legendary white sand beaches that lay just beyond the horizon.

- **Millertown** is the primary trading post on Oceana that hosts import and export from neighbouring towns, and across the Dune Sea. It is the last stop for proper supplies before one trek across Halcyon Road and is therefore consistently busy. The total amount of permanent residents, however, is unknown due to the persistent shift of kiosks, carts, and stands that pop up daily.

From tree roots carved from Gardenia's trees to sulphur from the Yellow Plateau's Sulphur Flats, there is nothing that cannot be found in Millertown's markets. Everything has a price, and everything can be haggled, traded, or negotiated for by any individual of Terrafirma V's inhabitants whether they be civilian, chop-shop owner, or Officer.

- **Tylan** is a small port at the base of the dune sea. It was a small refuelling port in its prime but now only lay waste to rotting ships and broken warehouses. Old forklifts and heavy cranes creak and groan in the wind as Dune Busters make their way through the abandoned port, wondering who, or what may live inside its abandoned buildings.

Caldura is a mountainous region on the west side of the Dune Sea. It is home to many trade posts and mining facilities but has seen a steady decline in all but local inhabitants since the planet's failure to Terraform.

- **Ricia** is a small town that borders the Halcyon Road passage through the mountains. It had provided safe passage and shelter to weary travellers since Terrafirma V's beginnings, even remaining neutral when the planet failed, and chaos began to boil over the land.

It is made up of an inn, a tavern, three gatehouses, and a small convenience shop. It has been family-run for more than a generation and is sustained by the travellers of Caldura and those from across the Dune sea.

The Inn is small, with only ten rooms on the second floor of its rickety, wooden frame, while a kitchen, dining hall, and stable for Skaali sit below. The family lives separately in each of the three gatehouses to keep watch for rogues and bandits that threaten to vandalise, or steal from their supply.

These gatehouses have been built over several decades from the rock of the mountain to its south-eastern border. They are infused with iron veins, making carving difficult, hence the length to build, and stand ten feet high, and four feet in diameter. With sheer cliffs on either side, the only way beyond Ricia is through it. Weapons are passed along to the exit gate of a traveller's choice, and all quarrels must cease until beyond its walls.

They host a single Tyrant for transport and assistance and threaten to feet any unruly guests to it should they become unmanageable.

- **Slumber** is a sleepy port on the edge of the Dune Sea. Its back faces the Caulduran mountains like the scene on a postcard; its port hub casts large, concrete docks into the sea, each one prepared to accept even the largest cruise ship or Skaali. Once home to the most magnificent lighthouse on Terrafirma V, it would guide ships safely across the sea from Oceana, until they reached their coastal destination.

It is now but a shell of its former glory; its streets no longer buzz with the busy travellers from across the way who would make their way eagerly to their transport through the mountains. It is now more of a camp. An outpost for dune busters to meet and share information on past bounties, or potential ones that may offer multiple rewards.

- **Solace** was established by the ICO as an outpost for Blimp service and repair but has since been deemed unfit for landing due to the intense sandstorms that sweep across its surface. It is now a deserted and isolated town, free from the laws and commitments of the ICO due to the winds that always threaten its perimeter. How many residents still live on the airbase, and in the few houses of the town itself, remains a mystery.

The Atolls are a valley region between the Dune sea and Caldura. Once a busy trading channel for cargo ships and sea-faring Skaali, it's water-less passages no longer see the tall ships sailing into its many ports. It is now filled with the broken blimps, rogue Skaali, and remnants of the old world. It is prone to dust storms, making traversing its depths difficult for even the most seasoned nomads.

Supra was a tropical continent with dormant volcanos at its back. It was a popular destination for tourists, but its volcanic eruptions became active once more as the planet began to falter, leaving the island paradise to become a dark and desolate place.

- **Xylia** is the main docking port for Blimps and other air crafts. The intense heat from Supra's volcanic mountain supply both the wind for push and the air for the rise to even the most gigantic Blimps on Xylia's massive airfield.

Once a military training facility and scientific research centre, all that remains of Xylia's past is its airfield, and Blimp warehouses that were built to endure the Volcanos should they ever become active again.

Residents here live inside bunkers just beneath the ground to avoid over-exposure to the intense volcanic heat above. Here, Blimps are crafted, repaired, and retired as per ICO command, and are left to be disposed of in the Volcano centres.

Though the workers and residents will call foul, claiming some Blimps to have been stolen, it is rumoured that they will sell them off, or trade the retired crafts to any buyer willing to pay the price for private transportation. Rumours of sky pirates around the Spura cliffsides have circuited among the ordinary folks.

Because Xylia was once one of the largest research centres on Terrafirma V, the population was made up of Chinese descendants since it was their technology that birthed the terraforming projects. Remnants of these ancient immigrants still remain in the form of hanzi characters across the underground cities and a local language blending elements of Chinese, Japanese, and English dialects.

Geneva is home to the delinquents and criminals of its only occupied space, Spurtown. The last island continent to be populated on Terrafirma V, it now only knows resentment and crime.

- **Spurtown** is the furthest occupied city on all of Terrafirma V. It is home to the lowest of the low; the criminals degenerates, and most vicious of the planet's residents. A small ICO office was established long ago in its small central locale, but its officers were easily corrupted, or simply disappeared from the city without a trace.

Illegal cyborg chop-shops are stamped on every street corner. Skaali are reprogrammed and used to fight one another, or serve as guard dogs to some of the more dangerous people occupying Spurtown.

Due to its isolation, regulating law and keeping the peace has proven difficult, even for the most determined ICO officers. Those running illegal businesses do their part to drive out new and aspiring officials; while those merely trying to get by do their best to deter other officials from stepping in.

Those not in the chop shop, or drug dealing business, live in slums; small hut-like buildings with only one large room in which to sleep, eat and try to relax.

Although the living conditions are not prime, even the homeless on the streets of Spurtown prefer outsiders to mind their own business, and ICO officials to stay away, but for what reasons they push the help away is ultimately unknown. Rumour has it a sizeable underground well still functions within its city centre, and each member of the community wishes to keep its existence a secret.

It would come to no one's surprise that such a sacred resource would be heavily guarded. As Spurtown is the furthest away from Aquarius, and the piping system doesn't always run a full supply of water to their region. Thus, having their own supply, and keeping it hidden from the rest of the world would prove to be in their favour for survival.

Spurtown's saving grace in the early days of Terrafirma V's establishment was their production facilities for the dual gun production that permitted both regular bullets, and advanced laser-scopes to be equipped on a single weapon. They were also the town to develop the technology for Rune Guns; guns powered by ancient glyphs carved onto their forms, giving them different levels, and types of power to anything from a small pistol, to a military rifle. Runes, despite years of use, would allow the weapon to continue functioning without issue.

Scientists were baffled by their creation, and without full ICO regulation, production on the arms ceased, and all were ordered to be destroyed. Importation from Kit'th was outlawed.

Of course, several made their way around the black market, while others mysteriously disappeared from the final production line. Unfortunately, due to their cryptic nature, and specified creations, many runes ended up corrupted, and destroyed the weapons they were attached to. Runes were enchanted by belief and trust; thus, the guns were only useful to their specified owner. Once the guns were outlawed, and many discarded, they became all the rarer, and extremely valuable. Not all buyers are compatible with the firearm they purchase, thus making their spending all the riskier.

When rune guns were outlawed, the people of Spurtown thoroughly believed that their production of the conventional dual weapons would increase, but they too began to decline. The people of Terrafirma V started to fear guns, regardless of the safety it brought them from rogue Skaali, or intruders, and abandoned the weapons alongside the Rune Guns. Despite this, Spurtown continued production as long as demand was met, including a contract with the ICO for their own military. But once the military base was established on Watchtower Plateau, production was moved, and Spurtown became the rundown town of resentment that it is known for today.

ACKNOWLEDGEMENTS

Many wonderful people went into the creation of the book. First and foremost, my dad, whose love of spaghetti westerns, science fiction, and ~~destroying~~ improving my dinosaur drawings with satellite schematics were the main influences behind this tale.

My husband, who maintained a steady flow of caffeine into the long hours of both night and day. To my kids, without whom this book would have been completed several months ago.

I'd like to thank Ellie of *Ellie Edits* for taking the time to read, provide feedback, and offer suggestions. I'd also like to thank her for making adjustments to my outline that helped to streamline my writing and the story I wanted to tell.

Finally, I'd also like to thank Justin Denks for the name of P'tato Sack Tennessee (Tate). Without his hilarious nickname for my husband, who is a native-born Tennessean, this character might never have existed to assist my errant Dune Buster.

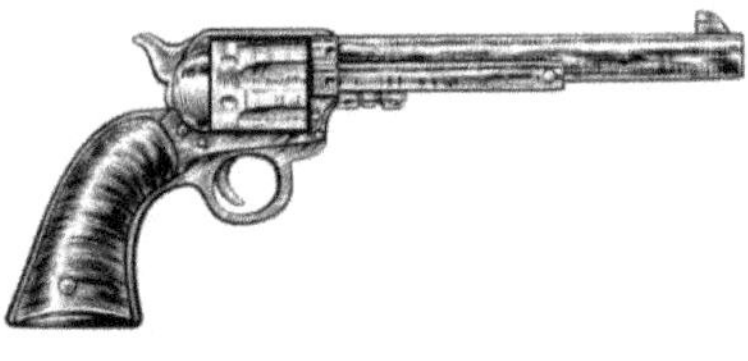

ABOUT THE AUTHOR

Sabine Elrod (Andrea Gill née Elrod) is an Imperial Dune Buster of the highest calibre.
She works hard to seek out and bring to justice the good, the bad, and the ugly.

Sabine enjoys binge-watching Netflix and pondering the existence of extraterrestrial life. When she isn't watching the stars, she enjoys reading manga and watching anime as well as playing MMOs and is a massive fan of all thing's dragon and dinosaur.

TO BE CONTINUED

BLEEDING GREY

-A SAND DUNES AND DINOSAURS PRE-SEQUEL-

Go back 15 years to see the story that started it all. Who is Carlson, and how did Grey become an Imperial Dune Buster? Who was Natalie? How in the hell did Tate get the name P'tato Sack Tennessee? All those questions and more will be answered in the exciting pre-sequel to *Dune Busters.*

JANUARY 19 2020

DEAD MAN WALKING

-A SAND DUNES AND DINOSAURS NOVELLA-

-TWO-

With his cyborg partners, Kato and Tweet, Grey is on the hunt to find and rescue Samantha Cowell but his enemies, Cilia and Zander, never quite believed Grey was dead and are on a constant lookout for him. Meanwhile, Camelia is now the head of High ICO and is working with Amerinetics Industries to introduce a new kind of pit-battle to keep the masses focused away from her shenanigans. One that is both as entertaining as it is deadly for more than just the participants.

JUNE 07 2020

CPSIA information can be obtained
at www.ICGtesting.com
Printed in the USA
BVHW040934120919
558270BV00010B/235/P

9 780578 529745